THE FLIGHT

GAITO GAZDANOV

THE FLIGHT

Translated from the Russian by
Bryan Karetnyk

PUSHKIN PRESS
LONDON

Pushkin Press
71–75 Shelton Street, London WC2H 9JQ

The Flight (*Polyot*) was partially serialized in 1939 in *Russkie zapiski*,
and first published in its complete form in Russian in 1992.

This translation first published by Pushkin Press in 2016

ISBN 978 1 782271 62 8

ИНСТИТУТ ПЕРЕВОДА

AD VERBUM

Published with the support of the Institute for Literary Translation, Russia.

Frontispiece: Gaito Gazdanov in the 1920s, Paris

Typeset in 10/13pt Monotype Baskerville by Paul Saunders

Proudly printed and bound in Great Britain by TJ International,
Padstow, Cornwall on Munken Premium White 80gsm

www.pushkinpress.com

THE FLIGHT

Events in Seryozha's life began on that memorable evening when, for the first time in many months, he saw in his room, above the bed where he slept, his mother—wearing a fur coat, gloves and an unfamiliar black velvet hat. There was a look of alarm on her face, so unlike the one that he had always known. He was unable to account for her unexpected appearance at this late hour, for she had left almost a year ago and he had grown used to her continued absence. Yet now, here she was, standing at his bedside. She sat down quickly and whispered to him not to make a fuss, telling him to get dressed and to come home with her right away.

"But Papa didn't say anything to me," Seryozha said.

She offered no explanation, however, and just kept repeating, "Come now, Seryozhenka, quickly."

She then carried him outside—it was a cold, misty night—where a tall woman in black was waiting for her; a few steps later, around the corner, they got into a motor car that immediately set off at a phenomenal speed, bearing them along unfamiliar streets. Later on, half dreaming, Seryozha glimpsed a train, and when he awoke it turned out that he was in fact on board this train, but something had imperceptibly altered; then, at last, his mother told him that he was going to live with her in France, not with his father in London, that she would buy him an electric train with all sorts of carriages and wagons, and that now they would never again be parted, although Papa would sometimes come to visit.

Seryozha would later recall that evening time and time again: his mother's unfamiliar, tender face, her hurried whispers, the alarming quiet in his father's cold house in London, and then the journey by car and by train. Only later did he learn that they had crossed the Channel by steamer, but he did not harbour even the faintest memory of it, for he had been sound asleep and had no idea how he had arrived at his destination. He was seven years old at the time, and this journey marked the beginning of myriad other events. After this, he travelled far and wide with his mother; one summer's day, however, towards evening, on a terrace overlooking the sea, where he and his mother were taking dinner together, Seryozha's father calmly strode in, took off his hat, bowed to Seryozha's mother, kissed Seryozha and said:

"Well, well, Olga Alexandrovna. We'll consider today the end of this little romantic episode, shall we?" As he stood behind Seryozha's chair, his great hand tousled the boy's hair. He glanced at his wife and broke into quick German. Seryozha did not understand a word of it until his father said in Russian: "Really, Olya, aren't you tired of all this?" Recollecting himself, he immediately switched back into German. A few minutes later, Seryozha managed to catch another phrase that he could understand—this time it was his mother who uttered it: "Darling, you never did understand, and you're incapable of understanding it. You're in no position to judge." Seryozha's father nodded cynically in agreement. Waves lapped beneath the terrace while a brown-green palm drooped motionlessly over them and the dark-bluish water glittered in the little bay, not far from a narrow road. Amid the silence Seryozha's mother swung her tanned leg, looking serenely and expectantly at the boy's father, as though studying him, despite the fact that he was just the same as always—tall, immaculate, broad and clean-shaven.

"German's such a wretched language," he said at last.

"Inherently so?"

He laughed and said, "Yes, even independent of the circumstances that…"

Seryozha's mother sent him to his room.

"Won't Papa be leaving?" he asked, immediately finding himself high up in the air in front of his father's smooth face with its large deep-blue eyes.

"No, Seryozha, I'm not leaving. Not again," he said.

His parents had a long conversation on the terrace. Seryozha managed to read half a book, but still they went on talking. His mother then made a telephone call; Seryozha listened, lying on the floor, as she said:

"*Impossible ce soir, mon chéri.*" And then, "*Si je le regrette? Je le crois bien, chéri.*" *

---

* Impossible tonight, darling… If I regret it? I believe so, darling.

Thus Seryozha understood that *chéri* would not be coming today, and so he was left feeling very pleased, since he did not like this man, whom, after his mother, he had also called *chéri*, thinking it to be his name, eliciting laughter from that dark face with its fixed grin, above which hung tight, thick curls of hair, as black as the Devil himself. *Chéri* never showed up again after that. There was, however, another man, somewhat similar to him, who also spoke with an accent, both in French and in Russian.

Seryozha's father did not leave that day, but stayed on for a fortnight, only to disappear early one morning without saying goodbye. After that, in Paris, at a railway station, he met his wife and child with flowers, sweets and toys; he carried the flowers in his hand, but the rest of it lay waiting in that same long dark-blue motor car that Seryozha remembered from London. They installed themselves in an enormous new mansion block, where Seryozha was able to ride a bicycle from one room of the apartment to the next; everything was going well until Seryozha's mother left once again, taking with her only a small *nécessaire* and showering Seryozha in kisses. She returned, in any case, exactly ten days later, but discovered her husband gone, finding only a laconic note: "I consider a period of absence to be necessary and in our mutual interest. I wish you…" Two days later, in the evening, the telephone rang—Seryozha's mother was not at home, although she was expected at any moment; Seryozha was called to the telephone and heard from afar his father's very funny (or at least so it seemed to him) voice, asking him whether he had been bored. Seryozha said no, the day before he and his mother had pretended to be robbers and it had been a lot of fun.

"With your mother?" enquired his father's odd-sounding voice.

"Yes, with Mama," said Seryozha and, turning around, he saw her. She had come in without Seryozha's noticing her light footsteps on the rug. She took the receiver from him and launched into rapid conversation.

"Yes, again," she said. "No, I don't think so… Of course… Well, to each his own… Yes… When?… No, just repaying kindness with kindness; remember, you met me with flowers… What, the flowers are for him?… The toys will do just fine… All right."

"Why are you always going away?" Seryozha asked his mother. "Are you bored here with us?"

"My silly Seryozhenka," his mother said. "My silly boy, my silly little fair-haired one. When you grow up, you'll understand."

Just as Seryozha, from his very first days of consciousness, could remember his mother and father, so too, clearly and abidingly, could he remember his Aunt Liza, her black hair, her red lips and an aroma that mixed the tobacco from the English cigarettes she smoked with her perfume, warm, silky fabrics, and that light acidity of her own. It was a very faint smell, but it was so characteristic of her that it was impossible to forget, just like her peculiar voice, which always sounded distant and strangely pleasant. Yet however much the lives of Seryozha's mother and father

11

were full of apologies, conversations in that incomprehensible German, departures, journeys, returns and surprises, Liza's existence was by the same measure devoid of any irregularity. Truly, she was a living reproach to Seryozha's parents—everything in her life was so clear, perfect and crystalline that Seryozha, lying in his favourite position on the floor in the hallway, once caught his father saying to his mother:

"To look at Liza, one could never think that she might suddenly give birth to a child one day, but then again…"

Seryozha's mother would always regard Liza with slightly guilty eyes; even his father seemed to shrink in her presence, and everyone would almost apologize to Aunt Liza for their personal imperfections, which were particularly ugly in light of her incontestable moral grandeur. However, an elusive memory dimly surfaced in Seryozha's mind: when he had been very little, Aunt Liza had taken him out for a walk, and with them had come a man who talked animatedly with his aunt. But this had happened so very long ago, and the memory of it was so indistinct that Seryozha was no longer sure that it had not all been a dream. Aunt Liza's natural state was one of quiet surprise. She was amazed by everything: the behaviour of Seryozha's parents, the very possibility of such behaviour, the books and newspapers she read, the crimes they contained; the only things that failed to amaze her were improbable and heroic deeds—for example, when a person laid down his life for someone, rescued a group of people or chose death over ignominy. She was slim, her skin was almost as smooth as Seryozha's father's, she was immaculate, and her hands were always cold and rather hard. One day, when all four of them—Seryozha, his parents and Aunt Liza—happened to be driving past a shooting stall in the street, Seryozha's father suddenly stopped the car and said:

"Well, ladies, shall we relive the good old days and have a shot?"

Seryozha's mother never once hit the bullseye; his father missed several times, although he generally shot very well, and only Aunt Liza, fixing the cardboard target directly in her sight, put five bullets right through it, knocking down ball after ball on the dancing jets of the fountain.

"Your hand's as steady as a rock, Liza," Seryozha's father then said.

As Seryozha grew older, he began to understand people better, and his instinctive judgements about everything gradually gained perspective; he began to suspect that Aunt Liza was unlike other people, since everything would change over the course of their lives, depending upon circumstances, events and influences; they might find absurd what only a year ago had seemed completely practical, and so often they contradicted themselves and changed on the whole so much that it was difficult to tell who was clever and who a fool, even who was beautiful and who ugly; in other words, the strength of their resistance to the outside influences that defined their lives was negligible, and they exhibited constancy only in very rare and limited respects. Seryozha knew hoards of people, for through his father's home passed the most varied stream of guests,

13

visitors, petitioners, friends, women and relatives. Aunt Liza differed from them all in that nothing about her ever altered. That complex network of feelings, knowledge and ideas, which for others was shifting and fluid, remained for her just as constant and as static as it had always been—as if the world were some sort of fixed concept. So thought Seryozha about Liza; so, too, thought others about her, and this went on for many years until an event that displayed the manifest fallacy of these notions took place. However, even a few years prior to these events, Seryozha, who knew Liza more intimately than the rest, had begun to doubt the accuracy of the image of her that he had created, when Liza and his father had an argument in front of him about a recently published novel. The novel recounted the story of a man who had dedicated his life to a woman who did not love him, a woman for whom he had left another woman, to whom he had been dearer than anything on earth. Seryozha's father defended this man. "You have to understand, Liza, the point is that he was drawn to the *vilaine*, whereas the other woman was almost totally irrelevant. So what if she loved him? That's all well and good, but really, he wanted something else, you understand?"

"I'm not saying that I don't understand the reason," said Liza. "The reason is clear enough. But the matter lies elsewhere: in the idiotic betrayal, in the futility of it. She deserved happiness more than that other woman."

"Happiness isn't deserved, Liza," said Seryozha's father curtly. "It is either given to you or it isn't."

14

"You're wrong; it is deserved," said Liza resolutely.

Seryozha listened. He was surprised by his father's soft, quiet voice, while Aunt Liza continued implacably to drive home her point, her eyes narrow and wild.

Seryozha asked, "Papa, have you noticed how pretty Aunt Liza is?"

His father became flustered and said that he had noticed it long ago and that everyone knew it to be true. Aunt Liza got up and left, leaving Seryozha's father looking embarrassed, which might have seemed surprising, for the argument had been an abstract one and could not have borne any relation either to Seryozha's father or to his aunt. That was the first time Seryozha had ever seen his Aunt Liza toppled from her immutable serenity.

In general, Seryozha would see his mother and father relatively infrequently—Aunt Liza was his constant companion. His father had affairs to attend to, business, trips away; his mother led her own completely separate life. Often for two or three days at a time Seryozha would be deprived of her rapid footsteps, only for them to reappear later; she would come into his room and say: "Hello, Seryozhenka, hello, my darling, I've missed you so terribly." She usually spoke to him in such warm, comforting terms, always latching onto what he was interested in at that very moment, playing with him enthusiastically, showing him kindness and tenderness for hours on end. She knew why some dogs had long tails, why cats were aloof, why horses have eyes on the sides of their heads and what the length of the average crocodile was. Aunt Liza knew all this, too, but her answers somehow never satisfied Seryozha, because they lacked something essential, perhaps this comfort and warmth. But Seryozha was happiest only after everyone had gone, and he was left alone in the care of the housekeeper. Such an event would usually be heralded by the arrival of Sergey Sergeyevich with some particularly intricate toy; Seryozha's father would give it to him, expressing his hope that Seryozha would behave himself and asking him not to get upset; a few minutes later Seryozha would watch from the window as his father's long motor car pulled away. Now he could do whatever he liked. He would shoot at a portrait of his grandmother with a bow and arrow, slide down the banisters, ride in the lift until his head hurt—up and down, up and down—spend all his free time lying on the floor, gorge himself on pastries, pour soup down the lavatory, eat handfuls of salt and refuse to wash. In the evening, as he lay on the floor, he would rub his eyes and be delighted to see green stars appear before him.

Later, as he grew older, no one curtailed his freedom, and so he began to appreciate that his parents had essentially nothing to do with him. The constant stream of people that had lodged in his memory not only never halted, but in fact seemed to grow in strength—and he lived apart from this. When he was sixteen, he invited Aunt Liza to the theatre for the first time. By now her authority had somewhat diminished; she would laugh at some of the things he said, and ask for his opinion—and so Seryozha felt himself almost her equal. Both she and Seryozha spoke of his parents as "them"—as though subconsciously setting themselves apart. They read together, listened to the same music, liked the same books. Liza was a whole fifteen years older than Seryozha. He began to see her in his dreams, in blurry, surreal situations; then, one night—it was late spring, sometime after two o'clock in the morning, and Seryozha was reading in his room—light suddenly flooded the whole apartment, and footsteps and voices could be heard; Seryozha's parents had returned from a ball, bringing with them a few people "to round off the evening" at home; a few minutes later there was a familiar knock at the door and in came Liza, wearing a revealing black dress that exposed her back, with her bare—cold, thought Seryozha—arms and a plunging neckline. Her eyes seemed bigger than usual beneath those erect lashes, and her excited smile was unlike the one that usually adorned her face. At that moment Seryozha was seized by an inexplicable urge, so much so that his voice broke when he began to speak.

"You've been reading too much, Seryozha," she said, sitting beside him and laying her hand on his shoulder. "I just came in to say goodnight."

And with that she walked out, having failed to notice the strange frame of mind Seryozha seemed to find himself in. After the door had closed behind her, Seryozha just lay there without bothering to undress; he felt slightly nauseous—it was a vague, premonitory and pleasant sensation.

And so, with incredible speed, in the two months that elapsed between that evening and Seryozha's departure for the coast, a deep and lasting change took place, which began when the entire idyllic world of Seryozha's lengthy, belated childhood crumbled, disappearing for ever. During this time, however, nothing altered substantially: his mother's voice would sound just as warm and tender as it had done before, whenever she spoke to someone on the telephone; his father would travel back and forth across the city as he had always done; and by evening, just as before, the enormous rooms of the apartment would throng with various people, and everything would be as it had always been. But all of a sudden Seryozha came to understand a number of things of which he had already been aware, but concerning which he had fostered an entirely incorrect notion. Snatches of conversation between his mother and father now became intelligible to him, as did Liza's tempered exasperation; he noticed many other things—that money was being thrown in all directions and expended in much vaster quantities than was necessary. He suddenly grasped how his mother lived—it aroused in him pity mixed with tenderness. Sometimes, when present during conversations in the drawing room, he would listen closely to what was being said, watch out for the most curious leaps of intonation and sometimes, wilfully closing himself off to the meaning of the phrases that had been uttered, listen to their musical excursions, as though it were some peculiar concert—with crescendos, diminuendos, monotone baritone notes, high-pitched women's voices that would gasp and break off, only to rise again afterwards to the deep, tuneless accompaniment of a croaking bass; closing his eyes tight, Seryozha could see distinctly before him a bass drum with a taut, lifelessly impassive skin—right there, where there was no drum, but a venerable old chap, a philosopher and professional advisory specialist in matters of international law.

Seryozha's father ranked among the few people who had acquired significant wealth through inheritance and who not only had resisted squandering it, but had in fact increased it. This was made possible by the fact that he was—generous, rash and magnanimous—in business astute and essentially cautious, and also primarily because he had been attended all his life by blind luck. He had enterprises in several countries, thousands of people worked for him, and his status could be credited to an acquaintance with every celebrity, as well as to the fact that his house was frequented by musicians, writers, singers, engineers, industrialists, actors and representatives of that particular sort of people who are always elegantly and becomingly dressed, yet the sources of whose income—if one were to trace them, which, in the majority of cases, would have required either chance or the unceremoniousness of a police investigation—are apparently almost always of the kind that can never be owned to. While Liza would regard these people with disgust, Seryozha's father would pat them on the back, and generally exude that broad, false candour and sincerity, the true value of which was known only by those close to him. When Seryozha told his father that he was being robbed, his father laughed.

"You don't say."

Then, still laughing and looking at Seryozha with his

lively eyes, he said, "Shall I tell you who's robbing me and by how much?"

He explained to Seryozha that that was just the way of things, that people would carry on stealing, regardless. This conviction, however, aroused in him neither distress nor surprise; he took it as a matter of course and sometimes amused himself by making fools of his household staff—as he did, for example, with his driver, who had robbed him of oil, petrol and a thousand other things, and invariably presented him with "bogus" invoices. He told the owner of the garage where everything was usually bought that it was setting him back too much money and that he felt compelled to change his suppliers—as proof he presented the invoices, the sight of which horrified the owner of the garage, who just repeated in a feeble voice, "*Oh, non, monsieur, jamais, monsieur,*"* and immediately brought the books, which showed entirely disparate sums of money; the difference was almost half. However, he said nothing about this to the driver, to whom the catastrophe only became apparent later at the garage, where they explained everything. He was already preparing to pack his bags, when that very day the car was ordered; Sergey Sergeyevich mentioned only in passing that the price of petrol seemed to have come down, while patting the driver on the shoulder and remarking, "*Ah, sacré Joseph,*"† laughing to himself the whole journey. The driver, on the other hand, after some

* Oh, no, Monsieur, never, Monsieur.
† You're quite a man, Joseph.

20

time, and following much hesitation and a clash of conflicting emotions, left, for the daily awareness that he was now unable to steal, and was instead forced to make do with his salary, reduced him to a nervous wreck. He was a simple man, of Auvergne peasant stock, insensible to physical fatigue, but mentally and spiritually defenceless against unforeseen and, in particular, unlawful predicaments. He was later caught stealing rather large sums of money and was on the verge of prison—from which Sergey Sergeyevich saved him—but it was too late, and the result was that instead of prison he was placed in a mental asylum, which he left a completely broken man.

Other such instances yielded less tragic results, but one way or another Sergey Sergeyevich did indeed know by how much he was being robbed and only limited it by including these sums of money as independent and naturally occurring items in his budgetary calculations, which contained, anyway, a great many items. He subsidized theatres, supported young performers whose talents he himself doubted, paid mostly everywhere and for everyone, as was necessitated by his position of great wealth, and performed his duty in exactly the same manner as he did everything else—with pleasure, with a smile, and with seemingly indiscriminate approval. He would say, for example, to the editor of a large tabloid newspaper that was going to carry some articles promoting one of his enterprises—having just donated a vast sum of money to the charitable aims of some implausible, fantastical organization that had lodged itself in the mind of the editor

21

only half an hour previously, blossoming there like some romantic mirage, the illusoriness of which was patently clear to any ordinary person—"I know, my dear chap, that your incorruptible integrity…" And the editor would leave feeling a complex mix of gratitude and pity for this naive millionaire, as well as the vague suspicion that if the naive millionaire was only making out that he believed, while in actual fact knew everything, then this endowment and these heartfelt words about integrity were just far too humiliating to endure. With a similarly selfless belief in the future he took on a singer of uncertain national-ity, although clearly of the southern variety—hair as black as boot polish, the whites of his eyes a dirty yellow, and hands of dubious hygiene. In all this he never gave more than was expected of him by the complex system of values he had built up over long years of experience and accord-ing to which, for example, subsidies given to people of southern extraction were always significantly less than those given to representatives of the northern races, for whom he entertained a sort of ethnic predilection. A never-ending army of cadgers passed through his life, an astonishing variety of petitioners, ranging from respect-able people with caressing baritones and complicated personal histories—never failing to include a few moments of pathos, most often inspired by reading not quite third-but second-rate novels—to those rasping, blurred figures, infinitely removed from any abstract notions and focusing exclusively on matters of primary importance, the cost of which wavered between two and five francs. A great many people wrote him letters with various propositions, from the laconically self-assured "not bad-looking" to the "strange allure" and even the "indomitable cruelty" of some of the more uncompromising female candidates for conjugal bliss, the very concept of which likewise ranged an appalling variety. His life, however, was not all letters and requests for money: twice had there been attempts on his life, and both times he had been saved by sheer chance, by that same blind luck that never failed him and led him out of even the most hopeless of situations, like the death sentence he received from a Revolutionary tribunal in the Crimea, in which not one man had been sober; the sentry of that poorly secured hangar where he was being held was killed by a stray bullet from a sailor who shot wide of the mark, allowing Sergey Sergeyevich to make a run for it and reach the quayside in Sebastopol, where not a single ship had been in sight— and only at dusk did their silhouettes loom darkly in the roadstead. Casting aside his jacket and boots, he jumped from the quay into the icy autumn water, and amid the cold, stormy evening he swam out to a British destroyer, to whose captain he recounted his story half an hour later, laughing at particularly inappropriate moments— for example, when he told him about the hearing at the Revolutionary tribunal. Two days later, at a cabaret in Constantinople, he paid for champagne for almost half the crew and sang Irish shanties that he did not understand, which did not matter in any case; he committed them to memory with the same ease as he did everything else. This sense of ease was by and large characteristic of his whole impetuous, lucky life. He never sat pondering important decisions; from the very outset the solution would appear clear and preclusive of any error, which would simply have been an obvious blunder. He grasped everything so quickly that he acquired a habit of not finishing his sentences. Just as a well-educated person, when reading a book, does not waste time on the gradual, sequential combination of letters and does not repeat the words to himself, but skims over the familiar image of printed lines with his eyes, everything passing by quickly and obediently, so too Sergey Sergeyevich found his way about business, the outcomes and the scope of any enterprise or initiative or trust, which, on the face of it, seemed to necessitate lengthy study. At any rate, he never demanded that others try to keep up with him in the conclusions he would draw, as if he anticipated dealing with cretins; and whenever one of his directors displayed a quick grasp of something, it would always pleasantly surprise him. Since, however, in both cases he would say the same complimentary, amiable things, those who did not know him sufficiently well would suppose that he was unable to distinguish a good worker from a bad one, and that it was just by sheer luck that he was surrounded almost everywhere by able staff.

For all that, however, he had never truly loved (just as he had never been totally candid), and both Olga Alexandrovna and Liza knew this. He was always good to his wife, as one would be to a best friend, but here—for the first time in his life—she had expected of him something else, the very thing she had read about in the novels he continued to deride, because it was clear to him that these books had been written by clumsy, not particularly cultured and, more often than not, primitive people; yet he knew without doubt that the finest pages of various literatures had been written on these very same subjects—and he understood and even loved these things, but here his impeccable sense of ease and his infallibility crumbled, and he recognized his guilt before Olga Alexandrovna, whom he had once, at the beginning of their marriage, been unable to answer, when, lifting her dark, tender eyes to him, she had said:

"You're talking about good relations. I, Seryozha, am talking about love."

Love truly was the most important thing in Olga Alexandrovna's life and the only thing that really interested and captivated her. Everything else had, as it were, only a provisional value, and was positioned as if functionally dependent on what really mattered. She had to leave, to go somewhere or other—because an assignation awaited her there; she had to read such-and-such a book—so that she could talk about it with the only person whose conversation she found stimulating; she had to have a pretty dress—so that she would be adored; she had, in general— any otherwise would have been impossible—to love and to suffer. She had married aged eighteen, but even before the marriage she had known three failed love affairs. She had fallen in love with Sergey Sergeyevich the moment she set eyes on him; it was at a ball, in Moscow, and then she told her mother that she would marry this man, which did indeed happen a few months later. She had never been good-looking, but was possessed of such a mighty force of attraction that was difficult and ultimately futile to resist. Everybody loved her—her parents, who would forgive her everything, her maid, her brothers and sisters; she obtained everything she wanted with a strange ease; children and animals loved her too. Even Sergey Sergeyevich, who held a condescending view of women, immediately felt such an attraction to her that he himself would laugh and joke about it, although resist it he could not. After their first kiss, she confessed that she loved him dearly and wanted to marry him. She was of diminutive stature; her hair was black; above her dark eyes were short little eyelashes that made her eyes seem larger than they really were: the first impression she made was one of rare youth and health— and indeed the blood coursing through her veins was abundant and unwearying; she knew neither fatigue nor illness, nor even minor ailments. She was unfaithful to her husband four months after they married, but it happened by chance and was insignificant. Following the birth of her son she stopped paying attention to her appearance for a whole year, spent all her time with the child, looking on avidly as he learnt to walk, and was wholly captivated by him. Later, one evening, having put him to bed, she paused in front of a mirror, carefully looked herself over, sighed and went into her husband's room to ask him how on earth he could still love her. He was writing at the time and, tearing himself away from the sheet of paper for a moment, said, "Despite it all, Lyolya," and continued writing, until she came right up to him and sat on his lap.

Then the routine argument about love reared its head; it was always Olga Alexandrovna, for whom Sergey Sergeyevich no longer felt that irresistible attraction that had brought him to marry her, who began these arguments; the airy, almost transparent mist that had suffused the first months of their intimacy now seemed inexplicable to him. And so began the period of his negative love, as Olga Alexandrovna called it; he readily forgave her everything, never became angry with her and satisfied her every wish, but in no way could he say that without her his life would lose its meaning.

"Well then, what do you think about adultery?"

"It's all a matter of temperament and, to a certain degree, ethics," he said.

"They're counterfeit, meaningless words," she said. "What is temperament? What are ethics?"

He extracted two volumes of *Brockhaus and Efron* from the shelves, handed them to her and said: "Read these and try to think. I know you're unaccustomed to it. But it is possible, Lyolya."

As she was leaving, he called after her: "And chance, too."

Later on, abroad, he was presented with a multitude of opportunities to test these theories on the causes of adultery, also because after a while he noticed that Olga Alexandrovna's outgoings had increased significantly. He quickly calculated how much she ought to be spending, not allowing for exceptional and unforeseeable expenditures, and saw that the amount of money disappearing was more than twice that sum. Then he spoke, casually, as always, of blackmail and of the general imprudence of writing letters. And since Olga Alexandrovna made a show of not understanding, he told her that he nevertheless knew everything and that she should not fear exposure. After a while, a man in a black overcoat, a black bowler hat, a pair of black shoes and a black tie turned up, whom Sergey Sergeyevich welcomed with his usual cordiality, while announcing that he had precisely five minutes at his disposal. When this man explained to him the purpose of his visit, Sergey Sergeyevich advised him to look elsewhere, since the matter would surely bring him nothing but misery. The man, undismayed, began mentioning newspapers. Sergey Sergeyevich stood up in order to stress that the meeting was running over, and said:

"You would do best not to try that—and believe me, I know what I'm talking about."

As the man was making his exit, Sergey Sergeyevich asked him with an inquisitive smile: "Would you like fifty francs for your trouble?…"

Never again did he receive this man or his successors, nor did he reply to the many letters that arrived, and so the matter was settled, when he said to his wife—fragmentarily, as always, and without explanation:

"I do wish you would choose more respectable ones, Lyolya."

He articulated this phrase, wanting to give his wife some friendly advice, though knowing in advance that she would fail to glean his meaning. He had long known that her

choice could in no way be guided by any rational considerations, and that she selected men not according to their
merits, but based on some obscure combination of physical
attraction and an intuitive presentiment of their own moral
constitution, in which these same ethical considerations
more often than not played no role whatsoever. Sergey
Sergeyevich also understood why he himself was unsuited
to his wife. The reason was partly that he found talking
about his own feelings tedious—he would listen to her for
a few minutes out of delicacy, and then say: "Yes, Lyolya,
I know," and indeed he would know everything that she
had planned to say. These people—these others—were so
often emotionally primitive: they could never fathom their
emotions, and every one of Olga Alexandrovna's affairs
was like a new and illuminating excursion into sentimental
lands, where she played the role of the guide—as Sergey
Sergeyevich had once said of her during a conversation
with Liza. Generally speaking, not all was well at home,
but the only one not to notice this was Olga Alexandrovna,
and although Sergey Sergeyevich pretended not to notice,
he in fact knew everything right down to the smallest detail;
Liza was aware of this, and with good reason, and now
Seryozha sensed it as well.

Sergey Sergeyevich's family rarely spent the summer together. That year, almost like clockwork, everything came about at the very last moment. Olga Alexandrovna, after several days of especial anxiety and having resolved many agonizing questions about whether or not she was within her right to act as her desires dictated, suddenly left, indefinitely—for Italy. Prior to her departure, with beating heart and burning cheeks, she had gone to Sergey Sergeyevich. Despite the fact that Olga Alexandrovna's entire life had been made up of these departures and betrayals, and one might have thought by now she would have accustomed herself to them, each time she experienced them just as forcefully, as though in the first flush of youth, and wracked herself as always, for she was doing something depraved and illicit, and through her actions she was doing wrong by her husband and Seryozha. However, her object in sacrificing all these fruitless emotions seemed to her so wonderful that there could be no doubt as to her final decision. And just as she had a profound understanding of her duty as a wife and mother, so too were her delusions about an imminent departure fresh and unfading. Each time she would leave for good, for a world of uncertainty, condemning herself, perhaps, to a semi-impoverished existence. If it turned out otherwise, it would not be on her account.

Yet as she set off for the apartment, she suddenly remembered that it was Thursday, Sergey Sergeyevich's day for receiving visitors. So she telephoned him and immediately heard his flat voice reply: "I'm very busy, Lyolya... Yes... I need at least an hour... You can't?... Very well, I'll be with you shortly."

He walked into the room. She had already donned her hat and gloves, and was wearing a travelling dress; in her hands she carried a *nécessaire*. In her eyes Sergey Sergeyevich once again saw that troubled look that he knew so well. Yet because he saw it, his face did not at all alter, just as his smile and his voice did not alter either.

"Going somewhere, are we, Lyolya?" he said.

"Yes," replied Olga Alexandrovna, but this "yes", despite her best intentions, sounded flat and unintentionally theatrical.

"Far away?"

"To Italy."

"A fine country," said Sergey Sergeyevich dreamily. "But then, you know that just as well as I do; indeed, it isn't the first time you've gone there. You've been out of sorts lately; I think it's an admirable idea, it's sure to cheer you up. I'm delighted for you. Well, all the best. Do write."

He kissed her hand and left. She stood for a few seconds, then sighed and began making her way downstairs to the entrance, where a motor car was already waiting for her.

Neither Seryozha nor Liza was at home—they had been out since morning.

Sergey Sergeyevich returned to his apartment, where a familiar visitor awaited him—the celebrated actress Lola Aînée, who had come to ask him to finance a music hall she was planning to open. She was a very old woman, of an age with Sergey Sergeyevich's mother, yet she remained firmly convinced of her irresistibility; she had undergone many surgical operations and spent hours daily on massages, her appearance and her *toilette*. At first sight, particularly from afar, she really might have looked young. Sergey Sergeyevich glanced momentarily at the motionless skin on her face and those long black eyelashes, starkly curled heavenwards, and recalled that only a year or two ago this woman had married a man more than thirty years her junior.

"*Toujours délicieuse, toujours charmante*," said Sergey Sergeyevich, greeting her. "*Je suis vraiment heureux de vous voir.*"*

She smiled, revealing a fine set of teeth. Yet she felt none too well—as she had done now for many years. These days she was tormented by haemorrhoids; it was as though she were sitting on red-hot coals, and whenever she laughed or blew her nose, a sharp pain beginning in that very place shot through her whole body. When the pain abated, she would start to feel deathly tired and struggled not to let her head drop down onto her chest. Occasionally this would prove beyond her, and she would lapse into slumber for a second. Opening her eyes later and starting, she would explain that

* Always delectable, always enchanting… I'm so pleased to see you.

32

she suffered from such momentary *éblouissements*,* which she attributed to strenuous work. Hers had been a long, tumultuous and, ultimately, difficult life; there was almost no one left alive who had witnessed her stage debut. But she would never pause to reflect on this. She never paused to reflect on anything. Her memory was cluttered with all the songs, cues, accents and intonations of her endless repertoire. Since she was essentially stupid, she had learnt nothing, in spite of her long career; she understood nothing of art and had blind faith in theatre critics. She truly believed the unfortunate *La Dame aux camélias* to be a masterpiece; but then, she had been a very close acquaintance of the author's and believed him to be a genius. She went into raptures over Corneille's tragedies, which, among other things, she could not understand on account of her lack of culture; however, it was with no less enthusiasm that she regarded many contemporary plays, which were wholly unskilled and devoid of even the remotest connection to art, whose authors were situated on the level of her mental faculties—with the sole difference that while her mind was static, theirs exhibited a certain primitive dynamism. Her life had passed in plays and romances, each one of which she recalled, despite their monstrous quantity. In her youth she had indeed been rather pretty, and in fact it was this incontestable animalistic radiancy of hers that had determined her career. She had come to Paris from Normandy as a sixteen-year-old girl with the intention of

* Swoons.

becoming a parlour maid, and even before her departure her elderly aunt, who had spent many years in Paris, taught her how she ought to behave, how best to rob her employers, how to talk to suppliers, and generally provided her with a great many pieces of advice, which Lola—her real name was Marie—intended to follow to the letter. Yet it turned out differently, for she immediately stumbled upon a man who was utterly alone, a passionate lover of the theatre. He was reasonably wealthy and headed the theatre column in one of the right-leaning newspapers. Since even in those days he was beginning to grow old, and seeing as a tempestuous life had worn him out, signs of this weariness and also of a certain naivety born of his enthusiastic but limited mind began to tell in the style of his articles and reviews, which acquired a conversationally declamatory tone. "*Est-il possible que ce soit ainsi? Allons, allons!*" or "*Mais si, mon pauvre lecteur, mais si!*"*

Progressivists were simply, in his opinion, *des gens de mauvaise volonté.*† Deep down, however, he was a good man with a pure heart, which was all the more astonishing given that he had spent his life in the theatre. His love for Lola was so peculiarly and unexpectedly intense that it did not at all correspond to his physical abilities. Because he was very much in love, there was not a single virtue he failed to find in Lola, and so he decided that the only thing worthy of her was the stage. He was a very influential man, closely

* Can this possibly be so? Come, come!... Oh yes, my poor reader, oh yes!
† People of ill intent.

acquainted with all the actors and directors of the theatres, and so, thanks to him, Lola, following several months of rehearsals, debuted at a small theatre on the outskirts of Paris. Since then, her career had been unstoppable. Her first benefactor soon died, after a sumptuous dinner with champagne and wines of the very best vintage, the cruel perfection of which his already flagging body was unable to withstand. He died immediately afterwards, scarcely having managed to get into bed, and Lola, covering her naked body with an overcoat, set out in search of a doctor, who arrived and said: "*Il n'est plus, mon enfant.*"* She stood by the bed, her overcoat flung open, and the doctor, unable to resist—suddenly, for the first time in his life—the overwhelming, uncontrollable urge, began kissing this submissive body in absolute ecstasy and at that very moment whisked Lola away to his apartment, where she remained for some time.

Such were the key events in her life; they had happened so infinitely long ago—more than half a century. Thereafter everything had followed according to a set formula that had been established once and for all: plays, benefactors, benefactors, plays. When she was twenty, she met her first lover: that is, the first man for whom she felt any strong physical attraction. But he, too, died soon after, throwing himself from the fourth floor of a stairwell in a drunken stupor—he was a decorator by trade. He was the only man she had ever loved. The rest of them—with those stock phrases

* He is gone, my child.

that forever reminded her of lines from a play, with their absurd, pitiful furore, and others, some truly remarkable people in their day—left her indifferent: *elle les laissait faire.*[*] Among them numbered politicians, writers and musicians, but none could even remotely compare in terms of allure with her dead decorator, a Corsican by birth, who with his firm hand would deliver a resounding smack on her naked behind, and who had smelt so pleasantly of cheap wine and the strong sweat of a peasant's unkempt body. As time marched on, however, several journalists constructed an entirely disparate image of Lola, which bore no resemblance to her at all. She let them write as they pleased—and so there appeared discourses on the plastic arts, on Spanish theatre, on Italian painting and even on Russian literature, of which she knew nothing at all. Little by little a reputation for erudition formed around her. Once, having had a little too much to drink, she reproached an old friend of hers, an expert author of short articles about classical ballet: "*Tu m'as traitée d'érudite, tu croyais peut-être que je ne le saurais pas?*"[†]

The expert author of short articles about classical ballet was unsure how to take this and decided in the final analysis that it must have been a joke. The years passed, but her life remained exactly the same: dawn, rising late, love affairs, those same words about love, divinity, ecstasy, restaurants, wine, divans—and despite that most robust of

* She let them get on with it.
† You called me erudite; perhaps you thought I wouldn't know?

constitutions, by the age of forty her heart began to play up, mysterious pains appeared in her stomach region, and a renowned doctor prescribed a more measured pace of life. Sometimes she would suddenly think that it was too late, and she had wasted the past twenty years in a struggle with age and ailment. Little by little it reached a stage whereby she was forbidden everything she enjoyed. She could no longer eat or drink to her heart's content; she could no longer take very hot baths—she could no longer do anything. But even with this did she make her peace. She had long been in possession of a certain fortune, and she could have headed off to the south, where she owned a splendid villa near Nice, but she refused outright to forgo the stage, to which she had become too accustomed over the course of fifty years. Most recently she had started performing in the music hall, and so now, having resolved to open her own theatre, but grudging the money for it, she turned to Sergey Sergeyevich, whom she knew just like everyone else. She explained to him that it would be a magnanimous gesture on his part, for which a substantial Parisian audience would be grateful to him, but that, essentially, it would be an extraordinarily lucrative investment at the same time, since the music hall would immediately be a sell-out. She told Sergey Sergeyevich that she already had ideas for a revue, which could be called *Ça à Paris*—"*Il y aura des décors somptueux*,"* and she showered Sergey Sergeyevich with a whole cascade of words, unpersuasive in their lush

* The staging will be sumptuous.

37

banality, as if they had been borrowed from that wretched language used to pen newspaper reviews of opening nights. It was that same style employed by her first benefactor, countless examples of which she would have occasion to read her whole life. They included *"décors somptueux"*, *"tableaux enlevés à un rythme endiablé"*, *"le charme étrange de mademoiselle"*, *"la voix chaude et captivante de monsieur"*,* and so on. Lola was unable to speak using any other words; no one ever explained to her that this language was poor and inexpressive. She herself had no inkling of this. Sergey Sergeyevich listened attentively to Lola, occasionally intoning *"merveilleux"*, *"admirable"*, *"il fallait le trouver…"*† and mused that had Lola been younger, she would have been able to arrange all this at once and would not have turned to him. Now he had to find a pretext to avoid having to fund this enterprise, which would have been a ludicrous waste of money. Therefore, as soon as Lola had finished, he said in a thoughtful and convincing tone:

"J'aime beaucoup votre projet, madame. Oui, je l'aime beaucoup." He paused for a second, as if thoughtfully imagining all the splendour of the project. *"Une salle pleine à craquer et la foule en délire, la même foule qui vous a toujours adorée."*‡

He paused again, then sighed and added:

---

* Sumptuous staging… scenes dashed off at a fiendish pace… the strange charm of Mademoiselle… the warm and captivating voice of Monsieur.
† Marvellous… splendid… we've got to find a way.
‡ I like your plan very much, Madame. Yes, I like it very much… A room full to bursting and the cheering crowd, the very crowd that has always adored you.

"Unfortunately, I leave for London tomorrow, for several weeks. As soon as I return I'll telephone, and, believe me, I should be both delighted and proud... you understand..."

With a deliberate, quick motion, Lola rose from her chair, which creaked gently, and throughout her weary body flowed a multitude of pains, mingling with each other in a single sensation of haziness and light-headedness: her legs, now suffering pins and needles, cracked at the joints, her haemorrhoids ached, there was a throbbing in her right temple, yet her face retained that same "dazzling" smile, the very one that had figured in every photograph of her and seemed so strange, because it should have accentuated her false dentures, which were made of the highest-quality material. She held out a trembling hand, its nails painted bright red, to Sergey Sergeyevich and made her way to the door with lively little steps, which only two people were capable of appreciating fully: her doctor and Lola herself. On the way home, she recalled Sergey Sergeyevich's words about *la foule qui l'a toujours adorée*, and again she smiled. She truly did believe that they adored her, truly did believe in her theatrical calling, her sole reason to suffer and to live, since everything else had vanished already. It was for the sake of this that she accepted the humiliation, the rejection, for this—for the illusion of her unfading youth—that she had recently married a man who, despite his best intentions, at certain moments could not hide his disgust at her—and she would feign that it slipped her attention. All this was done for *la foule qui l'adorait*, which in actual fact was as non-existent as her youth. Yet Lola never credited this, for to do so would have been to admit that all that remained for her was death, which was more terrible than all her ailments combined.

The next visitor, who detained Sergey Sergeyevich for only a few minutes, was a famous playwright, director and actor, all in one, the author of countless plays, a full-bodied man of fifty, affected like a coquette, who was forever changing his facial expressions and tone of voice, was extraordinarily satisfied with both himself and his successes, and was so convinced of his superiority over others that it even came across as good-natured. He was completely impervious to art, in the sense that everything professing true skill, true understanding and true inspiration did not exist for him and failed to leave any impression on him whatsoever—so alien and far-removed was it from his own works, in which everything was determined once and for all, having been reduced to the sole theme of adultery, with rather copious but not infrequently amusing variations. Occasionally, however, his characters would touch on general themes and even social ones, but these would always fall flat, so much so that he was given to expressing a conviction that the public had no interest in them. He arrived happy and beaming, although, generally speaking, he had no great love for Sergey Sergeyevich, because he thought the latter regarded him with insufficient reverence. Though he would forgive him: "*Avec sa fortune, il peut se permettre…*"* He offered Sergey Sergeyevich a ticket to a

---

* With his fortune, he can afford to…

ball that he was organizing in aid of impoverished artists. Sergey Sergeyevich apologized, saying that it could not be, since he was going away, but he would naturally take a couple of tickets and offer them to his friends, and, not wishing to place the organizer at any risk, he would pay for them up front. In addition, he asked that the gentleman accept a modest sum that... He then wrote out a cheque, handed it over and, without taking a single ticket, shook the hand of his guest and bid him farewell.

Sergey Sergeyevich's final guest was a very young actress. She too had come with a personal invitation, to the premiere of a play in which she was starring. She was in particularly high spirits, for before coming to see Sergey Sergeyevich she had gone to the doctor, who had assured her that the syphilis she had recently developed—she was only at the start of her career—had been completely remedied, leaving no trace. She told Sergey Sergeyevich that everything was "*épatant*",* that the other actors were "*tous de chics types*",† and that she was very happy.

"*Alors, mon petit*," said Sergey Sergeyevich, "*qu'est-ce que tu veux?*"‡

She explained that invitations by telephone or post were, to her mind, ineffectual, and so she had decided to do it in person.

* Marvellous.
† All fabulous people.
‡ Well then, little one... what is it that you want?

"Thank you so much. I'll try to be there." He considered it unnecessary to explain to her that he was going abroad.

Liza and Seryozha returned only towards dinner. Sergey Sergeyevich said:

"Well, my children, I'm glad to see you. I was beginning to think I was some sort of impresario. Just imagine, three visitors, and each one a theatrical type."

Sergey Sergeyevich immediately noticed that something was amiss with Liza: several times she had started laughing—which was unusual for her—and her eyes sparkled, their movements more rapid. However, Sergey Sergeyevich did not enquire the reasons for this. Seryozha was in high spirits following his walk, but this was understandable: he was like this every time he returned from the Bois de Boulogne.

"People are beginning to leave," said Sergey Sergeyevich. "The day after tomorrow I have to be in London. Lyolya left earlier today."

"Mama's gone?"

"Lyolya's gone?"

However, while Seryozha asked this in a voice expressing at once shock, upset and surprise, Liza articulated those same words as if she had meant to say: "Just as I thought. Very nice of her, but of course not entirely unexpected."

"Italy?" asked Liza.

"What makes you say that?"

"Well, I said Italy, but I might as well have said Australia or Turkey."

42

"Oddly enough, you've hit the mark. She has indeed gone to Italy. I'd imagine we'll receive a letter from her in a week's time. I've no reason to doubt it will turn out all right, as ever."

"Yes, as ever," said Liza.

Seryozha listened to this insignificant conversation, which he now understood differently from how he would have done only a year ago, when he had known nothing, but now those same words masked another meaning. They meant that Sergey Sergeyevich did not want to accuse Olga Alexandrovna of anything, and that he had already forgiven her for everything, while Liza found such action unbecoming and unworthy of him. Thus Seryozha understood it, but he was wrong.

"What about you, Liza?" said Sergey Sergeyevich after a brief but alarming pause occasioned by thoughts about Olga Alexandrovna's departure. "Will you be going?"

"Yes, I think so," said Liza in her usual slow voice. "I think I'll go. I think."

"We know you think, Liza," said Sergey Sergeyevich patiently, "but what exactly is it that you're thinking?"

"Liza and I have decided to go to the Midi," Seryozha quickly put in. "Tomorrow."

"Am I not invited?"

"You're going to London," said Liza, shrugging.

"One can also get there from London."

"Come from London," she said in a tone of voice as if she had wanted to say: "Fine, if there are no two ways about it."

43

"Your invitation seems less than enthusiastic."

"Darling, one cannot always go through life with enthusiasm. You of all people should understand this—you've never shown an ounce of enthusiasm for anything."

"Oh, but I have," said Sergey Sergeyevich, as though himself astonished by the thought. "But, of course, as you so profoundly put it, one cannot always go through life with enthusiasm—it wears one down. Just give it a few years."

"Leave my age out of it…"

"Liza," said Sergey Sergeyevich calmly, "your temper's getting the better of you. Have you noticed, by the way, that a bad temper and good taste are opposed to one another and strive for mutual destruction?"

"I have," said Liza drily and ironically.

"And you haven't drawn any conclusions from this?"

Suddenly Liza, eyes wide with rage, said quietly, looking Sergey Sergeyevich straight in the eyes:

"I cannot go on like this any longer, do you understand? Always nice, always joking, always this forgiving wit of yours—and a complete absence of passion, blood and desire."

"God, what dreadful things you say," said Sergey Sergeyevich in that same heroic tone of voice with which he would tell his hunting tale: *The day, as I recall, was overcast, calm. My dog, which I'd bought—just imagine!—completely by chance from a peasant and which turned out…*

"I can't bear it, I can't bear it!" Liza screamed, and, getting up from her place, she went to her room.

Sergey Sergeyevich and Seryozha were left alone. The former began whistling a serenade slowly, paying attention to the pitch and the purity of the sound. He whistled the tune right through to the end and said:

"When you're down in the Midi, advise your aunt to take as many baths as possible; it'll calm her nerves. *À part ça*,* how are things with you?"

"Not bad," said Seryozha. "I was training for the hundred metres today."

"What was your time?"

"Twelve and a half."

"A little on the slow side," said Sergey Sergeyevich. "I suspect you're losing time at the start."

---

* That aside.

Arkady Alexandrovich Kuznetsov, with whom Olga Alexandrovna had travelled to Italy and whom she had met about a year previously, was a stoutish man of forty-seven with dull eyes and a small bald patch, who dressed in a somewhat antiquated fashion and carried a cane with an ornate handle; his complexion was slightly jaundiced; he was short of breath; he walked slowly, and his voice was unexpectedly high-pitched. He never exercised or played sports, and on account of this his hands and body were soft, like a woman's. He was a writer by profession—and it was to this fact that he owed his acquaintance with Olga Alexandrovna, for he had met her at a literary evening, where a middle-aged poet with desperate eyes and a haggard face had recited the most naive verses, of which the majority described nature and a love of the earth.

Naturally, it was Sergey Sergeyevich who had bought the tickets to this evening, so fateful in Olga Alexandrovna's life. At dinner he had said to her and Liza:

"Ladies, you should, at least once in your life, go and hear some poetry."

He then explained that the poet they were to hear was *un brave homme*,* with six children and an interminably

* A decent man.

46

pregnant wife, and that the man was hard up. All this had come so out of the blue that Olga Alexandrovna and Liza decided to attend the evening. The poet recited his verse, each one exceedingly like the last and so feeble that the audience began to feel somewhat embarrassed. What was more, the poet had a marked Provençal accent. However, having delivered his third offering, he looked to the audience and suddenly smiled such an artless, naive smile, unaware of its charm, giving everyone to realize that the poetry, of course, was unimportant, and what was important was that he truly was the sweetest and most ingenuous man, who most probably loved children dearly—and all this was contained in that astonishing smile.

"Oh, how charming!" said Olga Alexandrovna in Russian.

And the man sitting beside her turned his pale, jaundiced face to her with its dull, laughing eyes, and said:

"Indeed."

During the interval this man introduced himself to Olga Alexandrovna, apologizing for the remark he had permitted himself to make; Olga Alexandrovna had never heard of him, but Liza had read his books, and so the conversation turned to literature. He then invited them to a cafe, was very sweet, amiable and unassuming, and so Olga Alexandrovna went to the next literary evening with the firm intention of meeting him. Such an intention also guided Arkady Alexandrovich, and after a short while their acquaintance began to take on a precariously habitual form, in the absence of which, in some fatal way,

Olga Alexandrovna's life could no longer go on. When Liza asked Sergey Sergeyevich whether he had heard of Kuznetsov, he replied that he had, and to the question of what he made of him, Sergey Sergeyevich replied with his usual smile:

"A maniac with a pen."

Then, with his habitual kindliness, he began to talk of literature and writers whom he considered, every one of them without exception, charming people, but, of course, mad and misguided. Their error lay primarily in their choice of vocation; as far as Sergey Sergeyevich was concerned, the majority of them ought not to write at all.

"What do you mean by 'the majority'?"

"The term is, of course, diplomatic, Lizochka. However, on this occasion I can be more precise: ninety per cent."

"You're terribly harsh, Sergey Sergeyevich."

"Harsh? How so? I give them money."

"You give everyone money."

"Not everyone, thankfully. But to a lot of people, it's true."

"Where's your respect for a writer?"

"Liza, dear, don't play that game with me. You too could do with showing some respect. Perhaps you keep a diary? All right, then, just to make you happy I'll give you another utterly rapturous take on literature. So, why should I have any respect for writers? Take this Kuznetsov of yours: you know these sorry books he writes—they're all dust and vanity, so to speak, while he himself is such an interesting and intelligent man and understands all this perfectly well.

Lizochka, all his characters talk in that same intellectual, legalistic language that no living person speaks, but for barristers, solicitors and pharmacists. And all these characters of his—from a groom to a general—say exactly the same things."

"What, would you deny a man's right to pessimism?"

"No, I wouldn't. But what's important is the cause of… Suppose the man has chronic rheumatism, or kidney trouble, or a liver complaint—there's pessimism for you."

"You astound me, Seryozha, with such a crude physiological explanation."

"Of course, it isn't quite so simple: it passes through a multitude of stages along the way; only I'm omitting them. Or here, suppose he's impotent."

"Well, I shouldn't be too sure about that."

"No, that, of course, was merely by way of suggestion. He's really the nicest chap. I know him; I've met him a handful of times, a little melancholic, a little limp, but on the whole quite charming. Perhaps he's on the rocks? Why do you mention him, anyhow?"

"We met him at the literary evening."

"Oh! What of it?"

"He seemed to take a shine to us," said Liza, walking out of the room. Following her, Sergey Sergeyevich's leisurely voice, in which this time one could hear a genuine smile, said:

"To listen to you, Lizochka, one might think you were a saint."

There was no more talk of Arkady Alexandrovich.

Only one day at dinner, Sergey Sergeyevich mentioned in passing that he had been reading a book by Arkady Alexandrovich, *The Last Stage*, and that he found it remarkable: such intellect, such understanding; he said it with such innocent and unsuspecting conviction that Olga Alexandrovna looked at him with gratitude in her eyes, and only Liza, without raising her head—she was eating an artichoke—uttered: "Your acting skills are wasted, Sergey Sergeyevich!"

Meanwhile, relations between Olga Alexandrovna and Arkady Alexandrovich were beginning to take on a rather definitive character. Olga Alexandrovna had read all of his books; in reading them, she seemed to hear the intonations of his touchingly high-pitched, childlike voice, and all his characters' many travails, which were brought about by the most varied of circumstances, caused Olga Alexandrovna to return to one and the same thought, which she once revealed to her sister, saying that one had only to read these books to know just how much suffering this man must have gone through in order to write them. Indeed, Arkady Alexandrovich's books were marvels. They betrayed an indefinable beauty that was forever restive and growing, never-ending; everything was clever, tender and melancholy, and no one but Olga Alexandrovna could see this. Olga Alexandrovna began to see to his clothes, to make sure that he wore a warm coat—it was cold outside—that he did not catch cold, that he went to see the doctor. And so Arkady Alexandrovich in turn, in his forty-eighth year, fell in love for the first time in his life. It struck him one morning, when his wife, a tired woman with mercilessly bleached hair, heard him singing. She was so astonished that she left her bedroom in a nightdress and walked down the hallway to the bathroom, where she saw Arkady Alexandrovich bare to the waist, his odious, white, flaccid body and—in the mirror—his unexpectedly joyful eyes. "Have you gone mad?" Arkady Alexandrovich, continuing to sing, paid her no attention whatsoever. At last, when she repeated her question, he turned to her, laughing, and said:

"Don't try to understand what you're incapable of understanding."

"I'm capable of understanding that you're old and a fool."

"Enough. Leave me in peace."

She then recalled several things to which, until now, she had attached no importance, and, amassing all this information, came to the conclusion that some change must have taken place in her husband's life, one that was both manifest and significant yet escaped her. Firstly, he had stopped asking for money. Second, he had ceased bemoaning his lot. Third, he had attended a concert given by Kreisler. A whole host of astonishing things had entered into his life and changed everything. Normally Lyudmila would have had no time for such considerations; she was much too absorbed in her own life to linger on them.

Lyudmila was an exceptional woman. Throughout the many years of their life together, Arkady Alexandrovich had earned almost nothing; everything they had was the result of her labours. What was more, they had a decent apartment, one that was well furnished, and everything was always paid on time, and she and Arkady Alexandrovich lived in complete happiness and security. She despised her husband down to the depths of her soul, yet kept him on like some legal fiction that had entered her budget along with the gas, the electricity and the telephone. In her own affairs, she would often invoke his name, mostly without his knowledge. He was also unaware that he would always figure in her accounts as a tyrant and a despot, a man of morbid jealousy, from whom she was forced to hide absolutely everything. For indeed she did have things to hide. Her most recent affair had been a veritable success: her admirer had given her the sum of ten thousand francs to pay for the burial of her only child, a charming little girl of eight years, whose illness and death she had recounted in harrowing detail; real tears had welled in her dark-blue eyes. Listening to her tale, so appalling in its plainness and persuasiveness, her admirer—no longer a young man, and a father himself—could not hold back his tears either. She implored him not to telephone for a week, to give her time to bury her daughter; thereafter, she would have only one consolation in the world—his love. Later she would call or write to him herself. And so she left, clutching the bag of money she had acquired through her labours. Only in the motor car did she begin to recover her senses, and her face gradually took on its usual appearance, which is difficult to convey: coldness, a certain moral lassitude, and only in her eyes something approaching a glimmer of hope. Her particular sort of charm was not lacking in allure, particularly for those no longer in the first flush of youth. One could like Lyudmila or not: her plans might go awry if not, but when she was liked, she would achieve her aims. She was possessed of what she herself called an iron fist. The power of imagination she would demonstrate, for example, in the case of her daughter's funeral, was truly remarkable: she had never had any children, but if she had, they could have fallen ill and died in all good conscience, since with the money she had received for their treatment and interment, one could have treated and killed off an entire family.

Lyudmila's brothers were consumptive—in the final stages of tuberculosis—and undergoing treatment in Swiss sanatoriums, which they had to leave, since they had no money to pay their bills; she had a great many relations in Russia who were forever starving, sisters who had been stricken down by paralysis and were condemned never to get out of bed again; she had signed promissory notes under terrible circumstances, and they had been presented for collection, because she, Lyudmila, in response to a creditor's brazen suggestion, would not hesitate to slap him in the face, while later she would weep feebly at home, in her apartment, the rent of which had gone unpaid for a long time. And yet she had a distinctly Germanic exactitude and fastidiousness about her in matters of finance, paying for everything down to the last penny and doing it as though she were performing a redemptive act; she despised dishonest people and those who did not pay their debts.

She had but one blind and unremitting passion in life, for the sake of which she was ready to forgo everything:

music. She herself was a magnificent pianist and would spend evenings alone in her apartment playing Bach, Beethoven and Schumann in the grip of a cold, selfless sensuality. Only in these hours, far from everything else, alone in this illusory, swelling world of polyphony, did she feel truly happy. Then she would stop playing and pause, gazing fixedly into the black mirror of the piano; and the unfinished melodies would continue to ring out silently, conjuring up a whole series of regrets, presentiments and reminders of what had never been. In these moments she would resemble a man who shudders from the memory that his life has been squandered, or a woman befallen by the most terrible catastrophe. Next she would lie down in her cold bed with the white-and-bluish sheets drawn tightly around her, smoke a couple of cigarettes and doze off drowsily, with the intention of repeating it all the following morning. She knew nothing of attachment, or love, or pity; when, around once a month, in the morning and always in her nightdress, she would cause a scene because her husband had not hung his overcoat in its proper place, or had thrown an unstubbed cigarette end into the waste-paper basket, Arkady Alexandrovich would look on, terrified, at her wild hair, her pale lips, shaking his head and preferring not to think about how it was possible that life could be so monstrous and absurd.

And just as Lyudmila was bereft of love and pity, so too was Arkady Alexandrovich devoid of self-esteem and morals. He understood these concepts and knew perfectly well what they were, and his characters' conflicts would more often than not have an ethical basis; however, none of his personal feelings corresponded to this understanding. He was not an actively unscrupulous man and would never have acted dishonestly where his family and friends were concerned; yet he possessed neither courage nor any will to independence whatsoever. He understood theoretically that it was wrong to live off the money of a woman who despised him and, into the bargain, a woman who earned it in such an unseemly fashion, but how could he act otherwise? He could never imagine suddenly having to work in a factory or in an office, having to leave his beautiful, warm apartment and take a cold room in a cheap *pension*, getting up at seven o'clock in the morning— it was so horrible that he simply had to reconcile himself to anything in order to avoid this. It was necessary for the sake of these most moral attitudes, which were fit only for literature, and for which there was no place in life; otherwise, to live would have been much too painful and distressing. And when people, in taking him to lunch and offering him a loan of one or two hundred francs, spoke ill of his friends, he would not defend them, for a defence would mean that there would be no more lunches, no more money. He never actually gave this any consideration; it came about of itself, so much was it plainly necessitated. Before, when he was young and embarking on his literary career, he believed that he could change everything—both life and art—and he was unafraid to utter these words; later he began to sense that to speak in such terms—"life and art"—was simply unmannerly in the society in which he moved—respectable people, rich businessmen with the hearts of patrons of the arts (but not actual patrons of the arts, as are people with the hearts of students but who are themselves not students), famous politicians or writers—in a word, everyone whose more or less stable, entrenched position admitted no desire, no necessity, not even in most cases the very capacity for abstract thought or the evaluation of different artistic concepts. Little by little, he too came to resemble these people; however, as with people of limited intelligence, he too failed to notice this, just as he failed to notice the error of his ways, and so fell to thinking that young people understood nothing and laboured under a delusion. In literature he immediately found his own voice, the one he would always employ—one of slightly weary scepticism, always guaranteed to make an impression: "All is corruptible, all is transient, all is insignificant and vain." And since none of this required any fortitude of thought, everything was written with ease and simplicity, and Arkady Alexandrovich felt genuine satisfaction, verging on joy, from this automatic deployment of ready-made attitudes, though the fates of his characters were most often tragic. Despite this, however, he enjoyed no literary success. He could trot out dozens of satisfactory explanations, but the main reason, which escaped Arkady Alexandrovich, was that he was incapable of experiencing or understanding the temptation to commit a crime, debauchery, great passion, the compulsion to murder someone, vengeance, irresistible desire, gruelling physical strain. He was a fat and flaccid man, living out his life peacefully in a rather nice apartment, and not once had his feelings been subjected to the cruel trials of mortal danger, hunger or war—everything transpired in refined halftones, and for that very reason it all seemed, essentially, unconvincing.

There had been several women in Arkady Alexandrovich's life. Lyudmila was his third wife. Still, he never felt capable of sacrificing anything for a woman's love, while this was precisely what they demanded, even in those instances where it was entirely unnecessary. He would leave them without any regrets. But even he needed a romance of sorts—and so he created one; he would say that he had been happy with his wife, who... And at this point he would go on to deliver an entire monologue, himself deriving a certain sad satisfaction from it. This woman had been his first wife, and her portrait hung above the divan at home: it depicted a slender brunette of the monastic variety, and the stylization lay, broadly speaking, somewhere between charm and chastity. Beside his wife's portrait was a photograph of similar proportions, in which Arkady Alexandrovich figured, dressed in a white suit and holding a bouquet of flowers in one hand and a panama hat in the other—at a cemetery, by his wife's grave. According to Arkady Alexandrovich's tale, which he had repeated so often that even he had begun to believe it in all earnestness, everything had been romantic and impossibly wonderful. They had met at a concert, talked at length about music, literature and art in general; she had known nothing of the baseness of life surrounding her, just as she had no conception of money; she had been made for art and for this one unique love. However, the people around her had been incapable of apprehending her charm. One day she came to Arkady Alexandrovich's apartment, with flowers, and looked so fragile and delicate in her spring attire. She then told Arkady Alexandrovich that her whole life belonged to him. And he replied: "My child, if I considered myself capable of making you happy…"

"You're the only one who can," she quickly replied.

Yet he took her hands, kissed them and said that she was too young—he himself was five years her senior—and that she ought to think carefully before resolving on such a step. It seemed to him that her delicate charm was incommensurate with the reality of a marriage that would entail the inescapable prose of everyday life with a man who was, perhaps, unworthy of her. But in the end he told himself that happiness was the rarest thing on earth, and that one ought to have the courage not to walk away from it. And so he married. Her pale face, white dress and ethereal veil in that tall church—he could picture it as though it were happening right now. For three years their life passed by—he would apologize for the trivial comparison—like a protean, shifting dream. He knew that this happiness could not last for ever; she contracted diphtheria and died a few days later. After her death, he went to his study, took out his Browning, placed it to his temple and pulled the trigger. A dry click rang out, but no shot followed. He then realized that she had removed the cartridges from the magazine;

she must have wanted him to live, perhaps so that on this earth the sorrow, which was the only vestige of her short sojourn here, and that blinding happiness she had given him should not die. He would speak of the sad rustle of the trees in the cemetery and how he would never forget the melody of this sound, a final melody to accompany her into the hereafter, in which he was ready to believe with all his strength of conviction, if only for the sake of her memory. Then he would pause for a moment and add:

"But don't let's talk about this. It's too distressing for me, and I wouldn't want to burden you with another's sorrow."

Such was Arkady Alexandrovich's tale of his first wife, or rather the romance he had created, which bore no resemblance at all to the actual history of his marriage. The romance, for example, entirely omitted any reference to her dowry; and, moreover, it was precisely this unmentioned dowry that served at once as both the reason for Arkady Alexandrovich's courting her and the deciding factor in it all. Arkady Alexandrovich had not attended the concert, since the tickets had been too expensive; he met his first wife at the house of some mutual acquaintances. There had indeed been some hesitation before the marriage, but this had come about for reasons entirely other than those featuring in the tale, which cast Arkady Alexandrovich's magnanimity and sacrifice in such a favourable light; the hesitation could be ascribed, firstly, to the young lady's thorough uncertainty about her love for the man and, secondly, and principally, to the fact that she had yet to come of age and was not in control of her capital—

almost a hundred thousand roubles, which belonged to her and constituted her dowry. However, she would come of age in a few months, and then nothing could impede the marriage. Arkady Alexandrovich indeed, for the first time in his life, displayed true perseverance in achieving his aim. His future mother-in-law, a formidable, miserly old woman who did everything in her power to see to it that her daughter married a rich man, hated Arkady Alexandrovich with every fibre of her being. He patiently bore it all, and in order to rationalize his indulgence, he constructed a theorem that excused the old woman's behaviour and her nerves, because she had suffered a great deal—which was incorrect: the old woman had known no suffering and lived the most untroubled of lives. Only, she found the prospect of losing one hundred thousand roubles to her daughter unbearable. The daughter, exposed on the one hand to the tempestuous exhortations of the old woman, and on the other to the quiet persuasions of Arkady Alexandrovich, hesitated for a long time, until finally Arkady Alexandrovich prevailed—and only then did the wedding take place. The only thing to hold any degree of verisimilitude in Arkady Alexandrovich's romance was that his wife had no conception of the value of money, which Arkady Alexandrovich now found entirely at his disposal—and so the now powerless old woman vanished like a phantom. Yet, Arkady Alexandrovich's wife never did love him; there were many indications of this, and each one constituted a world of its own. Nevertheless, since they were both of them possessed of calm temperaments, their life together was plain sailing, although perhaps a little dull. She died following an unsuccessful operation, which had been registered officially as an appendectomy. What was more, she had not removed the cartridges from the revolver, because Arkady Alexandrovich had never owned any such thing—and, lastly, the trees had not rustled on the day of her funeral, because it was the beginning of March and there were no leaves yet on any of the trees.

As strange as it may at first seem, Arkady Alexandrovich's tale enjoyed unfailing success among his female admirers. After laying a certain dialectical groundwork, the conclusion would readily suggest itself: in Arkady Alexandrovich's life there was an irreparable (in a certain sense) emptiness, and of course this emptiness could only be filled by another woman, one who bore a striking resemblance to the first wife—a little otherworldly, romantic, blind to any financial considerations—which is how every woman without exception views herself. It was only Lyudmila to whom Arkady Alexandrovich never told this romance. Naturally, however, he did tell Olga Alexandrovna, recounting even the programme of the concert.

For Olga Alexandrovna, Arkady Alexandrovich was an entirely new sort of man—she had never until now known such people. For a start, he was less primitive than his predecessors had been; secondly, she liked his gentle nature and that particular defencelessness about him: this man was unable to make demands, he could not contrive, he lacked the courage to tell his adoring wife that he no longer loved her, since he knew that she would never survive the blow.

"Tell her. Really, sooner or later she ought to know…"

"You don't know her," Arkady Alexandrovich replied. "Poor Lyudmila!"

It was, of course, Olga Alexandrovna who had devised the trip to Italy. She was to meet Arkady Alexandrovich in Nice, at a hotel on avenue Victor Hugo. From there, they would travel via Menton, Bordighera, San Remo and Genoa into the hinterlands of Italy. Naturally, it would have been simpler to travel from Paris together, but Olga Alexandrovna wanted to imbue the trip with her scripted sense of the unexpected and happy coincidence. She would travel to Nice alone; on the other side of the carriage window the sea would swell, the kilometres would fly by—and then the station, a motor car, avenue Victor Hugo—and in the lobby of her hotel, at long last, an unhurrying figure, so warm, soft and familiar. Olga Alexandrovna could no longer fathom how it was possible to love a man with broad shoulders, firm hands and muscles that moved monstrously beneath swarthy skin; the shoulders ought to be a little sloping, the skin touchingly white, the hands tender and soft. However, at first Arkady Alexandrovich had declined to accompany her on the trip, explaining to Olga Alexandrovna that, unfortunately, it would be impossible, since he had no money. "Silly boy," she said, patting him on the cheek, which twitched beneath her hand. "Silly little boy!" And although he continued to protest and object, it ended in his departing the Gare de Lyon in a first-class carriage two days before Olga Alexandrovna, having left a note for Lyudmila to the effect that he was going away for a couple of months and would write to her. Lyudmila, however, had been gone for two days already.

It was the month of June; along the way, Arkady Alexandrovich and Olga Alexandrovna stopped in Menton, and everything there seemed so wonderful to them that they saw no point in travelling farther. Besides, there was plenty of time—a whole life ahead of them. Despite the fact that Arkady Alexandrovich was stout, ill and no longer in the prime of life, despite the fact that he had long ceased to believe in anything at all, aside from comfort and a good apartment, despite the fact that love usually exhausted him and long conversations about the same things irritated him—despite all this, for the first time in his life he felt ready to sacrifice everything, even the nice apartment, for the chance to be with Olga Alexandrovna. Sometimes, after lunch, he would sit down to write his book, titled *The Spring Symphony*, in which he recounted in unaccustomed terms the love of two youths; in this book there was no hint of dust, decay or ashes, but rather descriptions of affirmative, lyrical things; and it read awkwardly, just as it is awkward to look at a fat old woman made up in a light gauze dress, prancing about a stage in the role of a young sylph. Arkady Alexandrovich was much too weary a man for an outward rebirth to appear decent. However, what mattered was that only now had he grasped the meaning of happiness, and only now did he sense how he ought to write, and Olga Alexandrovna, to whom he read all his curiously inept pages, was in complete agreement with him.

In the mornings, they would go for a swim together;

however, the disadvantage of this lay in the fact that while Olga Alexandrovna was an excellent swimmer, Arkady Alexandrovich could not swim at all. Standing up to his neck in the water, he would spread his arms, exhale and move about on the spot, as if gathering the strength to set off, but he would never move and just kept standing there, bobbing up and down. When Olga Alexandrovna appeared next to him, he would say:

"It's such a pity that Nature has bypassed man without giving him the means to fly or swim! Right now I'd swim far, far away!"

And Olga Alexandrovna, who would have laughed if any other man had said this, just as she would have laughed at his clumsy movements and lack of confidence in the water, would be touched by his manner, and lamented with him that Nature had wronged man.

Following Liza and Seryozha's departure, Sergey Sergeyevich was left in Paris alone. Olga Alexandrovna ought to be in Italy by now. There had been no letters from her, and Sergey Sergeyevich did not expect her return any sooner than a fortnight hence.

It was one of those rare periods in his life when he found himself almost entirely at liberty: there were no trips, no urgent commitments, no one asking for money or favours, and all this ceaseless movement around him ground to a halt for a time. He changed none of his habitual routine: as always, he would rise early; as always, he would make himself clean and presentable; and as always, he looked as though he had come fresh from the bath. However, on days such as these, he would read a lot, and it was chiefly on this pursuit that he spent his free time. It was an exceedingly rare occurrence, however, that he would read a book from cover to cover; most often, he would stop after the opening pages. Occasionally he would pick up novels that Olga Alexandrovna had praised, but after reading a few lines he would carefully replace them on their shelves. Liza's books were more interesting, but her favourite author was Dostoevsky, whom Sergey Sergeyevich had never been able to read without stifled indignation and a wry smile. But then, Seryozha's reading would always bring a smile to his face: it would always be Plato, or Kant, or Schopenhauer. All this would usually culminate in Sergey Sergeyevich's extracting a volume of Dickens or Galsworthy from the shelf and beginning *Oliver Twist* or *The Forsyte Saga* for the dozenth time.

On the second day of his holiday, once news had spread that he was in London—despite his almost never having left the house—he received a telephone call from an old friend from his days in Moscow, a certain Sletov, who said that he needed to see Sergey Sergeyevich on a very important matter, and, although Sergey Sergeyevich knew perfectly well what this matter was, he replied that he would be glad to see him. Half an hour later Sletov appeared.

"Hello, Fyodor Borisovich," said Sergey Sergeyevich. "Have you paid the taxi driver?"

Fyodor Borisovich Sletov was a tall man, very carelessly dressed, with a jaundiced, lined face, on which his rapturous blue eyes seemed astonishing.

"Just imagine, Seryozha, I was a little short, you see…" he began very quickly. "Yes, of course, you don't know yet. Everything's over. Everything, you hear?" He made a decisive gesture with his hand, as though chopping something invisible. He was speaking very fast, almost panting from the speed and agitation. "I haven't slept for the past three nights. Everything, you hear, everything. And who would have thought," he said, abruptly slowing his monologue and beginning to speak calmly, with embittered restraint, "that she, Lili, was nothing but a…"

He did not finish the phrase and shook his head.

"…a woman who didn't deserve your love?" queried Sergey Sergeyevich.

"There can be no doubt about it," quietly replied Sletov. "The letters, the evidence…"

"You're incorrigible, Fedya."

"Yes, yes, I know. I know what you're going to say… But no one, you included, understands a thing."

"That's a poor sort of wisdom, Fedya."

"But it isn't!" cried Sletov. "To you they're all fast women; you think there's something strange in believing that Lili, or Zhenya, or Olya could actually turn out to be an angel of virtue, don't you? Well, my friend, believe me: there are no two women on earth who are the same, do you hear? They're all different, every one of them."

"Possibly. However, they all act more or less the same."

"No, differently."

"That is to say, certain details, possibly, are dissimilar," said Sergey Sergeyevich, "but all the same, you still wind up here every time, just like today, and even that touching detail—that you haven't the money for the taxi— remains unaltered. And every time you have evidence and letters."

"Do you know what I mean by 'the creative principal in life'?"

"Where does creativity come into it?"

"Permit me to explain. Say I love a woman who…"

"Have you eaten?" asked Sergey Sergeyevich.

It was almost eight o'clock, and Sergey Sergeyevich

could hardly expect anyone else at this hour. Suddenly, a sharp and prolonged ringing came from the hallway.

"Well, Fedya, who on earth could this be? What do you think, judging by the bell? A man or a woman?"

"A woman of intent."

"I'd wager it's a man, and a brazen one at that."

The maid handed Sergey Sergeyevich a card inscribed: "Lyudmila Nikolayevna Kuznetsova"—and, added by hand, with a well-sharpened pencil: "On a most important personal matter."

"You know, Fedya," said Sergey Sergeyevich, "you should go and take a bath, shave, freshen yourself up a bit; meanwhile, I'll see to this woman."

"And I was just starting to get an appetite," said Sletov.

"Go, go, I'll feed you. Show her in," he said to the maid.

Lyudmila entered with assured steps, said "Good evening" in a businesslike voice, sat down and immediately lit a cigarette.

"Can I help you?" asked Sergey Sergeyevich.

"I believe," said Lyudmila coldly, "or, at least, I hope so."

"If you would be so good as to tell me to what I owe the pleasure of your visit…"

"You ought to know that just as well as I do."

"You see…" said Sergey Sergeyevich, reclining in his chair as though preparing to deliver a speech, "I have the misfortune—or good fortune—to be comparatively well off, and this has a most pernicious effect on the nature of visits paid to me by various people, whose aims are generally distinguished, I should say, by a certain monotony. I

68

should say that ninety-nine per cent of these visits are of the same unambiguous nature. In those cases when it is a woman who pays the visit, that ninety-nine per cent may be replaced with the number one hundred, without the slightest risk of error. In other words, I should like to thank you for the charming attention with which you've listened to all this, and to add that from the very outset I had no illusions about the reason for your visit."

"Do you always talk in this way?"

"No."

"You are aware that your wife has gone away, but you are not aware with whom."

"You see…" said Sergey Sergeyevich. He made as if to sink into thought, looked first at the ceiling, then straight at Lyudmila, and slowly said: "I take a dim view of a certain category of blackmailers, or, more precisely, those who invoke my wife's name. Any attempt by such people is doomed to failure."

"I have no interest in blackmail," said Lyudmila impatiently. "I know that your wife is my husband's mistress, that he's gone away with her—"

"Forgive me for interrupting you," said Sergey Sergeyevich. "I would suggest that in certain circumstances it's better to avoid such precise definitions."

"I'm unaccustomed to such farces. If the interests of your wife mean anything to you, it's your duty to show some—"

"You see," Sergey Sergeyevich went on, unable to hold back a smile, "it's possible, of course, that I'm under some misapprehension, but I believe I know my own duties well enough."

"Are you listening to me or not?" screamed Lyudmila.

"No, I see no need."

"In that case," said Lyudmila abruptly, getting up, "you'll be hearing from me."

"What, again?" said Sergey Sergeyevich. "It seems as though I've heard quite enough from you already."

Then he added in a thoughtful voice:

"Incidentally, I had expected you to be less amateurish."

Lyudmila, who had been about to get out of the chair, suddenly slumped back into it, dropping her handbag, and, covering her face with her hands, began to cry. Her shoulders shook with every sob.

"In French they call this *les grands moyens*,"* said Sergey Sergeyevich. "But the quickness of your change in tactics is commendable."

"You're a monster," said Lyudmila in a voice choked with tears. "You don't care that tomorrow I might have to go hungry."

"I very much like this 'might'."

"Don't you believe me?"

"Listen, Lyudmila Nikolayevna," Sergey Sergeyevich said patiently. "I wouldn't want you to persist in your delusions on my account. I know everything about you and I know perfectly well on what money you subsist. Don't misunderstand me."

* Overacting.

70

"You know everything?" said Lyudmila slowly, raising her eyes to him. "And you don't pity me?"

It was said with such sincerity, in a voice so far removed from any artifice or farce that Sergey Sergeyevich was transported.

"Bravo," he said. "*Ça, c'est réussi, mes hommages, madame.*"*

Lyudmila's face remained motionless; only in her eyes did there flash a fugitive, almost sincere smile. Sergey Sergeyevich proceeded to dash off a cheque. Lyudmila placed it in her handbag without looking at the sum and said in a faltering voice: "Forgive me, Sergey Sergeyevich. Goodbye." Sergey Sergeyevich bowed deeply—and she left.

When Sletov entered the study, Sergey Sergeyevich said to him:

"You were right, Fedya, it was a woman of intent."

"Young, old, beautiful, ugly?"

"Middle-aged, Fedya, not very beautiful, but interesting in any case and with a sharply expressed personality."

"Specifically?"

"A wh——," said Sergey Sergeyevich with his joyful smile. "Anyhow, tell me about Lili; I don't know a thing about her. Is she blonde?"

"Blonde—such a delicate shade that—"

"Yes, I know. Blue eyes?"

"Dark blue, Seryozha."

"Her mouth just a fraction on the large side, you say?"

"Maybe."

---

* Well played. My congratulations, Madame.

"Something childlike about her, the rest notwithstanding?"

"Yes, it's astonishing."

"Calls you 'my little boy'?"

"She does, Seryozha."

"Yes, altogether the same sort of woman as always."

"It astonishes me, Seryozha," said Sletov, "how you, with your indisputable intellect, can think that there is a definitive type of woman, among the thousands of them, and that they are all the same, right down to the expressions they use, the size of their mouths and colour of their eyes. Believe me, it isn't so; there's something unique in every one of them."

"I should say: something irreparable."

"Very well, irreparable. But when it comes to it, and you seize upon that one irreparable trait of hers, when she is, so to speak, defenceless before you, like a child, you'll see—it will make you cry sometimes."

"I do understand," said Sergey Sergeyevich, "but your tears won't suffice. All the same, tell me the what, where and why of it. Although, I'm aware of the why."

Sergey Sergeyevich spoke thus—candidly, without pretence or assuming any role—with only very few people. Sletov was one of these, because Sergey Sergeyevich highly valued his astonishing moral purity and his true sense of friendship. Moreover, Sletov's life, in which Sergey Sergeyevich could not help taking a close part, consisted in a sequence of tragedies, always of the same nature, for which Sergey Sergeyevich would always have to pay—in

72

the literal sense of the word—since Sletov had been living out of his pockets for many years already. These tragedies would involve Sletov falling in love with some woman—in which connection he would find no obstacle too great an impediment to their union; he would achieve his aims, rent an apartment, set himself up for good and live happily for a certain time, the average duration of which was calculated by Sergey Sergeyevich to be approximately six months. Then a drama would stage itself: either Sletov's sweetheart would prove untrue to him, or Sletov himself would fall in love with another woman. There would be an eruption, sometimes involving the threat of a revolver; then would come the parting, and later everything would begin afresh, with a new beloved. In brief, he resembled Olga Alexandrovna in both his nature and his inexhaustible belief in love with a capital "L". Love would swallow up all his plans and all his time, to the point where there could be no possible room for anything else.

By training Sletov was an expert in Russian legal practice, but in France, much as he would have liked, he was unable to find work in that field. One day Sergey Sergeyevich, in response to Sletov's request that he set him up somewhere, sent him to the provinces—to the suburbs of Marseilles—to manage the accounting department in one of his enterprises. Some time thereafter, however, trouble broke out in the office, and when Sergey Sergeyevich went there to investigate the matter, he found that the cause of all this was an affair Sletov had been carrying on with the director's wife. The director was a shy, young and very sensible man, who had recently married and had been living in perfect bliss until Sletov's arrival. Sletov had fallen in love with his wife; she had responded with reciprocal passion, and the three of them had held open discussions, accompanied by Sletov's tirades about free will and the director's wife's allusions to fundamental sexual theories about life; these theories, according to her, served as a unique, all-defining principle, something like the "Alpha and Omega" of the Gospels. There was no way out of the situation, although Sletov, foaming at the mouth, tried to convince her to leave her husband for him; things were further complicated by the fact that she was three months pregnant. Consequently, the director—who had become exceedingly attached to Sletov and harboured no ill feeling towards him, although he did continue to love his wife, who, with tears in her eyes, would tell him that she loved him, too, and would not for all the world consent to a divorce—took heavily to drink, and would turn up to work already drunk; figures and letters swam before his bleary eyes with a terrible absence of meaning and utterly incapable of holding his interest. He would sometimes cry in his office, no longer ashamed in the presence of strangers. Throughout all this, Sletov, together with the director's wife, would read Hamsun aloud and tell her about his life.

Sergey Sergeyevich patiently and benevolently heard out the confessions of each of the three interested parties; his face did not flinch when the director's wife spoke to him of the sublimation of sexual desire; he sympathized with her, telling her that he quite understood, that he did not number among those narrow-minded individuals who suppose that such maximally sublimated conflicts could be resolved immediately by the crudest, most primitive methods. He promised to do everything within his power, and that very evening he whisked Sletov off to Paris, where the latter made ready to shoot himself or throw himself under a train in the Métro.

"It isn't worth it, Fedya," Sergey Sergeyevich said to him. "I'm sure you will find something else unique and you'll see that I was right."

This was not difficult to envisage; and indeed, two weeks later, Sletov met a most elegant lady, the owner of a considerable fortune that was of a completely unexpected (as far as Sletov was concerned) mould: four major funeral parlours, to be precise. In recounting this to Sergey Sergeyevich, Sletov spoke of the unadulterated, mad (as he put it) thirst for life that this young woman had. "She's surrounded by mourning," he said, "but she has only one wish: to live, to live! Do you hear?"

He came close to marrying her, disappearing for several months—and the only thing that prevented him was her infidelity, upon discovering which he returned to Sergey Sergeyevich, as usual, with no money to pay the taxi driver, unshaven, dishevelled and exhausted.

"What happened, Fedya?" Sergey Sergeyevich asked him. "Really, you look deathly pale. Where have you come from?"

Despite all this, the man had never known the meaning

of debauchery or a love of convenience. After each of his affairs, he seemed to rise anew, keeping only vague, fleeting memories of what had gone before it. Each time he would fall madly in love, and each time he would be prepared to sacrifice anything for it. He had often absconded with his lovers, and he knew Europe rather well; he spoke several languages poorly and assuredly in equal measure, and had even taught himself a few tender terms of endearment in Hungarian and Dutch, which was to say nothing of his "intimate vocabulary", as he himself called it in all earnestness, of Yiddish, Armenian and Georgian. In spite of his lined, jaundiced face, the perpetual neglect of his attire, the incipient bald patch and the complete physical incongruity between him and the model of a seducer, he enjoyed great success among women, whom he infected with his ardour and the absence of any doubt whatsoever concerning the happiness that awaited them. Neither his age nor his long, woeful, piteous experience seemed to have the slightest effect on him. Anything that did not directly concern the principal matter in his life, namely love, simply escaped his notice; he lived as though eternally shrouded by a fog, in which, slowly gliding and steadily vanishing, floated all these many Lilis, directors' wives and owners of funeral parlours.

"It will be interesting to see what happens when you come to your senses," said Sergey Sergeyevich thoughtfully. "Or can you really stand to go on like this until the day you die?"

"Death is one of the aspects of love," said Sletov. "You

see, Seryozha, that well-known moment in one's intimacy with a woman is a perfect reflection of death. We are resurrected only to die again. This, of course, is a commonplace truth, but it is true nonetheless, there's no denying it."

"And you never grow tired of this?" Sergey Sergeyevich asked with curiosity.

"I see, Seryozha, that you do not know what love is."

"There is a cruel contradiction here," said Sergey Sergeyevich. "Just think about it, Fedya. What is value? The value of a feeling in particular. How are we to define it? By its exclusivity, by its singularity, if you will. The ramifications of this extend in all directions, into every nook and cranny of one's private life. But you have no place left for it in yours."

"Everything is singular, everything is unique, Seryozha."

"But *you* remain just the same each time."

"No," said Sletov seriously. "I am continually reborn."

"You know, Fedya, you ought to be a raconteur."

However, Sletov never backed down and never abandoned his beliefs. At times he would succumb to Sergey Sergeyevich's influence: the latter's ever-present calm assuredness that the question needed to be resolved one way, and not another, could not but impress Sletov. Yet he would refuse to move an inch when it came to his theoretical framework. Or, rather, theories did not exist for him as such; they were useful only insofar as they could, with a greater or lesser persuasive facility, express or complement his own private feelings. Any betrayal was always a catastrophe as far as he was concerned; it would seem as though it were happening to him for the first time in his life. He held an almost unconscious deep conviction that it was none other than he who had been the lifelong object of Lili's or any other woman's dreams; and so now, when her dreams had come true, she stood only to betray him if she found someone better than him—but this seemed impossible. This was not how he thought; rather, these thoughts never took on such a form in his mind, but it was how he felt, without even realizing it himself—unmerited insult, sheer gross injustice, a monstrous, unimaginable misapprehension. He was never able to comprehend the prospect of betrayal, and for that reason he suffered truly and greatly every time it happened. He told Sergey Sergeyevich about Lili, an extravagant American woman, even astonishing to a certain degree for her rare transparency and complete lack of inner thoughts or human emotion; she was the perfect blonde, with toned arms and legs, beautiful flawless skin, a healthy appetite and a body whose physiological functions were of the most enviable propriety; however, in all her life she had read barely a dozen books, which, more to the point, she had entirely forgotten. No moral questions played, or indeed could play, any role in her life. Sletov thought of her as a child, one that does not yet understand all the wonders of its budding soul—and by an unfortunate coincidence, in the love letter that left no doubt as to her betrayal, written in English, there was also a mention of a budding soul.

They dined together; Sletov drank five glasses of wine, then cried long and bitterly.

"Have you no shame, Fedya?" Sergey Sergeyevich said to him.

"No. No, I don't. There's iron where your heart ought to be; you'll never understand."

Sergey Sergeyevich's eyes suddenly turned pensive, and then he uttered a phrase that shocked Sletov somewhat, so much so that he lifted his head and looked intently at Sergey Sergeyevich.

"Has it never occurred to you, Fedya, that that may not be true?"

Sletov drooped his head, and when he raised it, Sergey Sergeyevich's face already displayed that old, long-familiar, joyous smile.

"Chaliapin is giving a concert tonight," said he. "It's time to get ready. Let's go, Fyodor Borisovich."

L OLA AÎNÉE RETURNED HOME at around two o'clock
in the morning, following an obligatory evening at
the Champs-Élysées, which had been put on by a famous
Parisian set designer, and which she would not have
attended, had she not planned later to call on his services
in staging the projected revue in her projected music
hall. She had smiled dazzlingly and joked throughout the
whole evening, although she drank very little, knowing
from experience that if she were to drink a lot, she would,
without fail, be taken ill. She left in a taxi, for ever since
her recent marriage she had been largely deprived of the
use of her own motor car: at the insistence of her husband,
the driver had been dismissed, and, in place of her comfortable old Delage, a Bugatti had been acquired, which
her husband drove. By and large, the motor was always
at his disposal, while Lola was now forced to rely almost
exclusively on taxis. Moreover, the Bugatti was forever in
the garage for repairs: either because of a routine crash
with another vehicle, or because the racing-model Bugatti
was unsuited to the relatively slow city traffic and the spark
plugs in its engine would get covered in oil. All this cost
an awful lot of money, and it was one of the reasons that
Lola's principal dream was now that of the death of her

husband. She knew not how to rid herself of him, and she feared him greatly, for when she first mentioned a divorce to him, he suddenly grew pale and said that if she were to start proceedings he would murder her. Lola feared death terribly and took great fright at this threat. She knew that he was capable of it; recently, as a result of the most savage inebriation , his reason had manifestly begun to leave him. She dreamt that he would be dashed to pieces, that the Bugatti would be run over by a lorry or a train at a crossing. Yet an extraordinary and peculiar run of good luck saw that he escaped almost weekly catastrophes unharmed, which seemed particularly astonishing, since he was forever drunk at the wheel.

He was thirty years of age, starting to plump out, and had thinning fair hair; he had lived a quiet life, full of hardship, until he met Lola. He had worked for an insurance company, earning very little money, and lived in a miserable *pension* near the Grands Boulevards. Everything had begun with several gushing letters that he wrote to Lola—about her beauty, about her talent, about the fact that these letters had no selfish aim, since he dared not even hope for an acquaintance with her. The only thing he wanted was for Lola to know that somewhere in the world there was a heart beating just for her. Lola had always been painfully susceptible to any praise of her talent and beauty, although one might have been given to suppose that she ought to know the value of such words. It ended with their meeting, and, on that very first night, she became his lover. She then decided to marry him and thus rest safely in the knowledge that there was a loving man who owed her everything and would feel something of an inextinguishable sense of gratitude towards her. She had borrowed this idea from the third-rate literature she very occasionally read. And so she married.

Nothing at all turned out as she had expected. For a start, he very soon developed a physical revulsion towards her. Whenever she would try to kiss him on the lips, he would always turn away, since he could not bear the constant foul smell emanating from her, which could be ascribed to her slow, ill-functioning stomach. She soon found herself in possession of other, wholly irrefutable evidence of this revulsion. It also turned out that he, this quiet and respectable Pierre, drank and, being drunk, would begin speaking in a common vernacular, which contained nothing shocking to Lola's ears, since this was her own native tongue, too; however, vulgarities that she had never heard from anyone would pass his lips. Furthermore, he had a string of mistresses, some of whom he brought back with him at night to the apartment, and Lola, through the light sleep of an old woman, would hear their voices, squeals and all the rest. He also allowed himself to make the most unflattering remarks in the presence of the maid, which was entirely improper.

It was past two o'clock in the morning. Lola was beginning to drift off, when suddenly the telephone rang. Feeling an inexplicable, rapturous presentiment, she picked up the receiver.

"Madame Aînée?" the voice said. "There's been an

accident: your husband has been seriously injured. He has been taken to the Beaujon Hospital."

"Thank you," she said, her eyes glittering.

She dressed at once and, having hailed a passing taxi, made her way to the hospital. By the time she arrived, Pierre was already dead. She insisted that they show her the corpse. What only a few minutes ago had been Pierre now lay hunched over on its side, the left arm twisted in one final movement, still wearing a gold wristwatch; at the cold wrist, the clock hand, dark blue and invariably accurate, continued its ticking race about the dial. Lola stood before the body; at this moment, she was truly happy. She fleetingly considered the wonderful publicity that would appear in advance of her music hall's opening night: the sudden death of her husband in tragic circumstances, which police investigations... With slight squeamishness, she undid the strap of the wristwatch, took it and placed it to her ear, although it was already quite clear that it was working—then she walked out of the room, covering her transformed, joyous face with a handkerchief. The policemen who had brought Pierre to the hospital told her that there had been a firefight between some pimps at the cabaret her husband had been visiting, and that a stray bullet had hit Pierre; the wound, alas, had proved fatal. As she left, Lola mused that there could have been no happier an omen for the opening of her theatre than this unlikely, attractive coincidence of her wildest dream and plainest reality. She returned home, completely drunk with happiness, and, purely for pleasure, from the necessity in some way to mark her happiness, took a second dose of salts—the first she had taken some time ago, before the telephone call, which had been nothing out of the ordinary, for Lola took it every evening—drank a whole glass of port wine, lay down and slept soundly, such as she had not slept for many months.

FYODOR BORISOVICH SLETOV had already installed himself for the night in one of the guest rooms in Sergey Sergeyevich's apartment; the latter bade him sweet dreams, saying that he needed a good night's sleep in order to be ready for new adventures, with all their possibilities—and, as always, Sletov replied that his life was over.

"It's been over so many times, Fedya…"

"No, this time… you know, after such a blow…"

"Thank God you're still alive," said Sergey Sergeyevich.

Suddenly Sletov turned to him—he was undoing his tie in front of the mirror—and said:

"You know, Seryozha, there's something dead about your face."

"You're no expert when it comes to men's faces, Fedya."

"No, Seryozha, I'm not joking. You know, that constant smile of yours, as if you're always happy about something—it's like a wax figure in a museum. Such jovial eyes and teeth that are too regular, like an advertisement for toothpaste, there's something very unnatural about it."

"What's to be done? Nature has wronged me."

"No, on the contrary. But something's missing."

"A heart, Fedya, a heart."

"That is also true."

"Well then. Goodnight, for the moment. And to think that at this instant Lili might be—"

"Don't mention her name. She no longer exists."

"Yes, Fedya. Life is over. Goodnight."

"Sleep if you can. I cannot."

Yet half an hour later Sletov was rattling and crying out in his sleep; then he sat up in bed and opened his eyes, but he could see nothing—everything was dark, and only from a distance could he hear the muffled sound of running water: Sergey Sergeyevich was drawing a bath.

Sergey Sergeyevich did not go to bed until much later. He slept six hours a day, no more, no less; he would drift off instantly, seldom dreamt, and never woke up during the night; yet in the morning, upon opening his eyes, he would regain in that very instant all his faculties. He did not know that half-state, familiar and pleasant to the majority of people, between dreams and reality. Since long ago, even in his Russian days, he had maintained the habit of keeping a revolver under his pillow and checking every night whether it was loaded, although for many years already his life had not once been threatened by any danger. He, however, was always ready for it, ready in theory, for there was no immediate physical danger, nor did he foresee any.

Sitting in an armchair and holding a book he was not reading, he thought how and with what means he might solve this intricate system of relationships that bound him to varying degrees with different people, and principally with Liza and Olga Alexandrovna. He sincerely wanted Olga Alexandrovna to find a man who approached her restless ideal of happiness—he had long known that he himself was infinitely and unequivocally far from this ideal. Besides, there was nothing left of his love for Olga Alexandrovna apart from those good relations, which she would speak of with such indignation. "What do they need?" he thought with sudden vexation. "Fedya Sletov, who's a good man, but a sentimental fool and nothing more?" Thus Sergey Sergeyevich conversed with himself: the doors to the room were securely locked and no one could hear him; in any case, he uttered only a few fragmentary phrases, the chief part of the monologue taking place inwardly. During those rare times when he allowed himself the luxury of such introspection, he was quite unlike his usual self. His face would ordinarily express disgust and ennui. He mused on the current affair between his wife and Kuznetsov, and shrugged, imagining this Italian trip. Perhaps, this time… But he had little hope: Sergey Sergeyevich knew Olga Alexandrovna too well. His thoughts then moved on to Liza, and he reproachfully and ashamedly shook his head. "The same family, the same blood," he said aloud. And his obedient, infallible memory conjured up the entire history of his relationship with Liza.

Liza was six years younger than Olga. She had arrived in the Crimea when Seryozha was three years old—this was during the second year of the war—having come to say awhile at Sergey Sergeyevich's dacha. She was almost the same then as she was now: that same oval face with smooth skin and almond eyes, those same sparkling teeth, with which she could lift a rather heavy suitcase off the floor, her hands clasped behind her back, leaving two wet semicircles on the leather strap, that same astonishing—for a woman—service at tennis, that same assuredness of her intrinsic wonder and that same unshakable will. She had grasped immediately that relations between Sergey Sergeyevich and Olga Alexandrovna were already not as they ought to be, and regarded her sister disapprovingly; however, as was her custom, she said nothing. The inevitable happened when Olga Alexandrovna went away for several days on a private matter. Sergey Sergeyevich had noticed how Liza was going about as though she were drunk, her eyes having lost their usual sparkle; and when, one evening, he embraced her and bid her goodnight in his usual, distant voice, he felt her body tremble. Her firm, cold hands grasped his neck with ever greater strength. She said: "Don't torture me." And then her hands suddenly grew weak.

Both she and Sergey Sergeyevich had been so secretive that no one, not even the maid, knew of their relationship. Olga Alexandrovna was too much consumed by her own private affairs to pay the slightest bit of notice to the relations between her sister and her husband. And so this relationship had gone on now for thirteen years. However, Sergey Sergeyevich had never been able to break Liza's will or to force her to do something she found unnecessary. He proposed that she live apart, but she just shook her head in response—although even the most resolute refusal could have been no more categorical. She was inconsistent in her affections for Sergey Sergeyevich: periods of scornful frostiness would be exchanged for fits of tempestuous love—yet irrespective of the state of affairs, her face, in the official family life of Sergey Sergeyevich, retained a classical equanimity, while he equally kept up his conventional joyous smile. Never would she yield to Sergey Sergeyevich in conversations with him. Once, when they were alone together, he said to her:

"There are some things you're incapable of understanding, Liza. You just come up against a wall."

"Do these things matter?"

"In a general sense, Liza, yes. You see, I cannot address any reproach of a personal nature to you; you're too perfect."

Liza looked at him ironically. His full lips were drawn out in a rapturous smile.

"Very well, what are these things?"

"You are utterly incapable of forgoing anything for the sake of others. There would come a point when the following would happen: if someone were to get in the way of your happiness, to put it rather grandly…"

Sergey Sergeyevich extended his right hand and with the index finger pulled the invisible trigger of an imaginary revolver.

"You think I'm capable of…"

Sergey Sergeyevich's smile grew even broader and he nodded several times.

"In that case, don't you fear for your own life?"

"No," said Sergey Sergeyevich.

"Because you think you're stronger than me?"

"No. Because it isn't worth it, and you know I wouldn't stop you."

The conversation had taken place after tennis. Several times Liza had tossed her racket in the air and caught it. Then she raised her eyes to look at Sergey Sergeyevich and said in a particularly quiet, insinuating voice:

"Therein lies your fault, Seryozhenka."

"Fault? In which sense? There are two in this arena."

"The latter."

"A delusion, typical of dear Olga Alexandrovna."

"And of any woman, Seryozha, if she's worth anything."

"In other words, you want me to wield a club and fend others off for you?"

"Precisely."

"*La charmante sauvage!*"* said Sergey Sergeyevich. "Poor, poor Immanuel!"

"Who's Immanuel?"

"Thus was called, Lizochka, a certain thinker from Königsberg, who falsely supposed—"

"…that his wisdom would be assimilated by your mistress?" said Liza, her eyes darkening.

"And what could a woman like that ever see in me?" said Sergey Sergeyevich with mock contemplation.

"Listen, Seryozha," said Liza, "I know you. I know that you're steeped in lies from top to tail. Even your muscles lie."

"A physiological phenomenon, which modern science—"

"And what's more, you're a clown."

"It would appear entirely inexplicable, then, why, in that case—"

---

* The charming savage!

90

"Because you know all you need to know, and you know what others know, only they think you don't."

"They do. But not you."

"No. I know everything there is to know about you, and you would do anything I wanted."

"There is something infinitely feminine and helpless about your charm, Lizochka."

Holding the racket in her left hand, Liza raised her right—half joking, half serious—and in that fraction of a second, with gentle precision Sergey Sergeyevich's soft hand stopped hers in mid-air. Then Sergey Sergeyevich lifted Liza's hand to his lips and kissed it.

"That's so typical of you, Seryozha," said Liza. "I'm sorry I'm so irritable."

"It's all right, Lizochka, I'm inured to it."

There had never been a serious argument between them, but only because—as Sergey Sergeyevich knew perfectly well—there were no grounds for one. Liza's suppressed furore would occasionally erupt in a purely physical way: she would pick a fight with Sergey Sergeyevich and feel beside herself with rage while he, pinning her arms to her body, calmly and slowly lay her on the floor, without ever causing her any harm. Her bites would leave deep and painful marks. One day, Sergey Sergeyevich nearly lost consciousness after Liza punched him in the stomach, which at that moment he had entirely failed to anticipate. He swayed back and forth, his vision dimmed; he could barely stand on his feet, and through the sudden darkness he saw Liza's rapt face and bared teeth.

"That wiped the smile off your face," said Liza.

"That's because you've distressed me. I wanted to see what lengths your destructive instincts could lead you to."

Sometimes Liza would go away—not like Olga Alexandrovna, but differently, carefully picking out all the necessary items for the trip—always alone, and she would usually be gone for a month or six weeks; however, in all this time she would never send word, and what she got up to remained a mystery. Then she would return—exactly the same woman she had been when she left, so utterly unchanged, even in her complexion, that one might have though she had not gone anywhere. There were times when she would take hardly anything with her: this meant that she was simply moving for a while to her own apartment, which Sergey Sergeyevich had rented for her long ago and about which, other than the two of them, nobody knew. Once, during one such period, she ran into Olga Alexandrovna in the street; the latter looked at her in astonishment and asked her whether she were not dreaming.

"No, Olya," said Liza with her usual composure. "No, you aren't dreaming. Shall I give you the answer?"

And so she explained that she had returned to Paris half an hour ago, deposited her things in the left-luggage office and gone to buy something before returning home. She added that she would be home for dinner, kissed her sister and disappeared.

Upon returning, Olga Alexandrovna told Sergey Sergeyevich that she had met Liza. "Just imagine, Seryozha, she'd just arrived and gone straight from the train…"

Then, perching on the arm of the chair in which Sergey Sergeyevich was reading a newspaper, she said: "You know, Seryozha... Hasn't it ever occurred to you that Liza might have a life of her own, one we know nothing about? I'm not talking about today—that's clear enough, it was nothing—but in general?..."

"We each of us have a life of our own, Olechka. Philosophically speaking, of course."

"Well, yes, but a different one."

"The older you get, the more profound you become, Lyolya."

"No, Seryozha, seriously," said Olga Alexandrovna impatiently. "Take you, you're as immaculate as can be. You have no vices, no passions; you're so kind, tolerant and good, without a single flaw; it makes one sick—although that's another matter. You don't have a second life. But what about her?"

"In this sense, Lyolya, she's more transparent than everyone. No, I think not."

"It astounds me," said Olga Alexandrovna, "that she hasn't got married, for instance. Really, it's unnatural."

"For some it's unnatural, for others it's natural."

"You're a machine, not a man," she said with a sigh. "A dear, sweet machine, but a machine nonetheless."

"It's a matter of reflexes, Lyolechka. Do you know anything about the theory of reflexes?"

"To tell the truth, very little. Are you going to give me a lecture on this?"

"If it would interest you."

"Go on, then, tell me," said Olga Alexandrovna.

Thus, the conversation about Liza really did turn into a lecture on reflexes. When Sergey Sergeyevich had finished, Olga Alexandrovna said:

"What an interesting man you could be, Seryozha."

"Not in your sense of the word, Lyolechka."

"That's just the point," she said.

Liza did indeed arrive for dinner, after which Olga Alexandrovna went into town, while Sergey Sergeyevich remained at home with Liza and did not ask her a single question—as was his wont. He knew, however, that Liza must have had a life of her own, but he never once referred to it and always attentively, with childlike trust in his eyes, listened to her tales of the weather in Switzerland or the waves on the Channel. Although Liza knew the true value of this trust, she usually gave herself over to its calming action. That, however, did not always happen, and there were times when it broke her. One day, after a trip to Switzerland, from which she, for the first and last time in her life, had returned anxious and cross, she was telling Sergey Sergeyevich about the snow in Megève having been powdery, which made for poor skiing and on the whole ruined the trip. He shook his head, all the while maintaining that blissful expression on his face.

"I know what you're thinking," said Liza suddenly, breaking off her monologue.

"That's not so difficult, Liza."

"No, I'm not talking about what you think I think you're thinking."

94

"All this Dostoevsky is spoiling your style, Liza."

"No, that's got nothing to do with it. You're wondering how many lovers I've had. Aren't you?"

"Don't cast aspersions on yourself, Lizochka," said Sergey Sergeyevich. "I think a rest would do you the world of good. Let's be off with you, little girl."

He took her in his arms and carried her, and then Liza, burying her face in his chest, suddenly burst into tears and began stroking his clean-shaven cheek.

Recalling all this now, Sergey Sergeyevich thought how his life had been built on tragic misfortune and how, for the most part, he had not been destined for happiness. Olga Alexandrovna, whom he had loved passionately at the outset and whom he still treated as a trusted friend—he never mentioned a divorce to her and always gave her to understand that, no matter what happened, she would always have a house, a husband and a son, and she could depend on this equally in those brief periods of happiness with another and in moments of disillusionment and despair— this Olga Alexandrovna had left him long ago, and he had been unable to stop her. Then there was Liza, whom he truly did love and over whom he also had no power whatsoever; one day she could leave him, just as her sister had done before her. "I would stand there on the threshold of my house as she forsook it, like a benevolent shadow eternally by her side. And this," he continued to think, "is what Fedya Sletov has been granted and I have been denied."

It was almost three o'clock in the morning, but Sergey Sergeyevich was still sitting in the armchair, gazing at the bright spot of lamplight in front of him, casting a regular, slightly diffuse circle onto the rug. "I don't know," he said aloud. "I can't see anything…" He stood up, took a few paces and muttered crossly: "…anything consolatory." Then he picked up a book, gripping it between his index finger and thumb, as though about to lance it into the air, but placed it neatly back on the side table. Next he gazed at the revolver for a long time, the black shimmer of its beautiful steel, shook his head and finally lay down to bed. A minute later, he was asleep.

Since early childhood, Seryozha had grown accustomed to the idea that the word "home" could encompass many different things at once. "Home" could mean London, a quiet street near Grove End Gardens in Hampstead, a bobby at the corner, the old church, the stone embankment of the Thames during his daily strolls; "home" could mean Paris, the proximity of the Bois de Boulogne, the Arc de Triomphe, the statue of Victor Hugo on a long-familiar square; "home" could also mean the crunch of sand beneath the wheels of Liza's motor car, an alley beyond a pair of iron gates and a squat house set amid a tranquil garden, right on the shore of a still bay, which seemed at times deep blue, at others green, although mostly neither blue nor green, but rather that colour for which human language has no word. This landscape never changed—it forever remained the same, come winter or summer, autumn or spring— much as the people who lived in Sergey Sergeyevich's villa never changed either: the gardener, always in that same large planter's hat, snipping away in the distance with his enormous shears; the Russian caretaker Nil, a former soldier and an old giant of a man, with a slightly flattened head and an accordion of unseen proportions, which he would play at night. And whenever a member of Sergey Sergeyevich's family arrived, from the suburbs of nearby Nice the cook would be summoned: a large, dark-eyed Italian who spoke in an astonishing idiom, a bizarre mix of the local dialect with French and Italian. And there was her son, too, a roguish, high-spirited youth, who would wash the car, repair the electricity and do odd jobs around the house, although he would always call himself the *chef mécanicien*,* and so everyone at home would jokingly refer to him as "Chef"—and so the name stuck. The suppliers, too, were the same year in and year out; they would always ring the one bell, which served absolutely no purpose but to quench the supplier's love of its simple melody. The greengrocer would arrive in his tiny vehicle with its thin forlorn wheels on narrow tyres, although arising virtually from the wheels themselves was a great white plywood cone with painted on it a bunch of bananas in a garish yellow colour, a sliced blood-red pomegranate and, somewhat off to the side of the pomegranate and bananas, a pile of fruits that were of a greyish-green colour and by their shape suggested something between potatoes and pears—in any case, something that did not exist in nature—and above all

* Head mechanic.

this, in assured green lettering, was written *"Fruits et primeurs de première qualité"*,* with an acute accent in the penultimate word. Then there was the baker, with his thin white hands and dark face, who drove his own car, the distinguishing feature of which was that there was a five-year-old hole in the exhaust pipe, from which fumes would come spluttering out, and when the car ground to a halt and the engine fell silent, there would come a strange, faint ringing noise from all its metal components returning to their places; from afar it would always seem as if little pieces of crockery were flying off their shelves, or that this were the peculiar swansong of the baker's car, which was falling to pieces, crying out as it did so; the most miraculous thing was that for all this, the vehicle remained intact. The milkman, who doubled as a bottle collector, was a young man and impossibly odd: he always went about without a cap, his black hair dishevelled; he had a leucoma in his right eye, was missing his front teeth, and always wore an oversized jacket, sagging trousers and enormous boots with upturned toes, usually with no laces. He lisped, and he would swing his weak arms, behind which billowed the broadest sleeves imaginable. His sole joy in life was bottles of different types and sizes: he knew everything there was to know about them. He was married to a beautiful, healthy woman who despised him, as did everyone else for that matter, and the *chef mécanicien* would say that he ought to duck when he passed below the telephone wires, so as not to get his horns

* Top-quality fruit and vegetables.

tangled in them. "*Tellement elles sont grandes, vous ne pouvez pas le croire!*"*

The milkman had but one friend and advocate—the old caretaker with the accordion; they sometimes took a stroll together in the evenings, talking animatedly, and the little milkman would run alongside the old man, lisping, swinging his arms and hitching up his sagging trousers. He loved the accordion and, listening to it, would say: "*On dirait de grandes bouteilles, qui font du bruit mélodique.*"†

As always, the butcher would come, a robust man who wore a very clean striped shirt, in a well-tuned automobile; from year to year the butcher grew fuller and rounder, and Chef predicted that he would die of an apoplectic stroke. But for the time being the butcher was still alive.

Seryozha found it astonishing that there had been no changes in the lives of these people; they never went anywhere, never read anything, and in all these years they had probably seen less than he had in a few months. He felt especial sympathy and pity for the little milkman and always had a chat with him whenever they met; however, the milkman was shy and would reply monosyllabically, smiling searchingly the whole time, his toothless mouth agape. But on the other hand, the old caretaker would chat happily, recounting the war with the Germans, weaving in tall tales that he himself truly believed: that he was impervious to bullets, that throughout the war he was never

---

* They're so big, you wouldn't believe!
† It sounds like great big bottles making a musical noise.

wounded and only once suffered a contusion—"though, really, a contusion doesn't count!"—that in the Ukraine witches milk cows, that he had served in the artillery and had seen all there was to see: he had worked in field hospitals for two weeks and seen how doctors butchered people, and how one soldier, he claimed, had his skull amputated and, what was more, survived—he was a strong chap, like him. The old man would call Liza "mistress" and Sergey Sergeyevich "master", and only to Seryozha would he speak with any familiarity, calling him by his given name, because he had known him since he was a babe in arms. He would speak Russian, but frequently lapsed into Ukrainian, and one day when Seryozha, who was nine years old at the time, brought him a large bar of chocolate, he thanked him, telling him he was a good boy, and added that the only thing left to do was to eat the sweet treat. "I don't need no woman, I can't dance no more," he clarified with a sigh. However, this was particularly coquettish of him, for the old man was as strong as an ox, and his solid white teeth sparkled beneath his grey whiskers when he smiled. He spoke of the Mediterranean with disdain, averring that the country, while on the whole not bad, could never hold a candle to Poltava province, and the climate here was inconducive to good health—he based this on the fact that he had never once worn his sheepskin coat, brought all the way from Russia, and so it was just "shrivelling away", as he put it. He would tell Seryozha about Poltava, about the Vorskla, which in summer glittered in the sunlight and in winter was so frozen over that you could ride sleighs over it, and about the dense, vibrant verdure of leafy trees; but then he would get carried away and talk of utterly fantastical things—how bears would almost daily wander into the farmstead, how he had killed a wolf with a stone, how he had a fabulous horse that would eat everything, and how one day he had fed it several pounds of *salo*. The people there, according to him, had been just like those found here, only they spoke a different language and were much more intelligent, and in his opinion the women were, on average, a little plumper than the ones here.

Seryozha knew all the inhabitants of the little village, on the outskirts of which Sergey Sergeyevich's villa was situated: all the shopkeepers, restaurateurs, all the Italian gardeners, all the random people who had wound up here God knows how and had stayed on to make a living—like the irascible old Englishman who was unable to bear the company of anyone and played tennis with himself, or the red-headed artist with freckles who went by the name of Yegorkin. For many years, Yegorkin had been painting the same pictures, depicting improbably garish peasant women riding a dashing troika through powdered snow; the one who was driving held a raised whip in her frozen hand, and what was most surprising of all was how lightly they were attired, with open necks and almost bare shoulders, so that when Sergey Sergeyevich saw one such painting for the first time, he asked the artist whether the sketch had been done during the thaw. Sergey Sergeyevich would always buy this artist's works, and he would invariably give them to Sletov, who in turn would give them away to his international acquaintances; and so one might have supposed that these paintings now adorned the walls of various apartments in every corner of the globe: in the state of Virginia, in Canada and California, in Sydney and Calcutta, in Persia, Turkey and Afghanistan, and, naturally, in all the capitals of Europe. The painter, who, as with the majority of artists, was a simple man and in his time had graduated from a Russian school—which he would translate into French most arbitrarily as *école supérieure*, although it had been an ordinary three-year college in Tambov—had at one time decided to conceive a passion for surrealism, having seen in Nice, at the Palais de la Méditerranée, an exhibition of some contemporary artist's work, and so to his usual troika racing through the snow he began to add, albeit around the edges, in the background, and even then sometimes from a far-off perspective, palm trees and a sea of the deepest blue, through which it was possible to discern some tailed monster with fins. However, Sergey Sergeyevich resolutely opposed this and had a long conversation with the artist, during which Sergey Sergeyevich persuaded Yegorkin to preserve at whatever the cost the distinct national character in his art and not to succumb to the influence of French painting, "whose contemporary trends seem, do they not," said Sergey Sergeyevich, "contentious". Sergey Sergeyevich particularly insisted that Yegorkin was, by calling, first and foremost a painter of animals, and not one of seascapes, with which Yegorkin, after some consideration, agreed. When Seryozha was young, Yegorkin would bring him cheap sweets (which the child would accept out of politeness) and bunches of mimosas, and would show him magic tricks, at which they both genuinely laughed. Seryozha always felt a little sorry for this shabbily dressed, very poor man, and Olga Alexandrovna shared that same sense of pity for him; only Liza never talked with him, and when she happened to glance at him, it was as though she were looking at an empty space. Sergey Sergeyevich said to her one day:

"Yegorkin, Lizochka, is a sphinx. Yes, a sphinx. Really, it's utterly incomprehensible how a man can dedicate his entire life to such terrible tripe as his pictures. It's easy to despise him, and so you oughtn't. Don't you think?"

The gates of the villa gave onto a rather narrow road that ran directly above the sea, which shimmered there three metres below. At the top of a path leading down, there was a large tree; below was a small bay paved with stone slabs, one side of which formed a little sea wall from which one could dive into the water. There was a dark-brown motorboat moored in the bay, beside which bobbed an ordinary pair-oar that Chef sometimes used to catch fish in particular spots known only to him, although their particularity existed only in his imagination, for there were no fish there at all, just as there were none in any of the waters nearby; or rather, they were so few that it was not worth mentioning.

It was the month of June, oppressive and sultry, when Liza and Seryozha arrived in the Midi. Chef was waiting for them at the railway station in Nice. It was around five o'clock in the evening; everything was glittering in the sunlight; there was a light breeze coming in from the sea. Seryozha's body ached slightly from the prolonged muscular strain, and there was a light throbbing in his head. That vague and wicked feeling for Liza, having begun on that memorable evening when for the first time he noticed her bare shoulders in her ball gown, had taken possession of him once and for all, and he was unable to break free of it. It had tormented him throughout the entire journey: he had barely slept a wink during the night, sensing near him, in the shuddering blue darkness, Liza's constant troubling presence. And so now, despite the heat, he felt cold and out of sorts.

"You know, Liza," he said as they were leaving the station, "I hardly slept a wink last night. I'm probably coming down with something, aren't I? I don't feel well."

She looked at him with her understanding and compassionate eyes, but what she said bore no relation to her gaze:

"Perhaps you really have caught cold."

"I must have done, Liza."

"It would be surprising," she said in response to her own thoughts, which did not, however, concern Seryozha's cold. "Once we're home," she said, "we'll get you fixed."

"In the sun?" asked Seryozha with a smile.

When they arrived, the Italian woman fed him bouillon, and after that he immediately fell asleep, lost in a soft silence, in the farthest reaches of which—he had grasped this as he was drifting off—that same quiet, though always troubling, presentiment awaited him.

WHEN SERYOZHA AWOKE in the early morning, all trace of his troubled state over these last few days had vanished. He listened. Downstairs, Nil was talking with the Italian woman in his strange French with its Ukrainian accent—in which all the verbs had but one form for every occasion, an indistinct conjugation—about how it was a shame that there were so few fish in the sea and that the big ones were taken to Nice from the ocean.

"What use is a sea if there are no fish in it?" Nil was saying. "Maybe you just don't know how to catch them. *Vous pas savoir attraper gros poisson, vous savoir attraper petit poisson?*"*

"*On saurait bien l'avoir,*" replied the Italian woman, "*s'il y en avait là-dedans.*"†

Seryozha washed, dressed and, through old force of habit, slid down the banister of the interior flight of stairs leading down from the first floor, where his room was situated, and went into the yard.

"*Bonjour, Monsieur Serge,*" said the Italian woman. "*Dieu, que vous êtes devenu grand maintenant!*"‡

"What are you doing up so early?" asked Nil, placing

---

* You not know how to catch big fish, you know how to catch little fish? [broken French].

† We could… if there were any there.

‡ Hello, Monsieur Serge… Lord, how big you've grown!

his enormous arm around Seryozha's shoulders. "Where are you off to?"

It pleased Seryozha greatly that Nil and the Italian woman were kindly towards him and so obviously loved him. He shook the woman's hand, asked after her recent health and enquired whether Chef was around. The woman said that she had been well and that Chef was washing the motor in the garage. Seryozha headed there: the garage was nearby, and he could hear the sound of a jet of water crashing into the automobile—there was a curious change in pitch when the jet landed under the wings of the vehicle.

"Hello, Chef," said Seryozha. "I'd like to go out on the water today. Is your boat working?"

"My boat?" said Chef in astonishment. "Of course it's working. How could it not be, when I've been looking after it?"

This boat had been made to order for Sergey Sergeyevich, and, as with everything he ordered or bought, perhaps with the exception of Yegorkin's paintings, it was of very fine quality. Chef abandoned the half-washed automobile, changed his clothes with the speed of an illusionist, and a minute later they were already sitting together in the boat, which was sailing across the smooth water of the bay, shooting up two white semi-transparent walls of spray. Then, having doubled the cape, they headed out into the open sea, where there were already a few reasonably sized, bouncy waves. The morning was clear throughout, and in the luminous fading blue one could make out the retreating outline of the opposite shore.

They were both silent. Seryozha sat reclining, now closing, now opening his eyes. Then Chef said in his easy manner:

"*Et bien, comment ça va à Paris?*"*

Seryozha could not help laughing. In Chef's imagination, while Paris was indeed a great city, it was also a homogeneous concept, and so it was sufficient merely to live in Paris in order to determine unequivocally how things were there in general. In reply to Seryozha's explanations, Chef nodded and then began to talk of events in his own life, telling him that he had a fiancée with a dowry, but that his mother would not allow him to marry, since he was too young. He spoke of a certain Jeannot, who, according to him, was absolutely unbeatable at any game, be it boules, billiards or even cards, and said that he, Chef, suspected him of cheating. Then he began to talk about the lonely Englishman, whom he had watched as the latter sat in his garden, talking with someone, and then grew angry and started shouting, although there was no one in the garden other than him; Chef had been unable to understand anything because the man had been speaking in English, but he was convinced that the old man had gone mad from drink, although no one had ever seen him drunk.

"That doesn't prove anything," said Chef. "Perhaps he had been drinking earlier, and only then, after he went mad, did he stop."

* Well, now, how are things in Paris?

When Seryozha returned, Liza was already taking her coffee. He asked her how she had slept. "Wonderfully," came the reply, but Seryozha detected a very slight but indisputable distance in her voice. It had slipped out unintentionally; Liza herself noticed it only several minutes later. However, while she understood the reason for it, Seryozha did not. Still, half an hour later they both set out for a swim and only retuned home once their shoulders began to ache from the effects of the quick southern sun. After luncheon, Liza retired to her room to read, while Seryozha went to Cannes with Chef to watch the motorboat race, and they returned only towards dinner.

It was already late evening when Seryozha and Liza went out together; they ambled down a deserted road, lit by a bright moon. It was very quiet. They walked in silence; a pale, thin strip of moonlight glimmered on the still sea, quivering on the dark ripples of water, the firm sand softly and rhythmically crunching underfoot; along the dark road, from which they were separated by an uninterrupted row of gardens, the noise of automobile tyres rushed by from time to time, their sound reminiscent of fading whispers.

"You know, Liza," said Seryozha, "it's like silent music, if such a thing could exist. I don't know how to put it into words. Do you follow me?"

She gave no reply. As before, her hand rested on his shoulder. He very much wanted to take Liza with his right arm, which had filled up with blood and hung limply by his side, but he did not dare to do that. Everything that had vanished that morning but had been going on for some time now—before their departure for the south and then on the train—now returned to him with even greater force. He saw in front of him the road, palm trees, the gates, the sea, standing stock-still, almost mockingly in their usual places, but everything was now different from how he had seen it before. As Liza walked along, brushing his side, he sensed the even movements of her body and closed his eyes; then everything ceased to exist, apart from this measured, inexpressible rhythm of her movements, far beneath which crunched the invisible sand, and the sound, with a magical precision, echoed this swaying of her body.

"Liza!" he had wanted to call out, but could not. Her hand then slowly drew away from Seryozha's shoulder and touched his cheek: her face, with its glittering eyes, approached Seryozha's; in the fickle light of the moon, Seryozha saw her mouth with its open lips. Every muscle in his body tensed; he could almost feel the distant touch of her lips, when suddenly he found himself being suffocated by her lingering, merciless kiss. Liza felt his body suddenly melt in her arms; she staggered, trying to support him. He had fainted. He became heavy and difficult for her to hold; then, stooping down, she took him with her left arm under his knee and lifted him as she had done many years ago when he was a little boy, while she remained just the same. She carried him several steps. Finally his eyes opened and he murmured, "Liza, Liza, what are you doing?" and quickly slumped to the ground. He was ashamed to look her in the face.

"My poor little boy!" she said. "Home, Seryozha, we need to get you home."

When they returned to the house, Nil was sitting on a stool by the gates. "The sea air's good," he said to Liza. "Truly, Madame, it's marvellous. But you, Seryozha, you look all pale from the moonlight. You're like a bride beneath her veil."

Seryozha went up to his room, leaving Liza alone. She undressed, wrapped her naked body in her favourite dressing gown of dark-blue silk with embroidered birds in flight, and sat down on the chaise longue. She was unable to calm herself. Even after drinking some iced orangeade, she still felt thirsty. The touch of her gown irritated her swollen nipples, so she threw it open and went out onto the veranda. Amid the diaphanous evening quiet, from somewhere far off in the distance, the muffled sound of a piano reached her. The air was balmy and still; down below, a dark flower bed sent up its particular evening fragrance. Liza did not think about anything in these moments. Without fastening her dressing gown, she went over to the staircase leading to the first floor, paused for a second, then, with brisk steps, almost at a run, headed upstairs.

Paris was almost empty during these summer months. Lyudmila, having spent several weeks alone in her immaculate—and also empty, following Arkady Alexandrovich's departure—apartment, having taken a rest from her constant state of suspicion, from the constant multifarious lies that constituted her everyday life and her relations with people, and having played on the piano all the many pieces of her vast repertoire, decided to go to the coast; she bought everything necessary for the journey, and had almost readied herself to travel to the railway station, when suddenly an unexpected incident changed her plans entirely. This incident occurred as she was leaving a large shop on boulevard de la Madeleine, when she ran into an old friend of hers, an Italian woman, who in her time had owned a modest *pension* in Switzerland, where Lyudmila had stayed several times. The woman was noted for having been the mistress of one of the kings of Europe for a very brief period some fifteen years ago—and ever since she had lived on her memories of this. However, in addition to the memories, the king, upon parting with her, bestowed on her a certain sum of money—insignificant for the State, but significant enough for a private budget—on which she had subsisted all these years. Her apartment was hung with portraits of the king in a great variety of poses:

on court, dressed for tennis; in an armchair, with a book; on his yacht, in a captain's hat; astride a black horse; astride a white horse; astride a bay horse. After this critical period in the woman's life, prior to which her biography had revelled in the utmost obscurity, she had travelled around Europe. However, just as it was unthinkable to imagine her in isolation from her glittering past, so too, to the same degree, was it a constant, inescapable reality of her current existence that she was in possession of a modest *pension*, in the running of which she would be assisted by one of her many cousins, who would alternate approximately once every eighteen months, and whose abundance in her homeland was seemingly inexhaustible. The *pension* was frequented mostly by personal acquaintances of hers, who would stay there for a comparatively brief sojourn and appreciated her discretion: in spite of her exceptional garrulity, the woman never said anything amiss.

She was overjoyed to run into Lyudmila, whom she had not seen for two years or so, told her that she had been in Paris for many months already and invited her to tea. On entering the hallway, Lyudmila spotted a portrait of the king that she did not recognize (ostensibly acquired only recently) in the new photographic style. The portrait almost looked like an icon: the king's face, which had evidently been subjected to meticulous retouching, was majestic and sorrowful, in the peculiar way that is characteristic of oleographs. Noticing Lyudmila's gaze, the Italian woman said that His Majesty—she always spoke thus of the king—had recently sent her this portrait. This was obviously untrue:

firstly, there was no inscription on the portrait; second, the king, although a man of no great culture, lacked the supremely poor taste that would have been required if he were to have actually sent her this portrait.

"What a melancholic face," said Lyudmila in an expressly detached tone of voice, so that the woman would take her pronouncement not for sympathy with her, but as her genuine impression—one might have thought that the king was pondering something or lamenting some unrealizable project.

"Yes, that's also my impression," said the woman. Both she and Lyudmila simultaneously felt a sense of satisfaction: Lyudmila because the woman had understood her exactly as intended, and the woman because she was dealing with a person of intelligence and sensibility. Indeed, the Italian woman regarded Lyudmila very highly and knew much more about her than one might have supposed. Before the maid served tea, the woman warned Lyudmila that a gentleman was expected, a very sweet but rather unfortunate Englishman, who regrettably spoke poor French and no Italian at all. He had come to the *pension* completely by chance. She wore a genuine smile that revealed all her teeth, which always made a slightly strange impression, for, with the exception of four front teeth on her upper jaw and an equal number on the lower one, all the rest alternated in a perfect, unbroken order: gold, white, gold, white, and so on to the end. This Englishman, insofar as the Italian woman knew, was still a young man. As the years went by, she had unwittingly and magnanimously raised the figure after which a man ceased to be young: at first it was thirty, then thirty-five, then forty, now forty-five and even over; after fifty they began to fall under the ambiguous expression "a youthful man"; by fifty-four it would be "an essentially youthful man"; and by fifty-eight, "an ultimately youthful man". This Englishman had recently lost his wife and was now completely alone in the world. According to the Italian woman, he was terribly sweet. Lyudmila immediately pricked up her ears and, although she had no plans yet, she had already made that customary unconscious effort that usually preceded their inception. Generally speaking, her face, despite its apparent woodenness, was possessed of a rare expressive faculty; while awaiting the English-man's arrival, she gradually imparted to him a character befitting his circumstances: that is, a slightly weary expression, distant eyes, a careless—as though forgotten in the air—hand, with a cigarette between long, slender fingers that betrayed a slight tremor.

Finally the Englishman appeared. He was a large man, with a full head of grey hair and a simple, ruddy face, a sort of gentleman farmer with the greater predisposition towards the gentleman, or so Lyudmila thought. He greeted the Italian woman, shook Lyudmila's cold hand and uttered a slow and completely incomprehensible phrase in French.

"Forgive me," said Lyudmila to the Italian woman; the Englishman listened with a tense face, trying to grasp her words. "Forgive me, Giulia. I'd very much like to know what Monsieur just said. I'll ask him in his own language."

The Englishman looked at Lyudmila expectantly. Smiling, the Italian woman nodded, and then Lyudmila, after pausing for a second and extinguishing her cigarette in the ashtray, said, addressing the Englishman in such a tone as if she were continuing a conversation that had been cut off:

"Sorry, I must confess I didn't understand what you just said."

The Englishman lit up, and the tense expression vanished from his face.

"I'm very, very glad," he said, "that Madame, thank God, speaks English. Is Madame French?"

"No, Russian."

"Russian!" said the Englishman in amazement. "You come from Russia? A remarkable country."

Lyudmila replied with a weary smile that she too loved this country but, alas, was deprived of the possibility to return there. Lyudmila had refined this conversation with various foreigners about Russia long ago; it would change depending on the nationality of her interlocutor— whether he was French or Dutch, German or English. With Englishmen, she would usually say that the Russian nature contained certain positive elements, essentially very close to those that had transformed her homeland into the undisputed great Continental power that it was. Although Russia was unfortunately tormented by fate and "adversity", yet she, Lyudmila, did not lose hope that some day—and undoubtedly that day would come—Russia would take up its rightful place in the world; she, Lyudmila, hoped she would live to see that day, after which she could die at peace. At this point she would strain her throat, her voice would softly tremble, and this was supposed to signify that, despite her reserve, she loved her homeland deeply, that she suffered alongside it, and that, more to the point, life was not so sweet for her. Lyudmila noted with satisfaction that the Englishman put up no resistance; he listened to her, his mouth nearly agape, and it was obvious that her words were incapable of arousing the slightest bit of doubt in him. The conversation went on for another half-hour, then Lyudmila got up, bid farewell to the Italian woman, who throughout the conversation had understood nothing and sat there with a permanent smile, so fixed and seemingly unflinching that the Englishman's jaw began to ache from unconscious sympathy, and several times he rested his chin on his fist. He said that he, too, ought to be going—and so he and Lyudmila left together.

The little rue Desbordes-Valmore, where Giulia's *pension* was located, was illuminated by the July sun; when at times a sultry breeze blew, the dappled shadows cast by the trees quivered almost imperceptibly on the pavements. The Englishman told Lyudmila that he was quite unfamiliar with Paris and his only chance of getting home was by giving the taxi driver a card on which was written the address of his *pension*. Lyudmila drew him into a conversation about England, and when it came out that he stayed in his house in London relatively infrequently and preferred his modest estate in Scotland, Lyudmila very nearly choked on her own saliva; at any rate, she placed her hand to her chest and began coughing, and when the Englishman became concerned, she told him with a meek and unfalteringly sad smile that she had never been able to boast of good health. During the conversation, which would prove decisive for future events, she succeeded in proving that he was mistaken to think American automobiles superior to English ones. "It isn't true," she said, and ultimately he decided not to trade in his old "Rolls".

Lyudmila had to make a great effort to keep up her tragic performance. It was not the obvious wealth of the Englishman that she found appealing, but the undoubted ease of acquiring it, which had, on such perfect terms, offered itself to her for the first time in her life. From that moment, it had become clear to her that she could not under any circumstances let the Englishman get away; to do so would have been absolutely unthinkable, since even a short-term, chance parting could change everything: on finding himself beyond Lyudmila's influence, he could, or indeed would, fall under the influence of factors she could not predict and against which she was almost powerless. She decided not to let him escape, and a plan was hatched immediately. Presently she would say that she wanted to take some fresh air—"My lungs have always been weak"— he would ask where they might go, and so they would head off to Versailles; there, in the park, she would be taken ill and would ask to be seen home. At home she would feel much better, and they would go to dine at La Tour d'Argent, and afterwards either to Bal Tabarin or to the Casino de Paris. Even the fact that it was the first day of

Lyudmila's monthly complaint could not hamper her plan, and it was indeed almost incidental, since her plan did not involve—in light of the fact that she was dealing with an elderly English gentleman—surrendering herself to him that evening or even the following morning; that could only happen at the end of the week, and so it was all the better. She immediately set about executing her plan. Leaving rue de la Tour, they turned onto avenue Henri-Martin. The conversation was academic: England, Russia, France.

"How hot it is!" said Lyudmila. "It's the curse of large cities."

"Yes, yes," said the Englishman.

He took not the slightest bit of initiative, and so Lyudmila began to talk about the Bois de Boulogne, the park at Saint-Cloud, and Ville-d'Avray, which she loved very much, she said.

"Where is all this?" asked the Englishman.

She told him, and he suggested going there. Lyudmila declined. After a few paces he said that, all the same, it would be rather pleasant to go for a stroll in the woods. Lyudmila consented. They hailed a taxi; Lyudmila gave the directions to the driver, a sad man with grey moustaches. It was immediately apparent from his accent that he was Russian, although Lyudmila avoided speaking Russian with taxi drivers, fearing a familiarity on their part, and so she tried to speak French with an English accent. She explained to him that he needed first to go around the lake in the Bois de Boulogne and then on to Versailles via Saint-Cloud and Ville-d'Avray—and so they set off. En route, Lyudmila mentioned in passing the necessary details of her private life which stood midway between classic English reserve in such situations and Russian directness, a national trait which she lost no time in commenting on to the Englishman, accompanying it with several observations of a general nature—with the purpose that her acquaintance should have no doubt as to the full correctness and decency of everything that even remotely concerned her.

Lyudmila was taking all these precautions partly just in case, but partly through the habit of always being suspicious; although, she understood perfectly well that in the given instance she could afford to be less cautious—with someone like this, she had nothing to lose. However, just as she discharged her financial obligations with exceptional diligence and now conformed to those unalterable precepts she had established once and for all, so too in dealing with her admirers did she always take great care over the smallest detail of her actions, as though it were a play that had to be acted out. Her interminable inward exasperation could to a large extent be explained by the fact that in dealing with living people, and not the dramatis personae of a play, she was forever, on account of some trivial, unwelcome disruption to her plan, having to refashion the text in accordance with changing circumstances. Broadly speaking, Lyudmila was characteristically single-minded and scrupulous in all that she did: she kept her word, always showed up for an appointment precisely ten minutes late, and one could generally rely on her. In all her maudlin commercial enterprises it was she who played the leading role, and not her partner. Throughout her conversation with the Englishman, she could breathe easily—everything was going so smoothly that she was on the point of asking herself whether it were not a dream.

When she was taken ill at Versailles, she staggered but remained on her feet; through almost closed eyes she realized with alarm that the slow Englishman had failed to grasp what was going on. This lasted only a moment, however, after which he placed his arm under Lyudmila's back, and then she, drawing away a little, let herself fall suddenly right into this arm—at her back she felt his phenomenally firm and supple muscles contract momentarily. It was a blissful sensation; among Lyudmila's few genuine feelings, love for an athletic male body occupied one of the top spots.

"Excuse me, I am not quite well," she said quietly, opening her eyes and smiling weakly.

When the driver accelerated slightly—after Lyudmila had been led to a taxi and they had set off for Paris—the Englishman shouted impatiently:

"Slowly, slowly!"

And Lyudmila immediately translated in a feeble voice: *"Allez doucement, chauffeur."**

The Englishman liked her apartment very much, but he was especially pleased to see the piano—to crown it all, he turned out to be a great lover of music. Lyudmila had not expected such blind luck, and tears welled in her eyes;

* Go slowly, driver.

she was so happy that she even exclaimed, "Oh, darling!" which she had planned to say, spontaneously and unexpectedly, only on the third day, as evening approached, possibly around six o'clock, following a conversation in which the Englishman had said that he would be only too happy to do everything in his power for her. For the first time in many years, the deviation from the plan had been instigated by Lyudmila. The conversation continued, already crossing over to that tone of instant understanding that usually precedes the most pivotal phase of a relationship; Lyudmila understood that she needed to "make the switch" and provoke *un coup de foudre*,* as she thought— otherwise she risked losing the advantage. Meanwhile, in her mind she feverishly hunted through her musical repertoire for something that might be of particular interest to her new acquaintance; she decided that after 'Old Man River' and 'Charlie Is My Darling' she would play some Chopin, whose lyric flights she greatly admired. This, however, could be deferred until the following day: today she would not play, on account of her weakness.

The next part of Lyudmila's plan witnessed no deviation from the script. They dined at La Tour d'Argent, then went on to Bal Tabarin, and afterwards Lyudmila drank some hot chocolate at Weber's. Finally, after it had gone two o'clock in the morning, the Englishman saw her home; along the way, in the taxi, he twice kissed her hand, which she permitted. As she sat there absolutely still, reclining,

* Love at first sight.

she wanted to throw herself around his neck. When they said goodnight, there was a rather drawn-out conversation which lasted almost ten minutes; the Englishman asked whether he might see Lyudmila the next day, and she assured him that it was quite impossible, but ultimately agreed, with the condition that he telephone first. Lyudmila passed through the hallway, dancing and humming to herself, as though she were suddenly twenty years old again. Then she undressed, got into bed and stretched out with delight; when she glanced in the mirror, she saw her deep-blue eyes, in place of whose usual sorrow was sheer joy.

The period leading up to the moment when the Englishman (MacFarlane was his name) would be in no doubt that Lyudmila, and only Lyudmila, could and should become his wife, and that it would be impossible for him to act otherwise—resting at home after a most hearty meal, Lyudmila had mulled over all these details at length and with great relish—lasted five days, precisely the same length as her monthly complaint. On the sixth day, in the morning, she took a bath and began getting ready for MacFarlane's evening visit; that day, he was to dine with her, for to do otherwise would have created an array of technical obstacles that were always particularly vexing and had a dangerous effect on the spontaneity and surprise of everything that was to take place. God knows how or why.

MacFarlane showed up half an hour before the appointed time; as always, he was very civil and amiable, although his eyes were those of a madman, just as they were supposed to be. After the meal, with long and deliberate pauses in the conversation, broken by Lyudmila's expressly anxious laughter, she went over to the piano without turning on the light—outside, dusk was quickly falling—and MacFarlane followed her. When at last he embraced her, her fingers remained on the keys, producing at the final moment the prolonged sound of three individual notes slowly fading away. Lyudmila felt the muscles in her neck tense as she let her head fall back during this first, impromptu kiss.

All the rest happened exactly as Lyudmila had envisaged it. His impeccable knowledge of intimate relations between man and woman, the fruit of long experience, could not fool her this time or any other. She knew that her future depended on the impressions left by her first night of intimacy with MacFarlane, and she would spare no effort in order to safeguard this future. Late at night, after MacFarlane had demanded several times that she give her outright consent to be his wife (in reply she had just stroked his round head with its terrible grey hair), she replied at last, smiling feebly, that she was very tired and would prefer to postpone the conversation until the morning. MacFarlane left with his head in the clouds; he was impossibly happy.

The following morning a telephone call disturbed Lyudmila's slumber. Not quite awake, she said in a sharp voice: "*Allô!*" But when she heard MacFarlane's voice at the other end, sleep instantly abandoned her and her voice regained the delicate charm that was necessary in her intercourse with the Englishman.

"My God, I'm still sleeping," she said, drawing out the words, which was, generally speaking, completely out of character for her, but came naturally when talking to MacFarlane.

He turned up for luncheon, which was followed by a discussion of their joint future. Until now, Lyudmila had only mentioned in passing that she was married to a man with whom she had nothing in common. Arkady Alexandrovich, in Lyudmila's descriptions of him, always had a strictly defined character, like the villain in a classic melodrama: a despot, a tyrant, a pathologically jealous man and—in the most catastrophic instances—a drunkard, possessed not of a single positive trait. He did not even love Lyudmila, but regarded her as if she were his property. However, now, for the first time in all these years, she altered the story slightly: MacFarlane would find it difficult to grasp—if she adhered to her routine version—what exactly was keeping her tied to this man. Therefore, although Lyudmila painted Arkady Alexandrovich in lurid tones, still she accompanied this with several lighter remarks that were designed to underscore not so much his only point of merit as Lyudmila's own kind-heartedness. In other words, Arkady Alexandrovich remained, fundamentally, a despot, and, it could be said, even a tyrant, but when all was said and done, he was a weak man, whom Lyudmila could not bring herself to leave. She could not imagine what he would do without her. In the last instance, Lyudmila had spoken the truth; this indeed was the state of affairs—until recently, in any case.

"Where is he now?" asked MacFarlane. "I think we should have a talk with him…"

"He isn't in Paris," Lyudmila quickly ventured.

The prospect of MacFarlane's meeting Arkady Alexandrovich did not suit her one bit.

"Then we ought to write to him at once," said MacFarlane.

It was decided that Lyudmila should write to Arkady Alexandrovich that very day, and after this conversation they moved on to the idyllic themes of the immediate future—Scotland, lochs, fishing, travel, trips to the Riviera. It was not without a degree of humour that MacFarlane spoke of his life in Britain, regaling Lyudmila with Scotch anecdotes.

Evening drew in unnoticed. It was like the previous one in almost every respect, with the sole difference that after dinner Lyudmila spent a long time playing the most lyrical pieces for him. MacFarlane, who was a true connoisseur of music, could not but appreciate her artistry, which only endeared him to Lyudmila even more, if that were possible, and again, late at night, he left, having dressed slowly and reluctantly. Lyudmila waved goodbye to him, not even lifting her blonde head with its dishevelled hair from the pillow.

The very next morning she telephoned Sergey Sergeyevich.

"It's Lyudmila Nikolayevna here," she said breathlessly.

"How kind of you to remember me," said the calm, mocking voice through the receiver. "Good morning."

"Sergey Sergeyevich!" exclaimed Lyudmila. "Sergey Sergeyevich, I have a colossal request to make of you. Everything depends on you."

"Colossal? What is it exactly?"

"I need my husband's address, immediately, do you hear?"

"I do," said Sergey Sergeyevich. "I'm afraid I do. You know, dear Lyudmila Nikolayevna, my acquaintance with your husband—I do not wish to conceal anything from you—has been until now rather superficial. I can't imagine why."

"Sergey Sergeyevich, for the love of God, you don't know how important this is to me!"

"It's possible, Lyudmila Nikolayevna, that it is important. Yet, however important it may be, it does not change the facts of the matter. In other words—and perhaps this may come as a shock to you—my correspondence with your husband has always been of a rather irregular nature. More specifically, it has never existed, and so, much to my dismay, I cannot give you his address."

"Sergey Sergeyevich, have you no heart? Your wife's address—you know it perfectly well. My God, I simply can't find the words."

"The state of your health is beginning to concern me," said Sergey Sergeyevich. "Take a sedative, refer yourself to the nearest pharmacy and—"

"Your wife's address, Sergey Sergeyevich. Surely you must know it."

"Indeed I do."

"Give it to me."

"I don't think that will be necessary."

"Sergey Sergeyevich, I give you my word of honour…"

Laughter rang down the receiver. Then Sergey Sergeyevich said:

"If that will be all, Lyudmila Nikolayevna. All that remains for me is to wish you the very best. Goodbye."

She could not permit, following her undisputed and decisive victory over MacFarlane, especially when everything she had dreamt of had almost been realized—riches, status, she had only to reach out and take it—she could not permit this curious bit of good fortune to slip away from her on account of the silliest of misunderstandings, for want of a single address, which hitherto she had not required. She grasped the delicacy of the situation: to go to Italy to search for Arkady Alexandrovich was entirely out of the question. She could, of course, have explained all this to MacFarlane, but she considered it necessary in every way possible to shield him from too intimate an acquaintance with her private life. For the first time in a very long while, she was at a loss. In any case, something had to be done. She knew that it would be difficult to get anything out of Sergey Sergeyevich; he was unlike others in this respect, as she had ascertained on the occasion of her first visit to him, although her undertaking then had met with success, but that had come about purely by chance, and the reasons for its success were not those she had intended.

She went out, hailed a taxi and set off for Sergey

Sergeyevich's apartment. It turned out that he was not at home. She stood on the landing, cracking her knuckles with impatience and generally going to pieces. A tall, unfamiliar man then went up to the door and, looking at Lyudmila with a certain degree of astonishment, rang the bell. The door opened, and he was about to enter the apartment without saying anything, when Lyudmila grabbed him by the sleeve. It was Sletov. She quickly said in Russian:

"Excuse me, do you live here?"

"Yes."

"Do you work for Sergey Sergeyevich?"

"No."

"Then what is your relation to him?"

"Are you from a detective agency?" asked Sletov with curiosity.

"No, I'm just a woman on the brink of despair," said Lyudmila, continuing to crack her knuckles. Sletov looked her up and down again; judging by her apparel, she looked more likely to be a philanthropist than a beggar.

"So you aren't after any money?" he asked after a moment of hesitation.

"No, not at all."

"Please, do come in," he said, recollecting himself. "Tell me what the matter is, and I'll relay it to Sergey Sergeyevich. What has happened?"

Greatly unnerved at first but soon calming down, Lyudmila began relating her story. Sletov listened attentively. She said she just had met the man for whom she had spent her whole life searching. Sletov's face was a picture of sympathy. She then explained that being forced to remain with her husband was absolutely impossible, that she needed to put an end to it, that life otherwise would not be worth living, and that if she did not manage to obtain what she needed from Sergey Sergeyevich, there would be only one option left... She extracted a small revolver with a mother-of-pearl handle. Sletov gesticulated wildly.

"For goodness' sake, you've gone mad," he said. "I'm prepared to help you in every way that I can. I understand you perfectly, but what does Sergey Sergeyevich have to do with all this?"

She explained even this point to him. Sletov shook his head.

"He won't give you the address; even the Devil himself won't be able to help you there," he said. "I know Sergey Sergeyevich well enough."

"I don't need the address," said Lyudmila, her eyes flashing. "I'll write the letter in your presence; let Sergey Sergeyevich send it, that's all I ask. I shan't even seal the envelope."

"That is a different matter."

In her large handwriting, Lyudmila then wrote out the letter and handed it to Sletov, who saw her to the door and promised to do everything necessary.

Sergey Sergeyevich returned half an hour later and found Sletov sitting in an armchair with a pensive look about him, playing with Lyudmila's letter.

"What are you doing, Fyodor Borisovich? Attending to correspondence?"

"In a manner of speaking, yes," said Sletov, "though only indirectly. You've just missed Lyudmila Nikolayevna."

"That was to be expected. So you're writing to her?"

"No, she has written a letter."

"To me?"

"That's just it. No."

"Ah, I see," said Sergey Sergeyevich. "She's asked you to send the letter to her husband?"

"Yes."

And so Sletov recounted his conversation with Lyudmila to Sergey Sergeyevich, adding that she had made a very sincere impression on him, that she was a woman who was very troubled and indeed, as she had said, on the brink of despair.

"Did she also tell you she was a virgin? No? Well, thank God for that, otherwise you would have believed her. However, this is something new; I seem to recall that time was when she used to operate rather differently. Give me the letter."

"What?" said Sletov. "You're going to read it? Someone else's letter, not addressed to you? Seryozha!"

"Trust me, Fedya, in dealing with notorious criminals, one cannot be guided by gentlemanly principles. From this woman, Fedya, we ought first to expect some underhand trick. Well then, what do we have here? 'Dear Arkady, you know how much I have done for you; you know how often I have had to sacrifice absolutely everything, even my own

130

self-respect. Being an intelligent and sensitive person, *tu dois avoir apprécié cela*.'* She's so distressed that she's even mixing her languages. 'I now ask you to send to me, without hindrance or delay, as soon as you receive this letter, your informed consent to a divorce. What is to be done? Our lives are on different tracks.' Indeed, one could put it that way. 'I shall take upon myself all the expenses incurred in the process.'"

Sergey Sergeyevich whistled.

"'I ask nothing of you other than this. I await your prompt reply. Send ahead a telegram stating your consent in principal, and then the paperwork. I wish you happiness. Your Lyudmila.' This, Fedya, as fortune-tellers would say, is what's called a turning point. But what poor man has fallen into her snare?"

"It's plain to see that she's being guided by love," said Sletov, blowing rings of cigarette smoke.

"God knows," said Sergey Sergeyevich. "Perhaps it's less absurd than it seems at first glance. In any case, she's clearly disturbed. To think, taking on all those expenses."

"It's love, I tell you, Seryozha. Love."

* You ought to have appreciated this.

131

THE TELEGRAM bringing news of Arkady Alexandrovich's consent to the divorce arrived three days later, and Lyudmila wasted no time in showing it to MacFarlane. After a further three days came the official paperwork; Lyudmila took it to her solicitor, explaining that she was interested in obtaining the fastest possible resolution to the affair and that money was no object. He promised to do everything on the shortest possible timescale, and she heaved a sigh of relief. MacFarlane proposed a trip to the Riviera, but Lyudmila demurred; she did not want to risk an encounter… while she was going through a divorce… She would prefer… MacFarlane agreed to everything. It was decided that they would go to the coast, and then take a trip around France. Early the next morning, they left Paris.

For Lyudmila, the life of which she had until now only dreamt was finally beginning. Beside elementary comforts, such as travelling first-class, expensive hotels, that is, those things she already knew from before—although they had always been patently ephemeral and, as it were, contraband—she experienced a sense of gratitude and even love for MacFarlane, to the extent that she was generally capable of such feelings. Of course, had it suddenly come out that MacFarlane was completely ruined, she would have immediately—although, perhaps, nevertheless, with a certain fleeting sense of pity—left him. Luckily, this was impossible. Here was a complex emotion, a large portion of which consisted in a purely physical attraction; having dealt her whole life with mostly elderly men—businessmen, industrialists, speculators, whose general characteristics almost always featured a large stomach, shortness of breath, a degree of physical infirmity—she was not precious in this regard. MacFarlane was a tireless walker; he loved nature, knew every type of tree, all the flowers and plants; he rowed, ran and swam well, and was second to none when it came to fishing; he never complained of any ailments, as invariably did every one of Lyudmila's former admirers. To top it all off—and again in contrast to his predecessors—MacFarlane was a man of culture. Lyudmila talked with him as she would with an equal. He was captivated by everything Lyudmila said and was especially touched by the fact that she felt at home with English literature. He did not suspect that a love of music, literature and art in general could be explained in some instances by spiritual wealth, and in others, conversely, by spiritual poverty; Lyudmila belonged namely to the second category of their devotees. However, one way or another, she and Mac-Farlane very quickly found a common language, the chief ideas of which were borrowed from Kipling and Dickens, his favourite authors. In one of her first conversations with MacFarlane, Lyudmila had told him that she had been raised on English literature. MacFarlane was amazed, as all the rest had been, by her fluent English; he could not have known that it was quite necessary in Lyudmila's line of work, which might have caused it to depreciate in value, even if it did attest to her undoubted linguistic abilities.

Lyudmila felt so marvellous now that little by little she was ridding herself entirely of her perpetual state of suspicion, of the fear of saying or doing the wrong thing—a single false move, a single misplaced remark… Not only did she fill her role, but it began to seem as though she had never lived otherwise, and that things had always been thus. She even wept several times without its having been prompted by so much as a request to defer a note of credit or the tale of the imaginary death of her imaginary daughter— she wept from sheer delight and from the fact that, at long last, her toilsome labours had met with deserved success. MacFarlane would call her "my little girl" and stroke her head. Every provision had been made, everything had been decided: three months later Lyudmila would obtain her divorce, by which time MacFarlane would already be in England, and they would be separated for a fortnight— only for a fortnight—and then Lyudmila, with the divorce in the bag, would go to the aerodrome at le Bourget, board an aeroplane and arrive in London two hours later, and the following day they would be married. Lyudmila was thoroughly happy.

LYUDMILA'S LETTER, which was perfectly unexpected and ostensibly ought to have cut straight to the point, did not bring Arkady Alexandrovich, however, the joy and relief that one might have expected. This was on account of the fact that through Arkady Alexandrovich's own actions Lyudmila had now shattered the image of his wife that he had spent so long constructing and cultivating for Olga Alexandrovna, an image that showed Lyudmila to be in no state to tolerate any idea of a definitive separation from her husband—so strong yet submissive was the quiet love she bore for him. It was, of course, possible that Lyudmila had sent this letter in the midst of a severe nervous attack, which, perhaps, betokened madness or suicide. However, for all that Arkady Alexandrovich knew well the theoretical improbability of such a supposition, it would have meant further the necessity of going to Paris to try to save her—this woman was, after all, willing to sacrifice everything for him, and if until now she had not done so, then it was only on account of his magnanimity. Moreover, Arkady Alexandrovich found the prospect of this journey thoroughly disagreeable. He spent some time mulling over the variety of ways in which he could explain Lyudmila's letter to Olga Alexandrovna, and so he decided to present it as an attempt by Lyudmila thus to cause something of an explosion—a mark of desperation, naturally, and, it could be said, a base act, although to a certain degree an understandable one. In actual fact, Arkady Alexandrovich could imagine rather accurately what had occasioned this letter from Lyudmila, who had never concealed from him that if she were to find a worthy man, as she put it, she would be especially curious to see under which bridge her former husband would end up. Arkady Alexandrovich even felt a certain slight and fleeting alarm—he was like a man who, while a train is in motion, crosses from one carriage to the next, over two platforms separated by half a step's distance, while beneath the quick air whistles, the passing rails flash and the gravel inaudibly scatters in all directions. However, when Olga Alexandrovna asked, "Aren't you going to tell me, Arkasha, whom your letter is from?", he immediately went to pieces and handed it to her, albeit apprehending that in so doing he was acting foolishly. Yet Olga Alexandrovna's reaction turned out to be entirely different from what he had expected; in her life, matters of an analytical and explanatory order played a role only when their outcome would grant her pleasure. For example: so-and-so was melancholic. What explained his melancholy? He was in love with Olga Alexandrovna. Wherever the explanation bore the slightest hint of abstraction or unpleasantness, Olga Alexandrovna could not kindle even the most abstract interest in it. She read the letter, handed it back to Arkady Alexandrovich and said:

"*Nunc dimittis*… Thank God. It's all for the best."

"Yes," said Arkady Alexandrovich pensively. "Maybe it

is for the best. Sometimes it seems to me… that it's perhaps better not to overanalyse positive turns of event. Analysis is like an alkali: a poisonous, corroding spot on the wonderful tapestry of life."

"You ought to write about that, you know. It's really very good."

"I don't know. I'm not so sure about it. The fact of the matter is that prose, owing to its elementary laws, ought not to indulge in excessive metaphor."

"But it's so beautiful and true, Arkasha."

"It's a curious thing," continued Arkady Alexandrovich with the same pensive air, "that certain seemingly obvious hypotheses don't hold up in practice. How should I put it? They need to be transformed, often almost irrationally, in order to be reborn, like a phoenix from the ashes. Incidentally, I haven't read to you what I wrote yesterday. Would you like to hear it?"

"Yes, of course!"

Arkady Alexandrovich extracted from a drawer several loose sheets of paper, sat down in an armchair and began to read:

He got up noisily from the table. The maid looked at him with terrified eyes. Without turning around, the minister scurried through to his study. He glanced at the portrait of his wife hanging above his desk and laughed bitterly. Then he took several steps, sat down in the leather armchair with the semicircular back and with a sharp tug pulled open the drawer of his writing desk.

The burnished steel of his revolver almost glistened in the brilliant light of the spring day."

"Does he shoot himself, Arkasha?"
"Wait and see. I'm just getting to that."

Then he slowly pushed the drawer shut. To die? the thought flashed through his mind. For what? Yes, of course, youth, the right to live, and so on—he knew it all. But a few years hence it would be as poor Don Carlos said to his fickle, charming Laura on that unforgettable night in Madrid:

> *...when thine eyes*
> *Are sunken and thy wrinkled eyelids darken,*
> *And hairs of grey appear amid thy tresses...*

But they did not understand this—perhaps it was better that way. The thought, however, brought little comfort.

"Well, that's all I've written so far. To be continued, as they say."
Arkady Alexandrovich, having begun his *Spring Symphony*, conceiving it as "a hymn to youth and modernity" (he had said so to Olga Alexandrovna), soon noted that positive descriptions were uncommonly difficult to execute, and in order to save himself from these for a certain time, he had introduced a character who was ambiguous to begin with,

the minister of a great country, a fifty-year-old man who was married to a young beauty and knew of her infidelity, in whose connection he would experience these dark thoughts. Moreover, he had been introduced into the novel purely because Arkady Alexandrovich felt a peace of mind in describing elderly people who had experienced misfortune; the minister, however, played no pivotal role and would have the good sense to end his life by suicide. The novel was to conclude in the most glittering apotheosis, without a single minor note. Then he intended to publish the book with a modest print run, on good paper. The novel would be preceded by the longest dedication to a woman identified only by three letters: O.A.K. The minister's appearance was so lacking in motivation that, despite the author's intent, he acquired a semi-fantastical aspect. Later, upon reading over what he had written, Arkady Alexandrovich mused with a certain annoyance that ministers who quote Pushkin, even when occasioned by their wives' infidelity, did not exist in real life. "Say some catastrophe were to befall me," he thought. "I shouldn't suddenly start speaking Spanish because of it." To Olga Alexandrovna, however, the minister seemed, yes, unfortunate, but charming nevertheless, and completely admissible as an incidental character.

Thus the conversation about Lyudmila's letter, which Arkady Alexandrovich so feared, did not take place immediately upon receipt of it, but was replaced for a time by the sad minister. The conversation resumed after lunch. Arkady Alexandrovich and Olga Alexandrovna were sitting overlooking the sea; a light breeze was blowing, the water sparkled under the sun.

"Now, Arkasha," said Olga Alexandrovna, "we need to talk. Essentially, everything has been said, and even more than that"—she stroked his hand—"it's been done." Her dark eyes smiled. "Now for the matter of the judicial process."

"I don't care about that," said Arkady Alexandrovich. "I say this at the risk of disappointing you, but isn't it all the same how the formalities are concluded? Or even whether they're done at all? What's important is that I've been waiting for this my whole life and now no one can take it away from me."

"Of course," said Olga Alexandrovna, smiling, "but, really, you're such a child, Arkasha. We're adults, we have to reckon with these tedious formalities."

"I'm in your hands."

"First, we need to send a telegram to Lyudmila Nikolayevna. Then the paperwork with your consent to a divorce."

"Very well."

"Then I'll write to Sergey Sergeyevich; naturally, he'll grant me a divorce immediately. And then, once everything is in place…"

"The church, the choir, the old priest…" said Arkady Alexandrovich dreamily. "And this time round a truly new life and real unimagined happiness. What angel was it that flew over Paris that evening—do you recall?…"

Arkady Alexandrovich almost unconsciously reduced

most practical conversations with Olga Alexandrovna to lyrical digressions; as a result, it was she who took care of the practicalities, while he devoted all of his time to what he called "the only thing worthwhile".

In his own way, he was no less happy than Lyudmila, and this could be put down, in part, to the very same reasons: the silent battle he had hitherto been forced to fight. There had been endless worries about money, endless homecomings where a hostile, scornful wife awaited him, conversations in which she asserted that the only justification for his position as a gigolo was his tawdry graphomania (in contrast to Olga Alexandrovna, Lyudmila had an excellent knowledge of literature, and her husband's failure as an author was all too apparent to her); and then there was the necessity of borrowing one hundred francs from a friendly manufacturer, a fat Jewish engineer in spectacles, who considered himself a patron of the arts and publicly supported serious literature (although he secretly preferred Artsybashev to other authors) and, moreover, had long given up reading, citing a lack of time, though he did have one undeniable quality in the eyes of his friends: that he would readily hand out sums of up to one hundred francs. Then there was the slow and arduous accumulation of money, in tens or twenties, acquired through sudden, unforeseen loans from various people, for a suit, a shirt, underwear, neckties—in brief, all that which Arkady Alexandrovich, with a weary tone in his voice, would call "the prose of life", and regarding which Lyudmila, in response to his complaints, once said: "This isn't the prose of life, Arkady.

This is just boorishness and cadging. I can't understand how you can have such scant respect for my name, acting like this." Arkady Alexandrovich had nearly choked with rage, but ultimately kept his peace.

All this was now at an end. In its stead, he had Olga Alexandrovna, who truly knew nothing of the value of money and spent it with her customary extravagance, and who was further moved by the fact that in contrast to her previous lovers Arkady Alexandrovich never borrowed from her or asked anything of her, being content with what she gave him. Moreover, he had already got it into his head that life with Olga Alexandrovna was in fact an unprecedented romantic symphony; truly, he had never tasted life's sweetness as he did now, unless one counted those distant times during his first marriage to the damsel of his romance. It was, however, not love in the pure sense of the word, but rather love as a function of his unconscious gratitude towards Olga Alexandrovna—gratitude for his lack of cares, for her fiery body, for the fact that she spoke to him seriously about his "lonely calling in art", for the fact that for the first time in his life he had found a woman who truly and unconditionally believed in absolutely everything, believed, above all, in the real life of Arkady Alexandrovich Kuznetsov—such as he had always been in his peaceful dreams but had never succeeded in being in actuality.

Arkady Alexandrovich's error was, however, understandable and based in part on the fact that, as it turned out, he had hitherto underestimated his physical qualities, which afforded him much pride and satisfaction. He told this to Olga Alexandrovna; it was not that he had previously supposed his life to be essentially at an end, but now... Having lost a little weight, he acquired a certain boldness in his stride, and his bronze face with its pale eyes seemed to have become slightly firmer. He even taught himself to swim a little (two or three metres) and this also granted him enormous pleasure. In addition to all these changes, which from afar were almost imperceptible, there was, nevertheless, a certain dangerous instability: that fragile world of whose vanity he had written all his life began to disappear, losing its former verisimilitude, and in its place arose a gaping void, which was only very gradually replaced by new things that would not have merited even a footnote in Arkady Alexandrovich's past life. Yet this unease was almost abstract and, naturally, could not obstruct the overall symphony.

It was Olga Alexandrovna's habit never to reflect on anything; to all appearances she had forgotten everything that had come before Arkady Alexandrovich. Together they would recall their brief shared past: their encounter at the literary evening, then meeting each other at a cafe, where they could not stop talking; then one day, as though in a dream, they had made their way to a modest hotel, for some reason near place de la République, where they were met by an obliging *garçon*, whose face they did not even notice (although, as Arkady Alexandrovich said, this person had really been the gatekeeper to their tender paradise), and finally they were together in this room with closed shutters and a cloudy mirror, in the twilight. Leaving Olga Alexandrovna after this, Arkady Alexandrovich had thought, without the slightest hint of chagrin, that of the money he had intended to use to purchase a suit a month previously, there were only ninety francs left— the rest had gone on the cafe. They recalled further how Arkady Alexandrovich had caught cold, waiting for Olga Alexandrovna at the place Saint-Sulpice (she had been held up because her taxi had collided with an omnibus); how another time he had been experiencing liver pain but still, despite the inhuman suffering, made it to their rendezvous. In the accounts of both Arkady Alexandrovich and Olga Alexandrovna, all this took on a decidedly heroic and triumphant aspect.

Next Arkady Alexandrovich began to quote various books he had read—he had an excellent memory—and Olga Alexandrovna's delight at his wit and erudition, which combined wonderfully with his singular personal charm and crystal-pure, almost childlike soul, grew and grew, so that one day she said to him, explaining this:

"You know, Arkasha, it's so marvellous that, well, I simply can't find anything to compare it with… I'm happy, I'm so pleased with everything. Only I must write, to find out how my little boy, my Seryozha, is getting on."

Then, for a fraction of a second, something like a fleeting regret flashed in her eyes, which neither Arkady Alexandrovich nor even Olga Alexandrovna herself noticed.

THROUGHOUT THAT SULTRY SUMMER, Seryozha hardly ever left Liza's side; he would fall asleep and wake up next to her, they would go bathing together, go for walks together, and they lived together, almost oblivious to their surroundings. One day, however, as they returned for dinner, they found Yegorkin in the dining room. He had turned up without considering that it might be inopportune, and ingenuously described how his situation would at times become unbearable, as he put it, because of the constant, inescapable loneliness. Seryozha studied his thin, sinewy neck with its prominent Adam's apple, his gnarled hands, his trousers which hung on him like a sack, and, in spite of his usual pity for the man, this evening he felt something akin to loathing for him. Liza said nothing at the dinner table; two or three times she said something to Seryozha in English, then immediately apologized offhandedly to Yegorkin, attributing it to an involuntary habit. As naive and ingenuous as Yegorkin was, never for one moment having suspected that he could in any way inconvenience someone (just as no one's presence could ever inconvenience him)—even he noticed by and by that the situation was painful and awkward for everyone. He stood up and, wishing in some way to smooth over the unpleasant atmosphere, said that he had in fact come to find out whether Sergey Sergeyevich would be arriving soon. Liza's face turned to stone. Seryozha replied that he knew nothing.

"I'd imagine you must at times get bored without him," said Yegorkin, as ever with his broad, artless smile. "Well, I must be going."

Liza nodded. Seryozha got up to see Yegorkin out, avoiding Liza's gaze.

"You know, Seryozha," said Yegorkin, "I'm looking forward to Sergey Sergeyevich's coming. I have some sketches, you see, and, well, I'd like to offer them to him."

It suddenly struck Seryozha that Yegorkin was probably in dire straits. He recalled how the artist had eaten at dinner—with deliberate slowness, but consuming everything down to the very last morsel of bread he used to wipe his plate. Liza had averted her eyes, while Seryozha had very much wanted to say that it was not the done thing. It occurred to him that today was perhaps the first day in a long while that Yegorkin had eaten a square meal, and he suddenly felt sorry for the man, almost to the point of tears.

"You're probably in need of some money, Leonid Semyonovich?" he said, overcoming his restraint.

Yegorkin smiled.

"I'm always in need of money, Seryozha. Only you don't owe me anything."

"No, no," Seryozha quickly put in. "You misunderstand me, Leonid Semyonovich. You see, Papa would doubtless buy the paintings from you, so does it really matter who pays for them?"

"No, I suppose not."

"Wait a moment," said Seryozha. "I'll be back shortly."

"Wait, where are you going?"

But Seryozha was already gone. He had run upstairs to his room and opened the drawer of his bureau. Of the thousand francs that he had changed the previous week, there were only two notes left: one for five hundred and the other for one hundred. He took the five hundred francs, but, heading towards the doors, stopped, went back, took the remaining hundred as well, and ran downstairs. In the bright moonlight he could see the artist sitting by the side of the road, watching the sea. On hearing Seryozha's quick steps, he lifted his head:

"What splendour," he said in a booming voice. "For all my years, I never tire of seeing it."

"Here, Leonid Semyonovich," muttered Seryozha, handing him the money. "Take this for now... If you need any more, just let me know."

Yegorkin slowly unfolded the money, then firmly shook Seryozha's hand.

"Thank you," he said as if deep in thought.

"I'm sure Papa will buy your sketches."

"Of course he will," said Yegorkin. "And if I brought him a piece of wood, he'd buy that, too, unless I'm much mistaken. Sergey Sergeyevich knows I appreciate it. Some people are given so much, others so little. Well, goodnight, Seryozha."

He walked off briskly. Seryozha went indoors. The sand crunched beneath his slow footsteps. He paused for a second and recalled the sound of his steps on that same sand—on that first night when he and Liza had gone out for a walk together and he had fainted after she kissed him. A whole lifetime seemed to have passed by since then. In order to comprehend the enormous, incomparable—as Seryozha thought—happiness, he doggedly sought an explanation as to how all this could happen and how it turned out that everything that had gone before this seemed like a prelude to his current existence. Everything Seryozha had known and loved before now seemed to be eclipsed by Liza's slender shadow, just as it had when one night she got out of bed and went over to the open window, and as he was beginning to doze off, Seryozha vaguely marked her naked body in the dark, airy bay window. He got up and walked over to her; beyond her back and shoulders, down which her black tresses cascaded, slowly and unexpectedly the sea, a tree-lined shore, the still evening leaves, a low star in the distant sky and a quivering strip of moonlight on the sea came into view. Even now, he could see what had hitherto separated the two of them: his mother, his father, the sensation of warm bathwater, long ago, when he was little and Liza's dark hands had lifted him out of there, her peculiar voice saying: "Now, then, Seryozhenka, it's time for bed." What else was there? There were strange childhood things: castor oil, salt, which he had been forbidden to eat but was so wonderfully delicious, then imaginary journeys through books and atlases: the Tierra del Fuego, Guiana, Tahiti, the banks of the Missouri, Alaska, Australia, Madagascar, Siberia and the Russian north. Then more books, a great variety of them, then the *lycée*, football, running, swimming, then walks through Paris with his schoolmates, the cinema, a silver-screen beauty with eyes half a metre wide and glycerine tears, then his father's visitors, among whom numbered the famous and the well-respected, music, the resonant air of the concert hall, and, after all this, as always, his mother, his father and Liza.

Seryozha always found his father inscrutable; to him it seemed strange how someone could lead such a life— always joking, laughing about absolutely everything, never worrying, never getting upset. There was a period when Seryozha thought that Sergey Sergeyevich—it was an uncharitable idea, but he did love him dearly—simply never reflected on anything; everything that concerned others, everything that would cause them to fall ill, age and die, would pass him by; having never known want or hardship of any kind, he simply lived with a sense of satisfaction, never making use of his leisure time, even for reading. This distressed Seryozha; he wanted his father to be on top of everything, while thus far Seryozha had only managed to uncover a competency in commercial matters and stock prices, things of which Seryozha had no knowledge at all. Although there was sport, too: specifically, Sergey Sergeyevich knew every world record. One day, however, Seryozha overheard a conversation between his father and a well-known, wizened old man about the development of religious philosophy, and it was quite clear that Sergey Sergeyevich felt just as at ease on this subject as he did on sport. After that, Seryozha gave up trying to understand who his father ultimately was. He knew that his mother called him a machine, that whenever Liza spoke of him either her irony or her temper would slip ever so slightly through her usual composure. What could they have against this charming man, with whom there was never a dull moment, and who would always agree to everything? Herein lay a paradox: the people who loved his father were essentially those who did not know him—the maid, Nil (who esteemed Sergey Sergeyevich greatly) and Yegorkin—while his mother and Liza regarded him coldly, which for them, generally speaking, was uncharacteristic. And why did his mother always remain a stranger to him? And when she would say, "We'll have to tell Sergey Sergeyevich," or "We'll have to ask Sergey Sergeyevich," why did it always sound as if she were speaking about a friend? And why was it that Sergey Sergeyevich, the master of his household and the owner of such a fortune, was looked upon by his friends not as an active participant in their lives, but as a valuable and, admittedly, rather pleasant advisor on various matters, but without whom, essentially, they would have got by? Seryozha very much wanted to talk to Liza about his father, but for the moment it was impossible, since it would have touched upon what was happening right now, and Seryozha feared this—all the more so because Liza had thus far not uttered a single word about what was ultimately the most tragic problem they both faced. The idea that Liza was his mother's sister was unable to ingrain itself in Seryozha's consciousness as it should have done; rather, it remained on the surface, and later somewhere deep, deep within him, where he sensed its disturbing presence and instinctively avoided thinking about it. Sooner or later, of course, the matter would have to be resolved, but until that point there was, perhaps, a long way to go.

So, for the first time in his life, Seryozha found himself facing the question of his own fate, of his role in events. Until now, he had almost been invisible in Sergey Sergeyevich's house as an independent entity—in the sense that his life and his presence could not in any way influence the general course of events or the relations between members of the family. Sergey Sergeyevich might have been discontented (though only in principle, since in actual fact he never showed his discontent); Olga Alexandrovna in turn might have quarrelled with Liza, and Liza might have been angry with Sergey Sergeyevich; however, the interests of Seryozha never factored in these situations. Irrespective of what went on, all three of them treated Seryozha with that invariable affection to which he had been accustomed since youth; only Sergey Sergeyevich occasionally poked fun at him, but only in those instances when he knew he would not cause offence.

Yet one day, that same Sergey Sergeyevich had listened sympathetically to Seryozha's forty-minute speech on the international situation. It happened as follows: Sergey Sergeyevich was walking past Seryozha's room, the door of which was ajar, and from within he could hear his son's booming voice:

"*Donc je crois, messieurs, que nous sommes tous d'accord en ce qui concerne ce côté du problème. Mais pour être efficaces, les mesures que nous envisageons…*"*

Sergey Sergeyevich knocked at the door; silence descended, and then a very different, almost childlike, voice said:

"Please, *entrez…*"†

"Who were you talking to, Seryozha?" asked Sergey Sergeyevich, taking a seat on the divan.

"Oh, it was nothing."

"Tell me, all the same."

"You see," said Seryozha confidingly, "I was imagining that I was the foreign minister, you know, making a speech at a plenary session of the League of Nations."

"Aha. On what subject, exactly?"

"Mainly on the international situation."

"Very well," said Sergey Sergeyevich. "If you can imagine that you're the foreign minister, then look upon me as the noble assembly—which is no more far-fetched. You give your speech, and I'll oppose it."

"You're serious?"

"Yes, I'm serious."

"All right, I'll continue. In which language?"

---

* Therefore, I believe, gentlemen, that we are all in agreement regarding this aspect of the problem. However, in order to be effective, the measures we envisage…

† Please, come in.

"Which country are you the minister of, exactly?"

"I hadn't actually thought about that," said Seryozha candidly.

"All right, it doesn't matter. Let's have you speak French, then, and I'll reply as a representative of the Foreign Office—that is, in French, but you must forgive my accent. Well, let's have it."

"*Tant que l'Allemagne,*" Seryozha continued, "*restera meurtrie, que les puissances européennes se désintéresseront complètement ou presque complètement de sa situation intérieure, nous ne pourrons aucunement compter sur elle comme sur un facteur de l'équilibre européen, ce même équilibre au rétablissement duquel nous avons sacrifié des millions de vies humaines et au nom duquel la plus atroce des guerres s'était déclenchée…*"*

"*Je me permets de rappeler, Monsieur le Président,*" said Sergey Sergeyevich with a pure English accent, "*que c'est bien l'aveugle et criminelle politique de l'Allemagne qui a provoqué la guerre.*"†

"*Messieurs,*" boomed Seryozha, "*nous ne sommes pas ici pour analyser les causes de la guerre ni pour chercher le coupable. La vengeance de l'Histoire, d'ailleurs, a été impitoyable. Mais je tiens à vous rappeler que nos efforts ne doivent pas être ménagés pour la*

---

* So long as Germany remains ravaged and the European powers have absolutely, or almost absolutely, no interest in its domestic situation, we shall not in any way be able to rely on it as an element of European stability, that same stability for the recovery of which we have sacrificed millions of human lives and in whose name the most terrible of wars was triggered…

† I would remind the president that it was the blind and criminal policies of Germany that provoked the war in the first place.

*construction de l'Europe nouvelle qui—je suis le premier à l'espérer—
ne ressemblera nullement à celle qui s'est ensevelie sous les ruines
fumantes, dans le sang et la souffrance."* *

Having debated the international situation from every
angle, Seryozha smiled, watching Sergey Sergeyevich as he
left, and was very pleased to have found a worthy opponent.

How long ago all that had been! Now everything had
changed: instead of historical and philosophical problems,
instead of the Sergey Sergeyevich, the Olga Alexandrovna and the Liza of former days, something new had
emerged, something infinitely more significant, more vital,
whose existence had unwittingly and irrevocably eclipsed
this whole precious and now distant world. Seryozha had
witnessed an instantaneous dissociation: everything seemed
to have remained in its proper place—the people were the
same, as was the mark on the floor of his room (which
had been made because the nanny at the time, stepped out
for a moment, leaving an electric iron there, and returned
only half an hour later), the smooth dark lustre of the
banister on the staircase, Nil, the Italian woman; yet nevertheless Seryozha, despite the outward semblance of all this,
felt as if these people and objects now surrounding him
belonged to a distant age, of which he could but regret

---

* Gentlemen, we are not here to analyse the causes of the war, nor are we
  here to point the finger. The vengeance of History has in any case been
  merciless. However, I would remind you that our efforts must not be
  spared in the construction of a new Europe that, I am the first to hope,
  will bear no resemblance to the one that is buried beneath smoking
  ruins, in blood and suffering.

the passing—and this regret was one of the elements of his happiness, this flight into an unknown land where God only knew what awaited him. However, in order to comprehend this happiness, he had to compare it with what had gone before it, and only then, only in so doing could he see the singularity of it. Liza's shadow never left him; even when she was not there, everything was imbued with her presence and the expectation of her return: the air was full of faint echoes of her voice, the music was full of her intonations, the water was suffused with her rippling reflection, and in the caress of the sea breeze Seryozha distinctly felt the approach of her lips, now forever half open, to his face. This constant intense presence of hers—the unconscious fatigue of which would send Seryozha into a deep sleep every night—required everything, irrespectively, to be sacrificed in its name. This avid happiness brought with it the permanent necessity of some sacrifice; to be worthy required the relinquishing of something very important and precious. And since no change in Seryozha's life had yet come about, a sense of having lost the world in which he was still living developed.

Seryozha, however, had little time to think about all this; most likely, these thoughts had not even managed to lodge in his consciousness, just like the notion that all this would end in what was, perhaps, the most significant decision in his life. He must have known this, but he did not think about it. He remembered the past and felt the present; it was impossible to foresee what would come later, if only because until then, in his current state, he had known nothing of the like; the life he was now living was entirely new to him.

The single, albeit insistent, reminder of what had gone before this period in his life was the memory of his mother, which could not eclipse even Liza's ever-present shadow. Seryozha adored his mother; although by now he knew that her private life was far from without reproach, this knowledge remained abstract and could in no way besmirch the image of his mother. She was still that same lovely, gentle mother, with her endearing quick patter and tender hands, and yet she was also the woman she was to others, strangers, who would frequently quit her house, husband and son—this woman bore no relation to his mother, although theoretically both she and his mother were one and the same person.

"Seryozha, my darling. Seryozha, my little boy. Seryozha, my little fair-haired one," he remembered suddenly. And when he then reflected that Liza was his mother's sister, he was gripped for a moment by despair, an unsettling, distant chill within him; what would she say when she found out about this?

THEY LAY TOGETHER on the sandy bank of a small backwater. High above was the path that led past their house; to the right was a sheer, almost vertical cliff face; to the left, a little cove. It had gone eleven o'clock, and the sun was high in the sky. Seryozha rolled over several times and, when he ended up next to Liza, he said:

"You see, Liza, you and I are alone now, nobody can hear us, and I feel the urge to tell you again that you're the finest, the most extraordinary woman."

"You're the silliest, the most mad," replied Liza, mimicking him.

"Liza, just look at how amazing it all is," he said. "What matters is that it isn't blind happiness. Just think, back there, in Paris, for example, tens of thousands of people suffocate, hate and die; a few thousand more are lying in hospital beds; more still are old men, and some have never in their whole lives known what love is. There are people who have never seen the sea. There's a whole world inhabited by other people. And next to this, but apart from it, in such infinite and undeserved happiness, here I am, lying next to you. Isn't it miraculous?"

Liza stroked Seryozha's wet hair.

"You're always so quiet, Liza. Why is that?"

"It's a good quiet, Seryozha, don't worry."

"I don't. But you know so much more than me, you're so much more clever…"

"No, Seryozhenka. We only know what has been. And what has been will never be repeated. When something new begins, you and I are equally defenceless. Later we shall know what it was, and we'll either rejoice in it or regret it. But now we don't know a thing, Seryozhenka; we feel. These are different things."

"No, I'm speaking objectively, Liza; not because I love you. Your whole life you've always been the same—just as pure, just as irreproachable and just as remarkable! You and only you. Do you understand? All your life, all your thoughts, everything, Liza, everything."

"My darling boy."

"I've always been selfish, Liza, you know that, but now it seems to me as though there's nothing I wouldn't do for you. If you and I were all alone, with no money, I would work for us both, I'd do everything I could—although not in the mines—and I'd be just as happy as before. I never knew there could be such things. You see, now I understand: Love came before the Creation, and I know why."

He smiled and shook his head.

"There's only one thing I don't understand: different people love one another, they marry, suffer, and so on. It seems ridiculous to me: how it is possible to love anyone but you? Not one of them has the slightest thing in common with you—which is not, of course, my personal opinion, but simply a fact that can be verified."

"That's only true for you, Seryozhenka."

"All right, it's true for me. But I'm an average man, like the rest of them."

Now Liza smiled.

"You aren't a man, Seryozhenka, you're still a boy."

"I was until recently," said Seryozha, blushing, "but I'm a boy no longer, as you can see, and you know that perfectly well. Liza, wait! Where are you going?"

But Liza had already stood up and gone into the water; then she floated on her back and swam, waving goodbye to Seryozha. Seryozha ran after her, dived in, and his head suddenly appeared from beneath the water at her shoulders. Liza then turned on her front and began to swim off; Seryozha swam beside her, stopped for a second and called in his sonorous voice: "You won't get away, Liza, you'll never manage, never!" When he shouted, he was two metres behind her, but then he caught up with her again, jumping in the water and turning a somersault like a dolphin.

As they reached the shore, they spotted Yegorkin, who, in a faded bathing costume, was standing up to his knees in the sea, splashing himself with water. From a distance Seryozha could see his gaunt body with its jutting ribs and a tuft of grey hair on his chest, poking out from under his maillot.

"Hello, Leonid Semyonovich. How are you? Have you come for a swim?"

"Hello, Yelizaveta Alexandrovna. Hello, Seryozha," said Yegorkin, straightening himself up and bowing. "Have you had a nice swim?"

"Thank you, Leonid Semyonovich," said Liza in a more cordial voice than usual. "We've enjoyed ourselves."

"I just can't seem to get the hang of it," said Yegorkin. "I'm afeared of the water. The minute I know there's nothing under my feet, terror strikes."

"I'll teach you," said Seryozha. "First, you need to learn to hold your head underwater."

"Good grief, Seryozha, how on earth will I breathe?"

"Just watch. You take a deep breath, then plunge your head in the water and breathe out through your nostrils. Like this."

Standing on his knees, Seryozha ducked his head under the water, and bubbles of air rose gurgling to the surface. Yegorkin, stooping over, watched intently.

"No, if I did that, they'd have to give me the kiss of life after," he said.

"But it's easy."

"I didn't say it wasn't easy, Seryozha. But dying's not exactly difficult either."

"All right, let's be off then, Leonid Semyonovich," said Seryozha. Liza had already taken a few steps in the direction of the house. "We'll lunch at home."

Seryozha waited while Yegorkin dressed, and together they went out onto the terrace. Meeting Chef along the way, Seryozha asked him to let his mother know that there would be an additional person for lunch. Yegorkin waited alone on the terrace while Seryozha went to his room to dress. Ten minutes later the three of them were sitting at the table.

"It's strange, the way things turn out," said Yegorkin. "I more or less grew up on the Volga, I've an aunt in Saratov who married a vet. I'd go down to the river with the lads,

160

they could all swim, but somehow I never could learn. So many years have been and gone, and still I don't know how. It can't be helped: I'm no swimmer, and that's that."

Liza remained silent. Seryozha said:

"So you lived in Saratov? And here I am, Leonid Semyonovich, a Russian, although I've practically never seen Russia. I remember the Crimea a little, as though in a dream."

"Yes, I know the Volga well," said Yegorkin. "My aunt was a lovely woman, just a bit heavy-handed."

"In what sense?"

"The meaning's clear enough," said Yegorkin, smiling his artless, simple smile. "She never touched us children, but her husband could be sure of getting it."

"For what?"

"He… Let's say he drank a little. Well, she was a nervous woman, but she'd still give him what for. She was forever shouting at him. 'You may be a vet,' she'd say, 'but you've drunk so much you can't tell a horse from a cow,' she'd say."

"Did he drink often?"

"No, once a month he'd drink for two days solid," said Yegorkin. "He was a quiet man, an angler, always fishing. And there's as many fish in the Volga as you could want. I'm no expert, but I once caught a fifteen-pound pike."

Seryozha laughed.

"What's so funny?"

"Don't take offence," replied Seryozha, continuing to laugh, "I'm just in high spirits today. You mentioned a pike, and it reminded me of a few fishing and hunting tales."

"A tale!" said Yegorkin. "That would be a fine thing! A tale indeed… I almost lost my life because of it."

"Because of the pike?"

"Of course because of the pike. The damned thing thrashed around so much that I fell into the water, dressed as I was."

"What happened then?"

"Well, I wouldn't let go of the rod and managed to grab onto a tree overhanging the water. Then the lads came and helped me out, and I reeled it in."

"Fifteen pounds—how much is that in kilos?"

"Almost eight."

"What other fish have you caught, Leonid Semyono-vich?"

"Lots, Seryozha, only I never fished much. My uncle spent his whole life fishing—knew every kind of fish, all their habits, all the places they lived, and how best to catch them. He was a real expert."

"You'd need devilish patience, I'd imagine," said Seryozha.

"Not patience, but character. Folks used to say that fishermen weren't quite all there. Not dangerous, of course, but a queer sort. Though to my mind it's better to go fishing than it is to sit in a pub."

"Undoubtedly, Leonid Semyonovich," said Liza, who until now had been silent.

Yegorkin became flustered, as he almost always did whenever Liza entered the conversation. She was the only person he knew whose presence almost pained him; every time he would somehow get into a muddle and begin to feel uncomfortable, although objectively he held her mind and her beauty in very high regard, as he was wont to say. She clearly belonged to another world, one that was inaccessible to him; and just as this difference seemed insignificant or unimportant to him whenever he was dealing with Sergey Sergeyevich, or Olga Alexandrovna, or Seryozha, so did it become all too apparent when dealing with Liza. He was unable to explain it, but this feeling of his had remained unchanged for many years already. Whenever he was in her presence, it would suddenly occur to him that he was perhaps not dressed as he should be, not saying what he was supposed to say, not sitting at the table just so—all in all, not the man he ought to have been in order not to feel this embarrassment. With Seryozha, on the other hand, he felt entirely at ease.

To change the topic of conversation, he began recalling how he had sold his first paintings to Sergey Sergeyevich:

"Do you remember, Yelizaveta Alexandrovna," he said, "it was the year that you and Sergey Sergeyevich first came here to spend the summer together. You must have been around seven, Seryozha, no more; although I met you only the year after. But Sergey Sergeyevich and Yelizaveta Alexandrovna spent a month and a half here together."

Liza's eyes widened; she obviously wanted to say something, but held her tongue.

"Back then," continued Yegorkin, "when I first set eyes on the two of you, I thought to myself: 'Can they really be Russians?' Then I followed you while you were walking,

163

listening, but you weren't speaking Russian or French. Must've been wrong, I thought. But then Sergey Sergeyevich suddenly said, 'It's all ignorant contrivance!' in Russian. It brought joy to my heart."

And so Yegorkin told the tale of how he first spoke to Sergey Sergeyevich. The day was overcast, which was rare for that time of year: Yegorkin was sitting by a solitary path, having set out his paints, working. The steps he had heard a few seconds before halted behind him. He turned around and saw a man wearing a white suit, the same man who had arrived several days earlier with a young woman in a gleaming new motor car, the same man who had been speaking about ignorant contrivance.

"Are you painting the sea?" asked Sergey Sergeyevich.

"As you can see," said Yegorkin, turning on his home-made stool with a sweeping gesture. One of the legs, however, was significantly shorter than the others, which made it very unsteady, and because of the sharp movement Yegorkin toppled over along with the stool. Sergey Sergeyevich helped him up, laughing all the while.

"Wherever did you get that stool?" he asked, smiling. "Its centre of gravity is off."

"The trick is to make it yourself," replied Yegorkin.

"What parts do you hail from?" asked Sergey Sergeyevich without any transition.

"Tambov province," replied Yegorkin.

"You've come a long way," said Sergey Sergeyevich. "Are you a professional artist or a mere enthusiast, as it were?"

Yegorkin explained that he was an artist, that at one time he had specialized in icons, which were in great demand among Russians—mostly icons of that most national of saints, St Nicholas the Wonderworker. Sergey Sergeyevich laughed.

"What's so funny?"

"Nicholas was a Greek," said Sergey Sergeyevich. "But it doesn't matter. Do go on. So, you say religious works are in demand?"

Yegorkin said he had painted the icons from memory, just as he had seen them in Russian churches. Then he moved on to portraiture, which, however, would satisfy neither him nor those who commissioned them: him, because he had been unable to achieve the necessary likeness, and the sitter—and in particular the women—because they invariably desired to look much more handsome in their portraits than they did in real life. One former lady writer had caused Yegorkin particular trouble.

"What was her surname?" asked Sergey Sergeyevich.

Yegorkin replied.

"I recall," said Sergey Sergeyevich. "She wrote some pornographic nonsense. Go on."

She had told Yegorkin that she was personally acquainted with Repin and Vrubel, that Yegorkin could not hold a candle to them and that his portrait was terrible and she would not pay, since he had not painted it as he ought to have done. She showed him a photograph taken twenty years previously, in which she was a rather attractive lady of forty holding a fan in her very crooked right hand;

she said that this was her true portrait, and set about convincing Yegorkin that his work had nothing in common with this photograph, which was self-evident. When Yegorkin said the photograph had been taken God only knew when, she flew into a rage and refused to pay; however, she held on to the portrait all the same. Yegorkin never received a penny, despite having spent much time and effort on the painting.

From Yegorkin's talk it became clear that his affairs were by and large in catastrophically bad shape, although he never thought to complain about it: for him it was just the way of things.

At the end of the conversation Sergey Sergeyevich remarked to Yegorkin that he himself was a lover of original art and that he would gladly acquire several paintings if there were any for sale.

"Good heavens!" said Yegorkin, beside himself with joy. "Take anything you want."

On the following day he brought five paintings to show to Sergey Sergeyevich, which the latter acquired on the spot for a very modest sum. But then, in hushed tones, he told the artist that he must always ask for more, that the people who buy paintings most often know nothing about art and judge it according to the price: if it is expensive, it must be good. Subsequently, however, Yegorkin successfully applied this principle only with Sergey Sergeyevich; the prices had a deterrent effect on everyone else, although one day a young student of one of the Californian universities, who had won a large sum of money at Monte Carlo and then spent almost three whole days in a state of inebriation, bought from Yegorkin on the second day of this profligate debauchery, without bartering, almost all of his paintings, after which Yegorkin left for Paris and stopped in a hotel, where he was robbed; he still managed to see the Louvre, only he had no idea how he would return south, but then he hit upon the idea of seeking out Sergey Sergeyevich, who gave him the money for the journey. Yegorkin had managed to keep the other half of his fortune back in the Midi, and, upon returning there, he proceeded to live on it for two years: he was an unassuming and undemanding person, who could never be called extravagant; however, like many such self-denying people, he had no idea how to manage his money.

Lunch had long finished, but still Yegorkin was recounting stories. Seryozha listened to him with fascination; Liza soon left and reappeared half an hour later, having changed into her clothes for town. Seryozha looked at her in astonishment.

"Have you forgotten that we have to go to Nice?" she asked.

"What, you're planning to go to Nice? I didn't think there was anywhere we needed to go."

"That just goes to show how bad your memory is. Go and get dressed. You'll forgive us, Leonid Semyonovich, I hope."

"Forgive me, Yelizaveta Alexandrovna, forgive me. I've outstayed my welcome. A very good day to you."

When Seryozha came down, Chef called him aside and asked his permission to go with them to Nice.

"Of course," said Seryozha. "Do you have business there?"

"I have a rendezvous," said Chef. "You ought to catch my meaning."

"Why me, exactly?"

"Because if you think I'm blind, you're quite mistaken," said Chef.

"All right, you can come with us," called Seryozha, heading towards the garage.

They took Chef as far as Nice, where he got out; then they drove on. When Seryozha asked Liza why she had wanted to go to Nice, she replied that she had not in fact planned to go, that she had thought up this trip to escape the eternal Yegorkin.

"Why don't you like him? He's a good, very simple man."

"Oh, he's simple enough, all right. But he vexes me."

"He's so funny, so ingenuous, and very kind," said Seryozha. "I remember he once came to play with me and brought me some sweets, although he never had any money. He probably went without food just to buy me something; it's very much in his nature to do a thing like that."

"I don't deny it. I just don't find his company interesting. All these ridiculous stories about the Volga, about a pike, about his aunt who was married to a vet. It's enough to make you cringe."

"Liza, you and I need to talk," said Seryozha. Liza's lips quivered, but Seryozha was oblivious to this.

"I'm listening."

"Liza, I have reason to think, you see… How can I say this?"

"*Nous y voilà, je crois.** Speak, my boy.*"

"You see, I think, that our relationship…"

"That's what I feared most of all," she said with a sigh. Her face turned pale; she found it difficult to breathe. Her spontaneous alarm passed on to Seryozha.

"Liza, what's going to happen about all this?"

"I don't know, Seryozhenka. I know only—and I won't hide it from you—that the worst is yet to come. Damn it," she said suddenly, raising her head, "I also have a right to my own life and I don't want to think about this. Don't let's talk about it, Seryozha. Kiss me."

Seryozha pressed her head to his shoulder and kissed it.

"We'll be a little more careful, that's all. And when the time comes to answer for everything, I'll answer for everything. Don't think about it."

"All right, Liza."

Late at night, however, after Seryozha had fallen asleep, Liza lay awake, turning over in her mind everything she had given her word not to think about, everything she had forbidden Seryozha to think about. Strictly speaking, the catalyst for these thoughts, as before, had been Yegorkin's gauche behaviour; he mentioned Sergey Sergeyevich at every opportunity, unaware of the degree to which it was agonizing for Liza. She knew that she loved Seryozha truly and powerfully. It even seemed to her as if that feeling

* I believe you've already begun.

of hers was unlike any other that had gone before it. She could not help being carried away by such a profound love for Seryozha, for whom everything existed only through her. Indeed, as far as he was concerned, there was nothing beyond her. At the same time, she asked herself whether she were capable of such a complete metamorphosis, of such total rejection of the past. Right now she did not doubt this, but what about five or ten years hence?

Until now she had never known such an all-encompassing, joyous love—everything had always been transient, accidental, fleeting, everything with the exception of her long-standing relationship with Sergey Sergeyevich, who was in fact ultimately not a man but a machine; at times she began to hate him because he was perfectly devoid of spontaneity, everything was thought out, nothing was unexpected—all these phrases, humorous rejoinders, humorous meditations. "A machine, a machine," she would say. Even physically, every muscle did exactly what it was supposed to do, with an accurate, almost calculated tension. In all this time he had never once caused her any pain, never once said anything that could have truly offended her, although, undoubtedly, had he so desired, he could have found the necessary words for this, and thus, without any effort, his gentlemanliness would always irritate her. "*Il n'a pas de mérite*," she would tell herself. "*Il n'a rien à vaincre*."* As with the vast majority of women, Liza dreamt of a singular love her whole life; it was an almost unconscious

* He has no qualities… He has nothing to overcome.

desire: to experience a feeling wherein it was possible to dissolve, almost to disappear, almost to die and forget oneself; however, for this one needed a mighty jolt, a gentle maelstrom, some overwhelming action, the impossibility of living otherwise. Then she would regain her femininity; her uniqueness, her love of independence would vanish, her unwomanly muscles would soften and become weak, and generally there would be total degeneration: the former Liza, with her habitual restrained ire (for all this had yet to come, while time was marching on), with her abortive love affairs, in each of which she had sensed her own superiority over the male, with the constant emotional headache that Sergey Sergeyevich inflicted—this Liza would have ceased to exist and another would have come to replace her, a Liza unlike this one and infinitely happier than she.

And now it had happened. Liza had long known about Seryozha's feelings; she was too much a woman not to have understood what he himself, of course, had not yet realized. And because Seryozha was drawn to her, at first she felt only sweet alarm, but the moment came when she could no longer resist her own desire—two nights after they arrived there. When she kissed Seryozha and he fainted, she knew then that the most wonderful, the most important phase of her life was now beginning. Besides her love for Seryozha, which went beyond any considerations of whether he was suitable for her or she for him, she could not remain indifferent to his romantic, naive adoration, to his utter singularity, to his vulnerability. Far beyond these feelings, in the very depths and silence of her being, lurked the dark, seductive taste of something illicit. It was not the obvious, outward consideration that an affair between an aunt and her nephew was, in itself, ethically inadmissible. No, it was something indefinable but almost physical, something like a sense of this love's incomparable astringency. No personal moral qualms could trouble Liza—and from this alone did she understand that she truly loved Seryozha. She thought about what was to come, and most of all she feared losing him. Despite all her power over him, she could not tell how Seryozha would react if he were to find out that she had been Sergey Sergeyevich's lover for many years already. More than that, she feared Sergey Sergeyevich's reaction, in whom, in this instance, she had not confided. Well, fine, she would explain to him that it was her happiness, her life, that without him she would die, that under no circumstances would she be parted from Seryozha. This would have no effect on Sergey Sergeyevich; he would say that in any other case he would have been happy for her, but now... On the other hand, it was impossible now to hide her relationship with Seryozha—she might have managed this, but Seryozha was so transparent that now everyone around him knew about it. What was to be done? Should they elope? That would mean ruining the boy's whole life; come autumn, he was supposed to begin his studies in London; he was still a boy. How would they live if they eloped? By giving foreign-language lessons—only for Seryozha, ten years later, with faded eyes and a poorly dyed patch of grey hair, to realize that he had squandered his whole life because of this elderly woman? Yes, naturally

Sergey Sergeyevich would offer to send money, but surely Seryozha would never consent to it. She felt a surge of hatred for Sergey Sergeyevich. This man knew what he was doing: neither Liza nor Olga Alexandrovna had any money of her own, and although Sergey Sergeyevich never denied them anything, they still had to ask him for money.

Liza feared Sergey Sergeyevich. She, even she, did not ultimately know what his typical official condescension masked. He was capable of much malice; he had every opportunity, but not once in his life had he ever used it against Olga Alexandrovna or Liza. Yet he always guarded them jealously, holding on to them throughout his life, able to release them at any moment; this threat, which he would never carry out (he would have laughed, had anyone ever suggested this to him), was within his power, but one way or another it was never enacted. Liza knew that his goodness stemmed rather from ambivalence than from anything else; he was never gripped by strong passions. She understood perfectly, however, that Sergey Sergeyevich—if one were to admit the possibility that hatred could suddenly flare up in him—could be more dreadful than any other man. And what an absurd idea: to have given his son his own name! Yet that other name—"Seryozha", so ostensibly like the first—carried intonations that were impossible to intuit; it seemed incredible that a single word could at first contain only resounding emptiness and expectancy, while the other one, his real one... What was it in that other one? A stream, green grass, a distant silver bell, a light breeze on the water's surface—the finest, purest love. The burden of

173

the past: was that not what Sergey Sergeyevich was forever mocking? With a strange clarity, Liza suddenly saw the Crimea glittering far away in the sunlight, Simeiz, the red clay of a tennis court, a white dress covering her naked body, Sergey Sergeyevich's white suit and his mocking eyes, which never under any circumstance lost their lustre, but remained bright, always catching what was going on—and it was in a fit of candour that Olga Alexandrovna, her own sister, as though she herself were unaware of this, had told Liza one day that she had asked Sergey Sergeyevich:

"Do you always see everything, understand everything?"

"Always, Lyolya, but with enduring benevolence," had been the answer.

"Do you always see everything, always understand everything?" Liza had asked him another time.

"I see your eyes, which is truly to see everything," Sergey Sergeyevich had said.

Then, several days later, holding Seryozha, who had just turned two, Liza said: "Is it possible that he'll turn out just like you?" And the child's quick eyes gazed intently at the aunt, and its small chubby hand gripped her cheek.

"I very much hope so," said Sergey Sergeyevich. "Just look how handsome he is."

Seryozha began to bounce up and down in his aunt's arms.

That was almost fifteen years ago. The burden of the past? Yes, then there was a musician from Berlin, flowers at a concert, a night in a hotel and a conversation that decided everything, that he was made for art and could not tie down his life... Only later did he learn that Liza was Sergey Sergeyevich's *belle-sœur*,* that he had let slip, perhaps, a lot of money, and so took to writing letters that she never answered, for to do so would have gone against her nature. Next came a Swiss student, such a marvellous skier, such a wonderful athlete and such a surprisingly poor lover, who knew this and was all the shyer for it—Liza always felt sorry for him. Then there was an Englishman, an officer in the navy, who died during a fire on board a merchant ship on which he was travelling as a simple passenger, returning from India to Europe, where Liza was waiting for him, having spent an excruciating week in a London hotel, on the ground floor, past the window of which, perfectly oblivious, had walked Sergey Sergeyevich one day, having come to England for a couple of days and gone out for a stroll with the former British ambassador at Constantinople, a keen walker—Sergey Sergeyevich knew him from his days in Turkey. Liza had retreated quickly from the window. Yet another broken life; it was September, and the weather was foul: rain and cold. Then she returned to Paris, to Sergey Sergeyevich's apartment, which immediately seemed empty and lorn, although Robert (for that was his name) had not only never visited it, but did not even know of its existence. At home everything was as it had always been: Olga, forever in love with some admirer, ringing up, going away, sending page-long telegrams; Seryozha with his sweet face and lovely, pure

* Sister-in-law.

175

eyes—he was twelve at the time and reading Wells's *The Time Machine*; and that emotional headache (she could find no other words to describe it) occasioned by Sergey Sergeyevich's presence. How many times in their long history had she tried to love him properly without ever succeeding? He understood everything too well, he was too good-looking, too kind, too well disposed, too scornful—and always resolvedly so. That ingenuous, almost puerile mixture of the motherly and the childlike within Liza could not reveal itself; when dealing with him, it would always seem inappropriate, and so, to protect herself from this, Liza always made out as if she too were scornful, like him, that she too took nothing seriously in her relations with him, that she too regarded everything with an Olympian indifference. Perhaps without desiring it, for many years he had slowly and mercilessly contorted her life and forced her always to play out the same comedy, always feigning, always unconsciously lying. This man's whole life was built on lies. Lying was a mark of his goodness; lying was a mark of his magnanimity; lying was a mark of his love. The only thing that wasn't a lie was his scorn. Yet it is indeed impossible to build a life, as it is entirely impossible to build a love, on this one negative quality. For all that, had it been blood that flowed through his veins—normal human blood, and not that ideal physiological preparation imbuing his strong, lithe body which knew no fatigue—he would have been the stuff of dreams. But this was not the case. It was impossible to interpret rationally: you could only intuit it, and only if you were a woman, and only if you were his lover. The sisters, Olga and Liza, knew this. Perhaps Olga had forgotten it; she had given up relations with her husband too long ago. Liza, however, knew that Sergey Sergeyevich did indeed love her—that is, Liza. *Seulement ce n'était jamais grand-chose*;* it was the incomprehensible paltriness of spiritual riches accorded to him by nature. And this too contained a riddle: Liza was certain that Sergey Sergeyevich would do everything in his power for her, and he could do an awful lot—why was it, then, that this left her cold? Was it that everything that came to others through hard work and sacrifice came to him easily and required no effort? Liza was certain that Sergey Sergeyevich had been faithful to her, but this was no achievement in itself: he did not have to fight temptation since he had none. He explained it to her; it was, he said, the result of lengthy physical training, of a well-functioning body—yes, probably just like the Swiss student's; yet the Swiss could in no way be compared with Sergey Sergeyevich: the former suffered from a physical shortcoming, the latter from one of the soul. Thus did he bring up Seryozha, who, himself, had never taken to sport; however, even at the age of five, Sergey Sergeyevich threw him into the water at a deep spot. Liza cried, "You've gone mad!" She got ready to jump in after him, but Sergey Sergeyevich's calm hand held her back.

"It's all right, Lizochka, this is the way to do it. I won't let him drown, you may rest assured."

* That had never been much in itself.

And indeed Seryozha floundered but managed to keep himself afloat in the water. But how could he look on calmly at his child's plaintive eyes, full of tears? It began to seem to her that Sergey Sergeyevich was bereft of human feeling; and, pondering this, she imagined that he, like the hero of some fantastical novel, was the fruit of an improbable and cruel fantasy, a being with a quick and uncommonly developed intellect, who would immediately grasp what cost others tears and suffering to comprehend. He required none of this. He understood, for example, that Yegorkin should be pitied and not mocked; Liza admitted this theoretically, but standing between a theoretical under-standing and her own feelings was a lifetime of experience, which she was unable to set aside; while on the other hand Sergey Sergeyevich had a glittering void containing not a single spectre. And thus it was in all matters.

Recalling Sergey Sergeyevich over the course of these years, Liza was surprised to think that he had never seemed to express excitement, anxiety or joy—no matter what happened. A very long time ago, when the Civil War was drawing to a close and Sergey Sergeyevich, after his ostensibly dramatic adventures and the total collapse of that world in which his life had really existed, arrived in London, where his family had long already been living, he turned up, clean-shaven and laughing, wearing a beautiful, just-pressed suit and carrying brand-new travelling cases— those gay dark-blue eyes, that dazzling white collar—as if he had just been away on a short business trip; and when talk of Russia began and Olga Alexandrovna said, "God, how awful, Seryozha!", he said (Liza recalled the phrase very well): "Yes, yes, such a pity about those poor, sweet generals."

After an attempt on his life in Athens, when the police detained the assailant—who had missed literally at a distance of two paces—Sergey Sergeyevich told Liza: "You know, it was so nice to see among those Greek brigands' swarthy physiognomies such a sweet-looking Russian face—the bulbous nose, the eyes of a desperate fool—an unadulterated pleasure."

"That's beside the point!" said Olga Alexandrovna to Liza. "Don't you see, Lizochka, that all he does is talk and pass life by, like some smirking lunatic who thinks he knows it all!"

To tie her fate to this man, everything, her thirst for true love, her eyes that wanted to melt in another's gaze, her powerful and lithe body, her hands with their long fingers and rose-coloured nails, to sacrifice everything for this machine?... And so, now that this Liza who was made for a glittering and incomparable love finally discovered what it was that she could no longer live without, it was as if she wanted to go to Seryozha but, suddenly, at the door, saw a familiar, broad silhouette, and a metallic, lifeless arm spanning the width of the door, barring her way. How many times had Liza been stopped in her passions by Sergey Sergeyevich, in her finest feelings, in her finest moments—just as she was, for example, when she quoted to him those favourite lines of hers, lying next to him and gazing into his eyes. "Do you remember this, Seryozha?

We are two horses; our bit is held
By one hand, stung by the same spur,
Two eyes we have, of but one gaze,
Of one lone dream, two trembling wings.

"How splendid it is, Seryozha!"

"Yes, indeed."

"Is that all you have to say?"

"It demonstrates a regrettable inexactitude; but then, in poetry—"

"Come, Seryozha…"

"No, it's true, Lizochka: how is it that we have two horses but only one spur? Only horsemen in the artillery have only one spur. And then there's the 'bit'; the bit is not the reins, Lizochka. The bit goes in the mouth of the horse, not in the hands of the rider, one spur or not. Why such thrift in equipment? Why instead of four spurs just one? However, the last two lines are inspired."

He did not care for anything grand, anything heroic, anything that reached the lofty heights of human inspiration. He would find something amusing in everything that would permit him to examine it from on high. "What is this? A defensive reflex?" he might have said. "Or cruelty?" When he spoke of something, his first words would be: "What a charming man! What a charming woman!" Then he would add a few words about the most regrettable shortcoming of this man or this woman, and it would transpire that the former was a villain and the latter a fool. "But still, they're the loveliest people." "Lovely", "charming"—these were his favourite words; however, no charm had any effect on him: it was utterly futile. For what did this man live? He lived—and suffocated the lives of others with his own. "Never, not for all the world! To find myself again in these tender embraces!" she thought. Not for all the world! He had ruined Olga's life, he had almost ruined hers, and he could yet ruin Seryozha—but this he would not manage. He must not know anything; otherwise this machine would be set in motion and there would be nothing she could do to stop it.

At the same time, had it been possible to breathe life into him, what a marvellous man he might have been! But she did not like to think about this. "What ever shall we do, Seryozhenka?" she whispered, bending over Seryozha. His eyes were closed, his breathing even; asleep, his face was that of a child. Liza recalled how she and her sister would leave the nursery on tiptoe after the boy had fallen asleep, and Lyolya would whisper:

"Sleep, my love, sleep, my darling, sleep my little fair-haired one."

And then Sergey Sergeyevich would appear, saying:

"Well, ladies, are we going to the circus or aren't we? Just imagine, Liza, the famous Italian juggler Curaccinello will be performing with flaming torches while reciting Raskolnikov's and then Svidrigailov's monologues from memory. Would you like to go and see it?"

And now, in place of this false, unreal existence— such a wonderful life with Seryozha. There were times when she wanted to cry out, to fight, to frolic, to run—in these moments she, who was usually so languid, would become unlike herself. One day, they stayed too late in the woods and had to hurry to dinner at the house, two kilo- metres away—down a twisting terracotta path—she and Seryozha ran all the way, and once more she felt as though she were eighteen, and again, as in those days, summer's smell of hot earth and scorched pine trees, vivid and intense, struck her face as the path ran smoothly away beneath her feet. Beside her, keeping up the constant, impetuous pace, was Seryozha, taking her arm at the turnings; then long jumps from little ledges, momentary flights in the still air, and the scent of one's own body, fresh and hot from the run. She loved everything: the constant shyness, Seryozha's awkwardness, his inept kisses and how he would get hope- lessly lost in her dress, while she could not hold back the laughter, hampering him in every possible way, taking him by the hands—her teeth would glisten in her moist smile. What foolishness—to have lived for so many years and know nothing of this. Together they dreamt aloud of how they would live on an island, in the forest, on the shore of a green lagoon with clear waters and sand at the bottom, how they would sleep in a cave, how they would take shelter there during a tropical downpour. They would spend the greater part of the day out of doors—in the sea or, after lunch, at Nice or Villefranche; in the evening, again, they would go for a stroll and, upon their return, everything in the house would be sound asleep. Only once did they spend the day without even going out onto the terrace. That morning Liza awoke because of the cold, got out of bed, went over to the window to close it and heard the powerful clatter of rain. As she lifted the wooden shutter, unending sheets of water streamed down before her; the rain was torrential. As far as the eye could see, everything was raindrops and damp fog; the wind howled softly and ominously. Amid this raw tumult, Liza could hear the shingle on the beach, and through the various noises came the rapid, simultaneous murmur of several streams; everything was there— the sobbing, the sodden squelch and smack of mouldering earth, and, cutting through the dank, leaden air, somewhere nearby a cockerel crowed. Liza could not step away from the window. Perhaps for the first time in her life, her perception of time had vanished; long ago, in the terrible abyss of vanished millennia, the very same event had repeated itself time and time again: that same violent whirl of rain, those same sounds, the noise of the vast earth and the shrill call of the cockerel—and if one were to imagine the mythical Titan, who fell sound asleep to the drumming of this rain and awoke, leaving the Stone Age behind and finding himself in the Age of Christ, everything would have been the same: the sheets of water, the damp fog, the piercing call of birds in a dank mist full of droplets. Seryozha awoke— however soundly he slept, he would always, after a short while, sense her departure—got up and went over to her.

"Look, my little boy," she said, placing her hand on his naked shoulder.

They both stood there, shivering from the morning cold, and, unable to tear themselves away, just looked out of the window.

"Do you know what it reminds me of, Liza?"

"What, Seryozhenka?"

"The creation of the world. That cosmic chaos, and there, a little above, the great shadow of the Lord of Hosts over this swirling, smoky world. Can you imagine it? All around Him, of course, there's no rain, but dryness; He's in a colossal waterhole—do you see? Just look, Liza, perhaps He's there? Peer into the distance, and you'll see that far away, in the air, floats a mountain range—but those aren't mountains, Lizochka, they're His resting stone hand."

"Over there, on the right, high up, Seryozha?"

"Yes, Liza, thereabouts."

"I was thinking about something else, Seryozha…"

"About what?"

"About time. What do you call it, that arduous flight?"

"Yes, if you will."

"So, do you feel at this very moment that time is no more? Do you understand how absurd Yegorkin, Chef, Paris and London are—none of these exist right now; only you and I, the sky, the earth, the waves in the sea and the rain. That we're cold and that I love you. Let's shout together: time is no more!"

They shouted this; their voices drowned in the noise of the rain. Then Liza said:

"You should sleep, Seryozha; go back to bed."

In a habitual movement, he picked her up in his arms and, as always, she said: "You're mad, you'll drop me. I weigh almost sixty kilos; you're mad, do you hear?"

But she put her arms around his neck and would not let go.

THE ENTIRETY OF THE immense world in which she had hitherto lived her life had been set in motion, only for it to vanish. Liza would now recall it, but only the most elementary images remained: coldness, ennui, emptiness, and the way in which every sound seemed to sink without an echo—this world was almost mute and lifeless, and no mighty breath could animate it. Music rang out, rivers flowed, snow crunched, the sea lapped, but it was as if all this were taking place in some long-familiar painting, on the mute spectrum of someone's silent, fading inspiration. Sometimes she began to think—in those distant times—that it could be ascribed to the absence of unrealizable desires of a material and geographical order: indeed, she was entirely free, she could do what she wanted, go where she pleased, dress as the mood took her—and for all this, Sergey Sergeyevich was by her side, ever ready to fulfil her wishes. There was nothing she had wanted for; of course the sunset over Lac Léman was more beautiful than the dawn in Paris; of course it was better at the Italian lakes than in London, but these were immaterial details that could not alter what really mattered. But there was nothing that really mattered, nor could there ever be.

Now she saw everything differently, as though looking through someone else's eyes—they retained their former dimensions, colours and sharpness of perception, but everything she now saw in those landscapes had blossomed and been transformed. The vastness of the distant sky spread out overhead, the water began to shimmer, and the black-and-white cliffs along the right-hand bank of Cap Ferrat towered as if for the very first time above the sea in their two-toned chaotic beauty. Above all this, amid the lush, almost wearying combination of different colours in the harlequin still, there was always the sound of distant music, lacking in melodic harmony—the wind in the trees, the sobbing of the water in the bay, the call of the cicadas, the roar of the waves crashing into the narrow clefts between the cliffs—but it was alive, never ceasing for an instant, and inexpressibly beautiful. Her vision grew sharper and more perceptive; she took in everything she saw, and she noticed everything—the shuffling gait of the old Italian woman who was going out to her vegetable garden, the muscular strength of the man who, some distance from the shore, was furling his sail in a light breeze, the casual suppleness of the monkey that was jumping about, tethered to a long chain in one of the nearest gardens, the impossibly swift flight of the swallow soaring upwards directly from the earth's surface to the belfry of the local church, the rush of a fish swimming away down below, the steady undulation of underwater seaweed, the smooth power of Seryozha's bronzed body in the water, when he, running off the jetty, hurled himself into the sea. She had the impression that her situation recalled the feelings of a man who is gravely ill, who cannot move and has to rest for long periods, without hope of ever getting up, but then, doing just that, feels his body revive, his fingers regain their magical, almost lost suppleness, and everything begin to live and run amok around him. Other sensations comprised that same disparity: from Seryozha's first tender caress, her head had begun to spin and her eyes had immediately clouded; this second life, the only one that was real, had begun that evening when she kissed Seryozha for the first time.

Despite the fact that she would almost always act prudently—in the sense that she tried to take into consideration every possible consequence of one action or another and take appropriate precautions that would eliminate any foreseeable obstacles or concerns—on this occasion she spared almost no thought for the aftermath, although in this instance it was more necessary than it had been at any other time. It felt too good, and her instinct—infallible at almost any given moment—which found the notion of a temporary perspective strange, prevented her from thinking about this. She felt, however, that the further she went, the more impossible a separation from Seryozha became for her. In any case, by ignoring what was to come, she knew intuitively that if any future sacrifice were necessary on her part, she would not let that be an impediment.

And so, despite Liza's unexpected and undoubted enrichment—in the sense that she experienced a great number of sensations and emotions that until then had been known to her only from books—it was impossible not to notice her privation in purely spiritual terms. Books, her beloved books, which she would occasionally attempt to read (these days her patience lasted for only half an hour, no more), now seemed boring to her. She could still appreciate their brilliance from a distance; their logical constructions still seemed persuasive to her, but they had lost their ability to comfort her, as they had done previously. In the end, it became clear that they essentially had nothing to do with her. "Art, Lizochka, was devised for those who are malcontent," Sergey Sergeyevich had once said to her long ago, whereupon she had vehemently opposed him, insisting that it was only his inner philistinism that led him to think so. Now she could not help agreeing with him. When one day they went with Yegorkin to see some mediocre exhibition in Nice, Liza had been unable to recall afterwards a single painting; all that had lodged in her memory were patches of colour, because the whole time Seryozha had been walking next to her, arm in arm, and his presence had absolutely consumed her attention. Even her appearance had changed. Before, it would happen that while walking down a street she would notice how people turned to look at her, but now, not only did it occur much more frequently, but among those who turned there were a great many simple people—workers, fishermen—who before would never have paid her any attention at all, because it was much too apparent that she was a lady who had nothing, and indeed never could have anything, to do with them. Now she had somehow become closer to them—perhaps because it was beyond all doubt, and because one could see in her eyes and face, by her slightly coarsened, weighed-down aspect, that it was the erotic that now occupied the lead role in her life—no man could have been mistaken in this regard. She understood this, but her understanding, as with everything that did not have any immediate bearing on her private life, was somehow abstract, extraneous and irrelevant. She was glad that at her age she felt no physical distinction between the woman she was many years ago, when she had held the young Seryozha in her arms, and the woman she was now; she did not think and did not remember that this was also due to Sergey Sergeyevich, who forced her to play sports and said: "You'll thank me later." However, on this point he was mistaken—at least for the moment. Liza felt no gratitude whatsoever towards him, to say the least. It pleased her that she was almost as strong as Seryozha, which never failed to astonish him—all the more so because the happy configuration of her body was such that her muscles did not show. Seryozha was surprised one day when Liza was held up on the road; he came out to meet her and found that she had a flat tyre and was changing the wheel.

"You're doing that yourself?"

"Of course I'm doing it myself, silly," she said.

"How did you unscrew the nuts?"

"Like this, Seryozhenka," she said, making a turning movement with her right hand.

"And you were strong enough?"

She laughed and then proposed an arm-wrestling match, from which Seryozha emerged victorious, but only after such effort that his whole face was left covered in beads of sweat.

"I was a little tired," she said. "If I'd been on form, you'd have been in trouble."

She enjoyed the sensation of Seryozha's supple resistance in the contest; in a similar exercise with Sergey Sergeyevich, she had met only with disappointment—therein she had found neither resistance nor suppleness, only a stiff, lifeless arm that she was unable to move, and it ended in her biting it, after which Sergey Sergeyevich calmly said:

"That isn't part of the game, Liza."

Liza had never before suspected herself capable of that unceasing physical languor which now almost never left her. Seryozha could but yield to it; for several days he lost weight and his face became drawn, in spite of the fact that he ate plenty and enjoyed several hours of unbroken sleep.

He had matured a lot in the first week; his features had become more defined, the slit of his eyes, ever so slightly darker but still very light against his bronzed face, seemed clearer. After Liza said to him, "Promise me not to think about this, Seryozha," he obediently submitted to her; for him there was no greater pleasure than to carry out her wishes, whatever they may be. However, even prior to this prohibition he would think deeply and intensely about everything, and now he was powerless to prevent, under the brilliance of the sun, at morning on the seashore, or in the soft, transparent darkness of the southern evening, the face of his mother occasionally materializing before him, just as lovely as he remembered it: those large dark eyes which had no eyelashes above them, her perfectly smooth,

190

wrinkleless forehead and the hint of eau de toilette that would appear as she leant over him. Strictly speaking, it was impossible to tell what Seryozha was thinking; it would have been inexact: his thoughts did not contain a single rational argument; there were a few visual associations that were at times more painful than any thought. To this day he had never succeeded in linking everything he thought, saw and felt to a logical system that developed gradually, as human life was usually depicted in the books he read. He did not believe that life was always conventional and artificial; he simply had the impression that he himself was incapable of such artistic representation. He knew a great deal and had read extensively for his age, and until recently he had imagined that, in theory, there was nothing in the world that he could not understand. He had taken umbrage one day when his father told him, in speaking of some mundane problem, that he could not comprehend it. He said this without offering any initial explanation; then Seryozha asked his father whether he thought him a complete imbecile. Sergey Sergeyevich patted him on the check with unexpected affection and replied that, on the contrary, he was very pleased with him, and that he could not have hoped for a better heir; however, this heir, according to Sergey Sergeyevich, was still too young to understand certain things.

"Not because, Seryozha, you aren't as clever as some rouged-up old lady who, truth to tell, is an utter fool; however, she is able to understand, and you aren't, even if she hasn't read even a tenth of those clever books that—"

"So what's the difference?"

"The difference, Seryozha, lies in emotional experience. Do you understand? It's difficult to explain and it would be pointless to try. In time you'll learn. You'll come across things you've read about a thousand times over, and then you'll see that to read is one thing, and to understand is another. What is every ethical problem? An attempt to systematize collective emotional experience—that's first and foremost—then comes utilitarianism, practicability, and so on."

Liza, on the other hand, would say this was not worth thinking about—not generally not worth thinking about, but that he, Seryozha, should not fixate on it; for him it was unimportant. As far as Seryozha was concerned, Liza had always been the embodiment of every virtue, and not only would this image of her no longer endure the slightest distortion, but it had even been reinforced. Of course, it was terrible that she was his mother's sister; but for this one minor point, everything would have been splendid, even from an ethical point of view. This aspect of the problem, however, was difficult for Seryozha, not because he personally experienced any discomfort, embarrassment or awkwardness on account of it—no, only because he could envisage the horror in his mother's eyes when she found out. He was utterly unable to imagine his father's reaction, but he knew that his father, too, would naturally take a dim view of it. With Sergey Sergeyevich, that was just what one could expect: a dim view. Where Olga Alexandrovna was concerned, the words would be savage: she would most likely be horrified. However, blood rushed to his face at the idea that Liza might suffer as a result of this; come what may, Liza should not suffer—she was so wonderful, so pure and so tender.

All these thoughts had occurred to Seryozha prior to his conversation with Liza—and at the time they had been agonizing and insoluble. Yet after the conversation he immediately felt as if a weight had been lifted from his chest: truly, he stopped asking himself questions about the degree to which everything was possible or impossible, as though between him and all these painful ambiguities stood an opaque screen, and only Liza and love remained—and nothing else in the whole world surrounding them.

THE FUNERAL OF PIERRE, Lola Aînée's husband, was exceptionally successful and, for the summer months, remarkably well attended. All Lola's many friends and acquaintances, the majority of whom considered her marriage to have been a *mésalliance* and had not even liked Pierre when he was alive, now suddenly gave the impression that he had been a wonderful man. Thus Lola's marriage, which had always come under fire during Pierre's lifetime, now acquired sympathetic sanction from society, and even received a few notes of approval. Lola had to hear out a multitude of condolences; most often people would say to her: "I didn't have the pleasure of knowing your husband well, but on the two occasions that I met him, he left the very best impression on me—and believe me, I fully share in your..." Lola would nod and reply: "My dear friend, I never doubted your feelings..." The funeral was attended by people of the most diverse ages, the majority, however, were elderly and had been lured there by a double-edged, contradictory sentiment: on one hand, it was an unpleasant thought that their own deaths, too, were already on the horizon and drawing ever nearer; on the other, in vanquishing these melancholy notions, there was a palpable joy that it was this Pierre who had died, and not them; these people would attend almost every funeral in order to obtain entirely irrefutable proof of their albeit temporary immortality.

At the beginning of the service, one of Lola's friends, a man of her own generation but still her senior, had a sympathetic chat with her and said that it would all pass. He was interminably old, but tried to keep his spirits up (although he did wear a corset which caused him no end of pain and creaked at the slightest movement); he was the author of a book that had enjoyed a certain popularity fifty-six years previously, in the January of that unforgettable year, an academic and an exceedingly respectable man who wore a discreet grey toupee atop his nodding head. Towards the end of the service, he came up to her again, adding this time that, as sad as it may be (tears were welling in his eyes, for he was tired and deeply moved), it was impossible not to observe that a great many of his and Lola's generation no longer numbered among the living. And now poor Pierre... With her face placid and downcast, Lola listened to him attentively, although what he was saying was entirely absurd, since Pierre could in no way be considered a man of their generation: as their fame had blossomed, Pierre had yet to be born. Moreover, Lola found the conversation about these distant times wholly unpalatable, for it reminded her of her age. She would usually reply to such things with the same unvarying line: "Yes, I scarcely remember it myself. I was really only a child back then." Her companion would be left to smile politely in response and recall inwardly that this child had had fifteen lovers by that point, all of whom would lavish money on her and were ready to fight duels on her account, according to the custom of that lost and exceptionally heroic era.

A mass of dark-coloured automobiles followed in the funeral cortège; the harmony was broken only by a light-grey cabriolet being driven by a very young man in a summer suit, hatless and with a truly pained expression on his face; next to him, however, sat an elderly lady, the very picture of mourning, wholly appropriate for the general scene—that is, somewhat old fashioned, with a solemn tranquillity. The appearance of the young man and his pained face could be ascribed to the fact that his aunt, having missed the official procession and, on account of her dreadful avarice, begrudging the money to hire a taxi, spotted him as he was turning at the corner of her street and insisted that he take her to the funeral: there was nothing else for it, and among those present he was the only man whose grief was entirely unfeigned.

"*Lola Aînée, ma tante?*" he said. "*Mais c'est une vieille toupie…*"

"*C'est une interprète remarquable de Racine et de Corneille,*" said his aunt indignantly, "*et il faut avoir une grandeur d'âme qui est inconnue maintenant pour être à la hauteur de ces rôles.*"

"*Pour la grandeur d'âme, ma tante,*" he murmured disconsolately, "*je vous l'accorde, mais celle des spectateurs est encore plus remarquable.*"

"Tu n'es qu'un imbécile," his aunt said coldly. *"Suis donc ce triste enterrement et tais-toi."**

The procession would sometimes stop at a crossroads; each time the young man very nearly drove into the venerable Rolls-Royce in front of him, and, instead of cursing, was made to swallow his words and, following his aunt's advice, respectfully remain silent.

Lola was very satisfied with the funeral, and she was truly glad that everything had come off so touchingly and well. The crowd accompanying her husband's coffin had been composed of devotees of her art; it was that same *foule qui l'a toujours adorée*, only more polite and reserved. Lola was so inane that no doubts in this regard ever surfaced in her head; those who attended the funeral had manifestly been guided by the most varied of reasons, which not infrequently found a particular personal basis outside any feelings of sympathy for Lola in her hour of deepest sorrow, which she never felt. There were several journalists present who, having immediately sought each other out, gadded about en masse, one of them, a writer of obituaries, telling his colleagues the latest anecdotes as they bit their lips, trying not to laugh; there were people—and a great many of them—who had nothing to do in life and seized on

---

* "Lola Aînée, Aunty?… But she's just some old cow." "She's a remarkable interpreter of Racine and Corneille… You need a greatness of spirit, such as is unknown nowadays, to reach the heights of those roles." "As for greatness of spirit, Aunty… I agree with you, but that of the audience is even more remarkable." "You're an idiot… Now just follow this sorry procession and keep quiet."

the opportunity to attend a funeral; there were those who found the notion of missing Pierre's funeral unthinkable, just as they would never miss a premiere at the opera or the races at Longchamp, and they composed by far the majority, but in the depths of their souls, the least stupid of them were indifferent to the premieres, and to the races, and to the funeral; there were those who came to settle their affairs, profiting by the fact that they could not later be accused of shamelessness—but what good fortune: "My dear friend, to think that you and I should meet under such terrible circumstances. What an awful death! By the way, forgive me, but those investitures that you so kindly…" There was also a very animated, very finely and sombrely dressed man of forty, with a beaming face whose expression was entirely out of keeping with a funeral; he was one of the first to go up to Lola and had a long conversation with her, greeting everyone earnestly and generally acting in such a way that no one present could possibly fail to notice him; he told everyone that his wife had regrettably been unable to come owing to illness; then he made an unexpectedly quick exit and got into the last motor car at the far end of the procession, where an uncommonly buxom blonde of around twenty-two awaited him and said: "*Alors, on est libre, c'est fini les condoléances?*"* The automobile lagged behind, then turned right and vanished.

One could never have said that Lola was unprepared for this funeral; she had tried on a great many dresses, and

---

* At last we're free. Have you finished with the condolences?

then, alone in her room, she had rehearsed that particular funereal walk and practised with determination, trying to give her face the necessary expression—the solemn service would not catch her unawares; after the funeral, much was said and written about the regal dignity of the illustrious actress and the noble comportment of her sorrow. What was more, it seemed as though no event in Lola's life had ever brought her so much happiness as did the funeral of her husband.

Everything at home changed immediately. The maid, who had lately been obeying Pierre's orders and not Lola's, now reverted to her ways from before Lola's marriage and lost the subtle disdain in her replies and general tone of voice, which had so vexed Lola. The Bugatti was sold post-haste, and in its place appeared a Delage just like the old one—with those same soft, firm cushions and those marvellous springs; travelling in it, Lola felt none of those sensations that had hounded her on the rare occasions when she had ridden in the low Bugatti—namely, as if someone had been dragging her down by the legs while the motor sobbed and roared after taking a corner, while in Pierre's unskilled hands the shuddering vehicle would gather speed by fits and starts. Once again her evenings were quiet; Pierre's many random female friends disappeared, and amid this heavy silence Lola, stirring, would from time to time hear the wind blowing through the trees in the garden overlooked by her bedroom window. The sound reminded her of distant, seemingly long-forgotten things: her childhood in the countryside, a rainy summer's evening, the resonant squelch of cows' hooves upon the wet earth, and that marvellous, beloved smell of dung, which was incomparable with any other smell. She saw herself as a fifteen-year-old country beauty, with firm legs, her feet in sabots, great black eyes and a strong white body, which knew nothing of the surgeon's touch back then. She drifted off, smiling at the memory of all this.

Lola was now totally free; she would spend whole days sitting in an armchair, and when she felt sleepy her head would drop onto her chest and she would doze off, since there was no one for whom she needed to maintain any pretence. She played solitaire, told her own fortune and even allowed herself, in the course of her first week of new-found freedom, to deviate from her strict diet—she ate roast chicken and beef broth, then one evening dined entirely alone at Prunier's, which was not far from her apartment. After a few days she became ill, and so it was then necessary to starve and take medicines, yet she bore all this with such ease that even she was surprised; of course, it could be ascribed to the rule of delayed happiness, the onset of which had occurred that evening when she received the telephone call informing her of her husband's fatal wound.

As soon as this first happy period had passed, Lola's former energy reawakened in her. She knew from long experience that she could not remain in the shadows, that her name had to appear in the newspapers as often as possible, no matter what the pretext. She scheduled several interviews; after successive readings of these one gathered that Lola did not intend, in the wake of her recent shock, to go to rest in the south at her villa near Nice, that she would remain in Paris where she was working intensely on the leading role in a play she did not yet want to name, that she had turned down a proposal from a leading American company, which had offered her a contract in Hollywood, that in the near future she would go touring in Central Europe, that she would go touring in South America, that she would go touring in North America, that she had engagements scheduled in Holland, that despite the rumours going about, she had rejected plans to go to Rumania and Greece. No one had been spreading any rumours about her, but this refutation of fictitious gossip was her usual ploy; none of these interviews or reports had any basis in fact whatsoever, apart from her convulsive desire not to be erased, not from the memory of her contemporaries—that was an irreversible fait accompli, since the majority of them had quit this world long ago, and those who still numbered among the living awaited death with trepidation and thought only of this—but from the memory of the society of the day, which had followed her for half a century. Then, after all these possibilities had been exhausted, Lola herself took to appearing in print, for which, ever since the days of her first benefactor, she felt almost as much of a weakness as she did for the theatre. Naturally, she never wrote anything herself (she would have been much too illiterate for this), and so she always had a regular collaborator, whom she would now have to pay in cash, which irked her greatly: only a few years previously, essentially not so long ago, she would never have used money to pay for services. Now she was forced to come to terms with the fact that times had changed. Her current *nègre littéraire* was a young man who was making a career for himself in the newspapers and wrote minor arts reviews; however, since the arts reviews brought in little money (he was unable to live on these alone), he also specialized in articles for government ministers, public figures, actors and singers; it was thoroughly unpleasant work, particularly because the majority of people who engaged him had absurd notions about style and would make demands that were all but impossible to meet without risking the readers' derision. Of all his clients, there was only one whom he greatly esteemed—an old senator who would say to him, "*Écoutez, mon petit,*"* and commission an article on some theme, but would not demand that it be written in one way and not another, and would not even read it before handing it over to the printers: he would read the beginning of it in the newspaper or journal, but even then he never found the strength to read it through to the end. He would stare at the nebulous letters, making out the first few phrases, and invariably say: "Splendid, my young friend, splendid." He would pay better than the others, and he was entirely uninterested in the printed matter bearing his name. In the circle of people who read his articles, he was considered a shrewd and audacious politician who diligently followed all the vagaries of current affairs. Carrying out such work

* Listen here, my boy.

had been unpleasant at first, but then Lola's collaborator became so used to it that he was entirely unsurprised when he learnt that the dismal bald man with the weary, haggard face, whom he frequently met in the editor's office of one of the large newspapers, was, it so happened, that same Mathilde Marigny who gave such ample advice to female readers on the most varied of topics, from facial and bodily care to amatory woes and dilemmas: "I think that my husband is unfaithful to me. Should I leave him and go with my child to a man who has proved his love for me many times over?…"

Lola met him with a businesslike air and said that they needed to talk; together they began to discuss plans for her appearances in the newspapers. The fact of the matter was that Lola had finally decided to realize her long-held dream: to write her memoirs. Her collaborator—Dupont was his name—coughed uncertainly: this sort of work was particularly disagreeable.

"I'm flattered by your faith in me, Madame," he said, "but—"

"Of course, of course," Lola quickly put in. "With your talent—"

"The fact is, I'm afraid… Ultimately, I just haven't the time—"

"But, my dear friend, it's so simple. I'll tell you everything—everything, you understand?"

"I think—"

"I assure you, it's a task that will bring you nothing but pleasure."

"I do not doubt it."

"Well, then. And you'll receive a cut from the publisher when the book comes out."

On this point, however, Dupont objected most categorically; he insisted on dealing only with Lola, yet however unpleasant this was for her, her hands were tied. A discussion about the contents of Lola's memoirs was due to take place a few days later. Their immediate tasks were to prepare for press, first, a long letter to the editor, in which Lola would express her gratitude to all those who attended her husband's funeral, and secondly an article, 'Why I Am Writing My Memoirs'. Two days later both texts were presented to Lola; she made a few corrections to them but was on the whole satisfied. The first piece, replete with expressions of restrained mourning, included a phrase that Lola found most pleasing, on the way in which people are accustomed to think of celebrities as if they do not live and suffer like mere mortals: "*Hélas! Nous ne sommes, nous autres, que de simples mortels, doués peut-être d'un pouvoir qui…*"* and so on; in brief, everything was done properly and with a most touching sensibility—everything, right down to the appreciation shown to the newspaper that printed it, for its "gracious gesture"… It was especially pleasing that the same issue also ran a last-minute article about Lola, written by a renowned lady author—only later did it come to light that this had been pure coincidence. By and

* Alas, we others are only mere mortals, blessed perhaps by a
capacity for…

by, 'Why I Am Writing My Memoirs' appeared in print, having been penned, with a certain indirect inspiration, by Dupont, who had clearly been on good form that day. "We represent a chronologically inconceivable combination of two seemingly so different epochs; this singular combination will be revealed only if we deign to shed our theatrical garb and appear before you, dear readers, just as we are in reality. You shall then be certain that the numerous fictitious dramas of a few historical women, which you have become so accustomed to seeing embodied in our interpretation, have perhaps not passed without trace; in a single turn of my head, I apprehend myself making one of Sappho's gestures and, with arm outstretched, the pose of Célimène…"

Lola immersed herself in work on the memoirs; admittedly, her part in it was only to provide a detailed narrative, which Dupont would interrupt very occasionally, saying, "Yes, I understand… Of course…", while taking it all down in his notebook. He depicted Lola's life as one full of constant wonder, skipping over any "delicate" areas: on this point Dupont had insisted, redacting from Lola's account any of the more risqué passages. Although this resulted in a somewhat curious situation in which it was stated that before her marriage to Pierre, Lola had known only platonic love for a few remarkable people, born of their mutual passion for art, and although it may have seemed unlikely that she had remained, essentially, a virgin until old age—to the extent that Lola herself noticed this and said so to Dupont—nevertheless, he insisted on such a redaction of the memoirs.

"Everyone will know you've had such liaisons," he said, "but what they'll appreciate is your discretion."

"No, you mustn't exaggerate like that," Lola rejoined.

"Everyone knows it's impossible," Dupont calmly objected, "but why make such a point of it? After all, one wouldn't set down that windows are to let light in, that they can be opened and closed; one doesn't waste time explaining this to the reader: one would hope that he knows all this himself. It's the same here, Madame."

On the other hand, Dupont frequently described the rising and setting of the sun in Auvergne, where a young girl, looking out from the terrace of the house in which she had been born, dreamt of Paris and happiness. Lola's family had immediately grown wealthy in the memoirs, and her parents had turned from ordinary peasants into representatives of the landed gentry. In Dupont's imagination there appeared—thereafter migrating to Lola's memoirs—a great many people who had never existed, but who were nonetheless very touching: an old teacher of French literature, who would say to her, "My child, cherish your amazing gift"; the mayor of the neighbouring town, who had wept when Lola appeared on stage one day during an amateur production; an aunt (the one Lola remembered as a wrinkled old woman with coarse hands, the one who had taught her how to conduct herself with benefactors in Paris), who had metamorphosed into a society beauty and retired to her estates in Auvergne to mourn the death of her beloved husband.

Upon reaching Paris, the narrative took on an entirely

pathetic tone. Here, in many respects, Lola's and Dupont's opinions coincided; they both regarded Paris as the greatest city in the world, and, for that reason only, they both believed that anything that happened in Paris acquired a special significance in itself—one that it would not have done had it happened elsewhere. The narrative focused primarily on theatrical premieres, Lola's successes, how one person or another, usually a government minister or a president, would arrive with an enormous bouquet of flowers and congratulate her on her performance. Much was written about people who had died, and could not refute anything categorically. However, despite his adulatory description of this theatrical life, Dupont couldn't but notice that everything was coming out rather monotonously and that his vocabulary of praise, among which the word "triumph" was repeated most often, had long been exhausted. And so he resorted to a new device—drawing simple people into all this; thus there appeared decorators and carpenters, who refused to take money from Lola for refurnishing her apartment, concierges, laundresses, chimney sweeps and cab drivers, who also drove her for free.

Lola's book was meant to create an impression of presenting the most fascinating memoiristic material and, at the same time, to be a stylistic masterpiece. Lola herself was very satisfied with it. Dupont had worked on it for many hours each day. The printed result, however, fared reasonably well, but was not a runaway success, and he was unable to comprehend the reason for this partial failure.

The reason was that he disliked and despised Lola—he himself was convinced of her utter lack of talent. For him, there could be no doubt about it. He had long known—throughout the course of his literary career, he had often found this—that there were many famous and respected people who in no way merited their reputations or their accolades. In the majority of cases it was even unclear how these misunderstandings—which purportedly transformed Lola into a fabulous actress, so-and-so into an eminent scholar and so-and-so into a great writer—could have come about and persisted for decades. In a very limited circle, among professionals, the appraisals were accurate and merciless, but they never, or almost never, reached the wider public, who believed blindly in everything that was written. Dupont harboured no doubts that they would believe Lola's memoirs, which were a fiction of his own devising, just as they believed everything else; sometimes, when he was able to set aside his immediate concerns, this astonishing lack of understanding on the part of the reader and audience greatly irked him—for he was still young. Moreover, it was patently obvious that Lola was a poor actress, who would fail even to understand the role she was playing. True, no one was moved to tears by her performances, but everyone accepted her great talent. How? Why? He could not understand.

He depicted her in relatively grand terms, perceiving, however, that no woman could live life as Lola did in his memoirs. Yet no one noticed this—no one at all. Even Lola, completely forgetting herself, would say to Dupont:

"I'm amazed, my dear friend, how well you've understood my life." He would smile politely in response, although he wanted to say that all he had done was to apply paint to a cardboard cut-out, and so her kind words were devoid of any meaning from the outset.

Little by little, however, Lola was captivated by the thought that her life had really been just as Dupont described it. She knew, of course, that the factual part of the book contained many inaccuracies—in particular, the first chapter, dedicated to her childhood, seemed especially vague, and what followed in the book bore no resemblance to reality whatsoever. Yet here, for the very first time, she found herself as though standing before her own psychological portrait. She had never spared any thought for the sort of woman she was, the ways in which her life differed from the lives of others—what is death? what is desire? what is passion?—all these questions that have forever concerned others had never even occurred to her. The "ego", about which she had occasionally read and which frequently figured in the plays in her repertoire, simply did not exist. She would react to something strongly only when it posed any palpable danger to her: she might view an impresario unfavourably if he failed to pay her promptly; she might hold an actress in contempt if she had obtained a role destined for Lola through her machinations or a love affair; however, in both politics and social life, as in everything else, that which did not immediately concern her failed to elicit any response in her at all—even when it was the most remarkable or the most scandalous occurrence. In almost exactly the same way, she completely lacked what intermittently appeared in other people and was termed "principles", "convictions", "opinions", "taste", all those words that were perfectly inapplicable to Lola. Dupont was convinced of this, having listened to her anecdotes at length, and each time that he left Lola's, he could not escape a strange and exceedingly unpleasant feeling, which he had no desire to reflect upon. However, in working on Lola's memoirs, he was obliged against his will to return to this, and then one fine day he felt as though absolutely everything had fallen into place. He was unable to work that evening and so went out, all the while thinking that he had never before come across such a remarkable case of spiritual poverty. He reflected on this, feeling something akin to horror: such a long life without a single thought, without any doubt whatsoever, without a second of understanding! Lola seemed like a cold and stupid animal to him, sufficiently well trained, but never having derived from this any human quality. Everything she said was trite and incorrectly expressed, phrases she had once read in a newspaper article or recalled from someone else's conversation.

Yet in her memoirs she had to seem different, and with a certain enthusiasm Dupont depicted this woman who had never existed, and her cardboard charm brought him a degree of satisfaction; she acquired the features of a chocolate-box beauty, appearing now in a field, now in a forest, now in the salons of Paris, now on the stage— with her permanently pained and, essentially, dead face;

only this was a happy corpse—in contradistinction to the real Lola, who instead of a soul had a cold void. Several times Dupont, in spite of the fact that he had worked as a professional counterfeiter for many years and had written the most varied things, ranging from political speeches of opposing content, to articles on archaeology, ballet, theatre, painting and music, all of which passed under the most diverse and predominantly illustrious of names; in spite of the fact that he, Dupont, had penned two thick political tomes and fifteen hundred leaders, not counting all the many speeches—in short, taking upon himself the political career of a certain wealthy individual who was no more literate or intelligent than Lola, and who could never have strung together a more or less coherent phrase and had not even the faintest notion of social doctrines, but published a newspaper and engaged in rather stormy public activity, until one fine day he died of a heart attack—in spite of all his experience, there were several points where Dupont had wanted to refuse to continue with Lola's memoirs. He would have refused, but his circumstances did not permit it: he was penniless, as ever. Sometimes he maliciously thought that in terms of intellectual worth he alone comprised one-fifth of celebrities—he was sure of this—while they, nonetheless, lived happily, enjoying the fruits of his labour: "Your last article, dear *maître*, despite the fact that we have seemingly become accustomed to the inexhaustible magnanimity of your genius…" This genius and the author of the article in question was Dupont, with whom they would scarcely have deigned to shake hands—while he, to whom

211

they owed everything, was forced practically to steal out of his apartment in order to avoid an unpleasant conversation with the concierge, for it had already been five months since he last paid his rent. Sitting in a cafe and watching the people around him with bitter abstraction, he dreamt of writing a book some day—in which he would exact revenge on all these people who were now exploiting him, by revealing everything he knew; then the reader would be convinced of the frailty and infidelity of all flattering epithets and so-called general notoriety. Of all his many clients, the only one he was truly well disposed towards was his senator, who was in fact a sweet old man. The rest he despised. Sometimes in his articles he permitted himself a few caustic remarks and lunges at them—that is, at himself—but the only people to notice these were colleagues among his profession, such intelligent proletarians like himself; for these people there existed no celebrity, no incorruptible people, none of the stuff that elicited such impassioned reactions in so-called social opinion, which these wretched and embittered people considered a manifestation of collective idiocy.

Lola insisted that Dupont immediately, irrespective of any chronological order, include her romance with Pierre in her memoirs. He was to begin with her performances where she would invariably see Pierre's pale face and those fiery eyes fixed on her: Pierre was very pale; with the last of his money he would buy tickets in the back rows, but never missed a single performance of hers, and so she could not help noticing these fiery eyes.

"Forgive me," said Dupont. "If he was sitting in the back rows, then how were you able to make out his face in a half-dark auditorium?"

"Very well," said Lola, "let's sit him nearer to the front. 'He was poor, but with the last of his money…'"

"No, that's impossible," said Dupont, losing patience. "How much money did he have, then, in order to be able to sit in the front row every night? It follows that he couldn't have been poor."

"But he really was poor," said Lola guilelessly.

"Yes, of course, I understand. But then we must do it differently."

"Very well," Lola consented. "Then we'll simply write that I noticed his fiery eyes and that every day he came to the theatre—we'll get to his poverty later."

Dupont was barely able to contain himself: never had he encountered such a stubborn lack of understanding for basic things; even the deceased government minister, legendary for his stupidity, had been sharper than this. He sighed and started to explain to Lola at some length why it was impossible to write this. However, Lola suddenly took umbrage and began saying over and over that it was just a caprice of his and that ultimately he could do as he pleased. Dupont supposed that for a long time already, perhaps for several weeks, she had been dreaming of this part of her memoirs—the wretched pageantry of that "pale face" and those "fiery eyes"—and that she was at pains to part with it. Yet here he was mistaken.

After an hour of heated unbroken debate, they agreed

on a situation, equally dubious, whereby Pierre was to receive a small inheritance—a pittance, some ten or twenty thousand francs—and that he, at the time when Lola noticed his fiery eyes, had spent it all in order not to miss a single one of her appearances. Lola was very satisfied with Dupont and paid him several compliments with regard to his intellect and knowledge of a woman's heart.

Lola, however, was living on the memory of Pierre more and more. It was not by chance that she was so keen to include him in her memoirs. Had she been capable of analysing and in any way dissecting her feelings, she would have realized that her memory was carefully avoiding all the unpleasant aspects of her life with Pierre. Having said that, almost all of it had been unpleasant: the little pleas-antness there had been was minimal, and yet it was this that she remembered. One night, unexpectedly even for Lola, tears welled in her eyes as she thought of him. After a while, even Dupont noticed a marked change in the expression of her eyes and face, the reason for which he could not fathom, although he spared little thought for it, for it was of no interest to him; it was with a sense of great relief that he observed Lola becoming more readily agreeable. She herself was unaware of this, and herein she suddenly came to resemble other women who stubbornly resist admitting that a new emotion can force them to see everything in ways they had not done previously—they have the impression that there is something humiliat-ing about this, something that belittles their exceptional nature, and however plain it may be, they go on denying it.

Lola had nothing to deny; no one ever mentioned this transformation to her. Nevertheless, it was beyond doubt that, owing to some extraordinary, absurd fortuity, a love of Pierre, which had never existed during his lifetime, now welled up inside her with seemingly perfect improbability. It was born of a deep, unconscious gratitude to this man for having died and, in so doing, returning to her the freedom and repose that she had forfeited for so long. Since he could in no way hinder her now and, having ceased to number among the living, had become an embellishment to this touching romance in her memoirs, she seemed to realize, perhaps for the first time, that it had been real. "If only you knew how much I loved this man!" she said to Dupont, and, moreover, she truly was being sincere. Then she said with conviction: "He had a few minor shortcomings, of course, but then who doesn't?" For the hundredth time Dupont noted with some irritation that nine-tenths of what Lola said was made up of commonplaces. "But how he loved me!"

Now, for the first time in many, many years, Lola began to live out this posthumous romance, so monstrous in its artificiality. "*Le pauvre petit!*"* she would invariably say when the conversation turned to Pierre. Little by little, Pierre altered completely in her memories and her anecdotes about him: he stopped drinking, ceased his revelry, became well bred, sweet and tender; and so his sepulchral allure only increased. "Sometimes I think," Lola would say, "that I am

* The poor thing!

one of those rare individuals who only love once in their lives. Yes, of course, I had liaisons, but who hasn't? Pierre was my only true love—and I cannot accustom myself to the thought that he is no longer alive. *Le pauvre petit!*"

Despite her extreme avarice, which had revealed itself in her, however, only in the last few years, as though it were a sign of old age, like grey hair or atherosclerosis—before this she had been extravagant and careless with money, which could be put down to her comparatively modest means—she commissioned a magnificent monument to Pierre with the inscription: "To my dear husband, from the simple and sincere heart of Lola Aînée."

And just as a man's face and the expression in his eyes change when it becomes apparent to those around him that he is going to die, so too was there undoubtedly a deep and lasting rebirth in Lola, which was particularly striking at her age. Dupont, who visited her every day, noted with astonishment that his former irritation had disappeared without trace, and he stopped viewing his routine visit to her as an unpleasant obligation. One day, as she was pouring him some coffee—he was writing in his notebook at the time—and stirring the sugar in for him, a thought, which before would have seemed utterly wild, suddenly flashed through his mind: this woman, in fact, could have been his mother. There was a sense that human traits had suddenly begun to show through her deathly face. In any case, not everyone who happened to meet her noticed the change that had taken place in her—for that they were much too unobservant and, as with the vast majority of people, thought too little and infrequently—but still they sensed it. When they would later say among themselves that each of them had found Lola charming, there was something more sincere in this, something that corresponded better to their real impressions than usual.

What had happened to Lola was the same as what would have happened to any other very elderly person who, in the final stage of life, during the long hours of senility, had recalled and re-evaluated his life, drawing certain conclusions, the only ones possible: that it was necessary, above all else, to forgive people for their involuntary misdemeanours, that one should not hate anyone, that everything was fragile and uncertain, except for this peaceful and pleasant reconciliation, this undemanding love and tenderness for those dearest to us, irrespective, even, of whether they deserve it or not. Lola now acted as though she had understood these things, but the difference was that she had given no thought to it; much as she had done throughout her entire life, she spoke and acted without thinking, deferring to some internal necessity, in essence never knowing why she was doing one thing and not another, but generally the right thing to reach her goal, which became clear to her only retrospectively, for at that time no thoughts had preceded this change in her mode of life or her relations with others.

This was Lola's final, belated blossoming. Anyone who wanted to get the measure of her and studied her entire life without knowing anything of these final months of her existence would have received an erroneous, single-sided impression of her. For this to have taken place, it was necessary for the many years of her interminably long life to pass by, for not a single one of them to leave any mark on her existence and, finally, for death, that most terrible and incomprehensible event, to draw abreast of her and, having delivered her from the presence of that odious man who had entered her life essentially by chance, at the same time suddenly to liberate the humane in her and what she would never have known, were it not for that death. It was like opening a window that had been closed for years, at night, in an ancient, remote building in a forest, on the seashore—only for a great many things that had been hitherto unseen and unheard suddenly to pierce the deathly silence: the dark-blue starry sky, the eternal rush of ocean waves, the call of an unknown bird, the rustle of leaves in the wind, the headlong flight of a bat.

This could not but entail a drastic and total reversal in her mode of life, and an involuntary and painless renunciation of all her former opinions. She continued to receive guests and go out of town, but these events became less and less frequent. As before, she would read the reviews of shows, premieres and concerts, but these opinions, which even a few months ago would have aroused her indignation, now left her ambivalent—as did any mention of her own name, which in former times she would have so eagerly anticipated. When someone once asked her about the fate of her music hall, she replied that matters were still up in the air, but then, on a sudden, she realized that she would never open any music hall, because the futility of it was now entirely apparent to her, although she had never before considered this.

Work on her memoirs, however, continued apace; Dupont, having succumbed to her current disposition, began to write in rather a different manner from that which he had until now been employing; and Lola— that same wooden Lola, who thus far had been so totally unreliable as a collaborator or an assistant—now dictated entire pages to him; naturally, a few finishing touches were necessary, but these final chapters were written predominantly by her. Their unexpected naivety surprised Dupont, and he often mused on the strange fate of this woman. At any mention of Pierre, her eyes would fill with tears, and the power of this total transformation, from scorn and hatred for him into compassion and love, was so great that if anyone were to have said to Lola that she was afraid and had not loved this man, she would never have believed him. As ever, for anyone in suchlike circumstances, when dealing with memories and finding himself at the mercy of a sudden rebirth, brought about by the manifestation of some powerful emotion, it was entirely clear to Lola that, despite facts, evidence, everything, it was impossible to refute: there had been no unpleasantness, no hatred—just love and sudden, merciless death.

Meanwhile, Lola's health—which on the whole had been fine until now, her maladies being entirely natural for a woman of her age—began to decline. Broadly speaking, there were no catastrophic alterations; everything seemed to be just as it was before, but she began to tire easily, and things that would not ordinarily have wearied her now occasioned momentary weakness. During her daily strolls in the Bois de Boulogne she would walk half of her regular distance; one day the driver, alarmed by her unusually long absence, set out to look for her and found her not far off, on a bench: she was asleep, with her head on her chest, her bag having fallen out of her hand, and her face so still that he was seized by the involuntary fear that she might have died. He stood there for several seconds, motionless, watching her closely, her chest rising and falling evenly. He coughed, but Lola did not stir. Finally, he decided to wake her; he called her name loudly several times and she opened her eyes and with a smile said: "It would seem we fell asleep?" Sighing, she slowly got to her feet and walked back to her motor car.

Time passed and it became quite clear that Lola, for all her most ardent desire, was no longer fit to appear on stage. She did not dwell on this, because, imperceptibly for her, and unconsciously, as with everything else that had happened to her, the stage had receded into the distant past, and she no longer recalled it. It was clear that she would have to leave her enormous apartment and live more modestly than before. All that remained was to put her financial affairs in order and calculate how much money had been spent and how much, in the final analysis, was left. She might have possessed a significant fortune, but she had spent much too lavishly, putting an end to it only in the last few years. After lengthy computations, she learnt that she was left with astonishingly little money—less than two hundred thousand francs. She had one last resort, which long ago she had decided to use only in case of extreme necessity, the source of which was rather unusual.

It had happened more than thirty years ago, during a brief affair with one of the most illustrious London bankers of the time, who, even then, was no longer in the first flush of youth but was nevertheless very much in love with Lola. He offered everything to her: his name, his life, his fortune, everything she could have wanted. Laughing, she replied that her name was better than any other, that she had no need of his life, and that the money he could offer did not tempt her either—she was rich enough.

"Very well," he said, "but have you thought what might happen to you later, when your name is forgotten and all you have left is old age and poverty?"

"I shall die young," she said, "and isn't it all the same what happens when I'm dead?"

However, his readiness to do all he could for her was touching; she became his lover—despite having no love for him—only in order to bring him pleasure. Two weeks later, as he was leaving, he told her that he knew she did not love him and he was powerless to do anything about it. "But you're better than you know," he added, "and I don't want you to think me ungrateful."

He explained to her that, whenever she desired, in a London bank, the address of which he gave her, on any day of her own choosing a sum of money would be paid out to her, which he would leave in her name.

"You're an incorrigible banker," she said. "You see everything in terms of cheques and banks. I don't need your money."

And so he left. He died of cancer five years later, and Lola never saw him again. Yet she knew that he had been true to his word—an advice notice was promptly sent to her from the bank, indicating that the money authorized in her name by such-and-such a man was at her disposal. Many years had passed since then, but only now did she recall this; and so, in order to escape financial worries once and for all, she decided to travel to London to withdraw what was rightfully hers—all because of one fortuitous event that had taken place over a quarter of a century ago.

I T WAS ALREADY mid-September; yellow leaves were lying on the pavements of the boulevards in Paris, and there was an occasional chill in the mornings. Sergey Sergeyevich had spent all summer with the exception of the first week and a half travelling: Sweden, Norway, Finland, several times to England; trains, motor cars, offices, offices, motor cars, trains. In the end, there had been no time to go to the Midi, as he had originally intended. Sletov had remained in Paris throughout the summer, hardly ever leaving; he had filled out slightly, recovered entirely from his sentimental shocks, and struck up several new acquaintances, not one of which, however, had amounted to anything. He had been living alone in Sergey Sergeyevich's apartment and had grown accustomed to this quiet, comfortable existence, and again, as in the days of old, he began at various intervals to dream of eternal things: work, an apartment, a wife, children, a comfortable little world, at the centre of which was none other than he, Fyodor Borisovich Sletov.

On the evening of the sixteenth, as he sat reading in Sergey Sergeyevich's study, he suddenly began to hear strange movements about the house—several doors opening and closing—and into the study walked Sergey Sergeyevich, who feigned surprise on seeing Sletov.

"Well, Fedya, still loveless?" he asked with his usual smile, while shaking Sletov's hand. "Don't you think that in this empty world…"

"You're an astonishing fellow, Seryozha," said Sletov, "and manifestly abnormal. I'm not sure whether you yourself realize this."

"I admit I had my suspicions, but most likely for reasons other than yours. How exactly do you suppose my abnormality manifests itself?"

"Just look: you can turn up out of the blue, from the other end of the earth, yet still I can know for sure that your first words will be derision. Do you see what I mean? No greeting, no expression of joy, only derision. Any other person might say: 'Hello, my dear friend! How are you? I'm so glad to see you,' and so on. Whereas you say: 'Hello! Why do you have that idiotic look about you?' Not literally, of course, but near enough."

"Well, fine, we'll discuss this later. What's the news, anyhow?"

"Actually, in fact, nothing. But do you know, there are certain things I think I've begun to realize for the first time in my life."

"Your memory, your memory," Sergey Sergeyevich was quick to put in.

"What about it?"

"It's deceiving you. You forget you've realized them before."

"No, I haven't."

"Indeed, you have. Each state of mind corresponds to a

224

certain conception of the world that… Do you follow? The one corresponds to the other, whereas you seem to think it's the first time because memory is connected to all this and it's only one of the factors, not an independent variable. Hasn't it occurred to you? It's elementary. But really, not a single encounter?"

"No, of course I've had them," said Sletov, smiling guiltily, "but without consequences, so to speak: you know, just sporadic, fleeting impressions."

"Personally, I shouldn't lose hope. On the whole, you've always been lucky."

"How so?"

"Because you, for instance, don't have to decipher correspondence, whereas that's what I must do presently."

However, Sergey Sergeyevich was unable to carry out his intentions, because as soon as Sletov left the telephone rang. He picked up the receiver and heard a familiar voice:

"Hello? Seryozha?"

"Is that you, my dearest?" said Sergey Sergeyevich. "Where are you calling from?"

"From a hotel. I'll be there shortly."

"Fine, I'll be expecting you."

Ten minutes later, Olga Alexandrovna walked in. Her face was very bronzed; her dark eyes betrayed a frosted tenderness.

"I'm pleased to see you," said Sergey Sergeyevich. His cheerful eyes neared her face; he kissed her several times on her cheeks and forehead. "So we've come back, have we? The Lord be thanked. And such a beauty, such an inscrutable creature. Is everything all right with your luggage?"

"Seryozha," said Olga Alexandrovna, "I've come to have a very serious conversation."

There was a strange intonation in her voice, which Sergey Sergeyevich could not fail to notice.

"Something really serious?"

"Yes, Seryozha: you must grant me a divorce."

"I hope, Lyolya, that you don't doubt my good intentions. Tell me what's happened."

Olga Alexandrovna explained to him that her life hitherto had comprised mistakes—"A simple classicism," said Sergey Sergeyevich—but that now it had reached a crisis point; she was not the woman she once was.

"You know, Lyolya, it's a thing of the past now—that other woman was really quite charming."

Still Olga Alexandrovna persisted. She spoke of the new life awaiting her, which demanded her full, uncompromising part in it. She could no longer live in two homes. She must marry. Sergey Sergeyevich would remain her friend, as always; there could be no doubt about this.

"You've really thought all this through?"

"Oh, many times—it's all been decided, Seryozha."

"It's a great pity. Very well, have it your way. But you've really taken everything into consideration?"

"Yes, yes."

"May I ask one question?"

"Of course."

"What will you live on? Is your future husband sufficiently endowed?"

Olga Alexandrovna's dark eyes glared at him with reproach; however, despite this, there was also another expression that defied description. She said nothing. Sergey Sergeyevich also said nothing. Finally, she said:

"No, Seryozha, whatever you may think, I could never be wrong about this."

"Ah, Lyolya, you said it yourself: your whole life has been a series of mistakes."

"Yes, but not of this sort."

"I suppose," said Sergey Sergeyevich, "that your future husband is a remarkable man, is he not?"

"Yes."

"Marvellous. But the others—and it's just the two of us, Lyolya, we can speak frankly—they, too, were remarkable. However, they all had one striking characteristic in common, one that you never suspected."

"Again, this ironic philosophy, Seryozha. Wake up! Understand, finally, that this isn't a joke. When you're dying, will you be so derisive then?"

"I don't know, Lyolya, I just don't know. But this characteristic is well worth mentioning."

"Go on."

"It consists in the fact that all these people loved, chiefly and most sincerely, not you, as it may have seemed on the face of it, but me."

"What are you saying?"

"Well, just that—me. That is, not me personally, if you

227

will, but me as the man from whom you get the money you give to them. Do you follow me? There have been no exceptions. I don't mean to disillusion you. You're planning to marry, however, for the first time in all these years. By all means marry, but don't tell your fiancé that you have no money."

Olga Alexandrovna sat there utterly dejected, unsure whether to believe Sergey Sergeyevich's words. What grieved her was not that she would soon be deprived of her means of subsistence, but that Sergey Sergeyevich could even mention this.

"This changes nothing," she said finally.

"On your part, of course. But how will Arkady Alexandrovich react to this?"

"We shall soon see," said Olga Alexandrovna. "I can tell you now that he'll react just as I have done. Hand me the receiver."

She pulled the telephone towards her and called Arkady Alexandrovich. He answered immediately.

"Arkasha," said Olga Alexandrovna in an agitated voice, "I've just been to see Sergey Sergeyevich. He has agreed to grant me a divorce, but won't give me any money. I'll be penniless. What will we do?"

After a brief pause, Arkady Alexandrovich's voice replied:

"I don't know, Lyolya. I know only one thing: I don't think this should alter our plans."

Olga Alexandrovna stared fixedly at Sergey Sergeyevich.

"We'll need to change the hotel to begin with," continued Arkady Alexandrovich, "but these are all details.

228

Money will perhaps, even doubtless, be tight. But I won't be afraid with you by my side."

"Thank you, Arkasha, I never doubted you. I'll be back soon; we'll talk then."

She replaced the receiver and, as before, stared silently at Sergey Sergeyevich.

"Clearly he's smarter than I thought," said Sergey Sergeyevich.

"You never did understand. You're incapable of believing in anyone's love. But now you'll see. I don't need your money."

"Listen, Lyolya," said Sergey Sergeyevich. "I hope you understand that I don't intend to deprive you of money. Only I doubt this episode is worth your leaving."

"If only you could understand!"

"Fine, Lyolya, hear me out."

And so Sergey Sergeyevich set about explaining to her that, in his opinion, it was not necessary for her to forsake her home because of a common affair. He said that Olga Alexandrovna was a dear old friend, that without her everything would be empty, that she could continue living as she wished, but ought to remain here.

"Just think, Lyolya," he said, "all the rest is incidental. I've always loved you—if I hadn't, could you really have lived your life as you do, never thinking of my interests or Seryozha's? He understands a lot of things—things that should never have been, Lyolya."

Sergey Sergeyevich knew that this was a sore spot for Olga Alexandrovna. She sat there silently, her head down.

"In spite of all this," Sergey Sergeyevich continued, "do you really not know that you're surrounded here by good intentions—intentions, Lyolya, that aren't spoilt by time, like other extemporaneous ones? Fine, I may not count, but what about Seryozha?"

"This is very painful for me," said Olga Alexandrovna, tears welling in her eyes, "but what's to be done? A new life is beginning now; this one is finished."

"And you accuse me of callousness," said Sergey Sergeyevich. "I don't want to accuse you of anything. Do as you will, if you believe you must. We'll all regret it. It would be folly, I think, to try to dissuade you. If you wish to go, then your current feelings must be stronger than those we so vainly, it would seem, expected of you. Go, I shan't stop you. But always remember," he said, raising his eyes to Olga Alexandrovna, "wherever you are and whatever happens to you, you can always count on Seryozha and me. I'd very much like to think that we could also count on you, but I believe that in this I would be mistaken."

Olga Alexandrovna sat in the armchair, weeping.

"Of course, there can be absolutely no material change," said Sergey Sergeyevich. "You shall live as you have always done. All that is mine is yours."

OLGA ALEXANDROVNA arrived back at the hotel with tear-stained eyes. Arkady Alexandrovich kissed her hand—he, too, was in a state of distress. Nonetheless, he immediately began to console her. When she rang, nothing could have been further from his mind than the blow that was dealt; however, for the first time in his life he rose to the occasion. Truly, he could not envisage life now without Olga Alexandrovna, and, in responding to her, he had been absolutely sincere. There was, of course, another reason for his unexpected noble-mindedness: he had not had time to grasp what was at stake; his often sluggish mind perceived this as a minor obstacle and had not managed in that moment to comprehend the magnitude of the problem. In any case, however, he had done the right thing: owing to a combination of several factors beyond analysis, as almost always when it is difficult to determine why, in fact, a man answers one way and not another, and why very often it is impossible to predict his reaction to a given occurrence. The onrush of a fleeting emotion, a chance agonizing sensation, the fear of the unknown, some dark instinct—all of these can determine and bring about entirely unexpected and uncharacteristic responses in a man. However, in the brief period intervening between the telephone call and Olga Alexandrovna's arrival, Arkady Alexandrovich, while pacing about the room, had time to think about many things. His first impression was that some irrevocable catastrophe had occurred; then, once he had calmed down somewhat, the situation began to seem less tragic. Firstly, it was still unlikely that Sergey Sergeyevich would deprive Olga Alexandrovna of an income; he would probably give her something on which it would be possible to live. But even then, if he really did refuse Olga Alexandrovna any support, there was another way out: an appeal to Lyudmila. Arkady Alexandrovich knew very well that it would be impossible to get even so much as one hundred francs out of Lyudmila by any conventional means. It was too late to stipulate any sum as part of the divorce proceedings— it would have been necessary to do that earlier, but back then, in the Midi, he could not have foreseen this. The only thing left was the threat of approaching her current fiancé directly—a threat he would carry out if Lyudmila refused him. Arkady Alexandrovich even had time to consider that it would be irrational to demand a large one-off sum: firstly, because such a request couldn't but seem odd to her future husband, and secondly, because after payment the threat would pass. On the contrary, it was necessary for Lyudmila to pay him monthly that to which he believed he had a right. In the case of non-payment: a letter to her husband and the ensuing consequences. Arkady Alexandrovich knew that all this was far from straightforward, that Lyudmila would make a desperate effort to contest this, yet the decisive final argument was nonetheless on his side. Naturally, Olga Alexandrovna would know nothing of this;

indeed, Arkady Alexandrovich himself could not conceive of this solution without an involuntary feeling of disgust. However, he could not imagine another way out: through long experience he knew well that the options available to him were limited. When he saw tears in Olga Alexandrovna's eyes, he took it to mean that Sergey Sergeyevich had been categorical, which still troubled him.

"What's to be done, Lyolya? We'll get by somehow," he said in a high-pitched, slightly pathetic voice. "We'll work…"

"No, no," replied Olga Alexandrovna. "That isn't why I'm crying. It's all been arranged."

Arkady Alexandrovich felt wild with joy; however, he did not let it show.

"What do you mean to say?"

"Sergey Sergeyevich said that there will be no changes, everything will be as it has always been. But he was so cruel, so merciless, as only he knows how to be. He spared nothing, Arkasha, nothing! He was uttering sympathetic words without so much as a smile; it cut me like a knife!"

Olga Alexandrovna then told him the whole story. Arkady Alexandrovich listened attentively and said:

"There's an impropriety here, Lyolya, a scandalous impropriety. People might think that I want to take something away from you. No, it's just that something else is being added to your former life, something that demands no rejection of the former one. It doesn't demand anything at all; it's ready to content itself as it is—all the more so as what we have now is so wonderful and unique! If you want

233

to live there, live there; if you don't want to marry, don't marry. Can this really change anything? Can this really change my love for you?"

"Oh, Arkasha, you don't know what a wonderful man you are!"

"No, no, I just love you, that's all."

"You know, never in my life have I witnessed such understanding, such a combination of mind and spirit as you have. My God, how many years I've lived on this earth without knowing you!"

"Why regret this? You have met me: that is what's important."

That evening Arkady Alexandrovich was especially affectionate and tender with Olga Alexandrovna. The brief panic he had experienced during her absence—which proved to have been in vain—had now, with redoubled strength, metamorphosed into an onrush of grateful love. Half an hour later he had completely forgotten his plan to blackmail Lyudmila, and if someone were to have expressed the opinion that he were capable of such a thing, he would truly have thought this person a fool and a scoundrel.

Some days later he telephoned Lyudmila, and after a brief interlude they met in a large cafe on the Champs-Élysées.

Both Lyudmila and Arkady Alexandrovich were astonished by the change they immediately observed in one another. Lyudmila noticed Arkady Alexandrovich's suntanned face, his sprightlier gait; he had lost a lot of weight and acquired what could almost be called, in comparison with his former aspect, a trim figure; he was self-assured and wore a finely tailored suit, and there was none of that evasive look in his eyes that Lyudmila had known for so many years. Arkady Alexandrovich, in turn, was struck by the markedly dulcet tone in Lyudmila's voice, the sincerity of her intonation, which was not directed at him but continued as a result of momentum, and then the absence of suspicion in her eyes.

"I'm glad to see you, my dear," said Arkady Alexandrovich in that perfectly unaffected voice, of which he could only have dreamt before, and kissed her hand. Lyudmila began speaking English, immediately apologizing, and saying that she had become unaccustomed to speaking Russian—"to the point, just think, where I often have to search for the words"—and that she had a familiar feeling of disappointment; for her complete satisfaction, Arkady Alexandrovich would have to have been destitute, shabbily dressed and humiliated. Alas, this was not the case. It violated a detail of a long-held dream, but in the abundance of her bliss she was ready to forgive Arkady Alexandrovich even this. The conversation, after the very insignificant practical questions had been exhausted, carried on to the most general of topics. Arkady Alexandrovich and Lyudmila simultaneously asserted that they essentially had nothing to talk about, and they both thought of the absurdity that these two entirely dissimilar people had lived together for so many years. After all, neither of them was stupid; both were sufficiently well-educated people, with a wealth of worldly experience, and one would have thought they ought to have found things to talk about. However, at that particular moment both of them were essentially so consumed by one aspect of their private lives, the result of which was an indisputable impoverishment of all the emotional and spiritual faculties that did not have any direct bearing on what they both held to be the most important matter. Lyudmila casually dropped in a few phrases, the point of which was to give Arkady Alexandrovich to understand that her future husband was a very wealthy man—wild sums of money were mentioned, along with God knows what else—and everywhere the pronoun "we" figured, right down to "we thought", "we supposed", "we paid". Arkady Alexandrovich did not know how to explain this behaviour: either Lyudmila was using every pretext available to underscore the existence of this "worthy man", or else she was truly indifferent to him and for that reason had lost her sense of *ridicule* and that intelligence in conversation which usually never failed her. Arkady Alexandrovich, in turn, responded with those same passive-aggressive tactics Lyudmila was employing, but, in so doing, resorted to counter-manoeuvres: never once did he say "we"; he made no mention of money or automobiles, but gave her to understand that everything was very luxurious by means of oblique, casual allusions to minor things—such things whose significance did not even suggest itself, but became immediately apparent. In this way, he emerged the victor from their covert duel and derived indisputable pleasure from this.

As it happened, Lyudmila would be leaving her apartment in several weeks' time. Arkady Alexandrovich promised to stop by soon to collect his books and a few other things. Then Arkady Alexandrovich paid; they left together and he headed towards a taxi.

"Can I drop you off?"

"No," said Lyudmila. "We're headed in different directions."

They bid each other farewell. Arkady Alexandrovich kissed his former wife's hand, cold as ever, and thought that, perhaps, they would never see each other again. While he was in the taxi, a chord emitted by the radio in a shop he was driving past suddenly struck him as strangely familiar. He then immediately recalled the last evening he had spent with Lyudmila, around three years previously, after a long and painful conversation; on that occasion, she had gone through to the drawing room and sat down at the piano. Arkady Alexandrovich had been standing by the door. She began playing the first thing that came into her head—an étude by Chopin—and Arkady Alexandrovich could now clearly see her fair-haired head and dark-blue eyes in front of the black mirror sheen of the piano, and he heard the motif he thought he had long forgotten. Those feelings he had experienced at the time now came flooding back to him: the sense of pity that life would slip away, just as this melody in the black mirror, too, would fade, and never, never… The rest defied definition: music, emotion and dreams, and that strange, almost immobile woman at the piano. There was also a sense of pity that all art, music in particular, leaves us without even the remotest, most illusory comfort. He pictured his entire specious, wasted life, and for the first time in recent months, that corruptible, transient world he had until now been writing about flashed anew before him and vanished in a momentary flight, together with the final phrase of that Chopin étude.

I T WAS THE postmeridian hours of a brilliant September's day; Seryozha and Liza were planning to drive to Monte Carlo. Seryozha was already dressed and waiting on the terrace for Liza, who was expected any minute, when suddenly the telephone rang. He went over to the apparatus.

"There's a call from Paris for you," said the operator.

Then a very familiar voice said:

"Hello! Is that Seryozha or Liza?"

"Hello, Papa, it's me," said Seryozha.

"I shouldn't have recognized your voice, you've such a queer bass. Is everything all right at your end?"

"Yes," replied Seryozha, faltering slightly. "Liza's just coming."

Indeed, Liza was walking over to Seryozha.

"Fine, put her on. Liza? *Mon amour*,* you need to come back to Paris."

"We were, in principle, planning to do just that."

"You've essentially got a few days left. Seryozha needs to be in London for the last week of September. But in any case, despite the pleasure that... By the way, there's a bit of family news."

* My love.

239

"More than a bit," Liza wanted to say; in conversations with Sergey Sergeyevich she would always slip into a sarcastic tone. However, she asked:

"What is it?"

"Your older sister is planning to marry Arkady Alexandrovich Kuznetsov."

"Have you lost your senses?"

"Not I, Liza, not I. But it gives rise to a whole host of interesting considerations, which…"

"What do you mean to say?"

"Nothing in particular, but who knows how things will turn out?"

Liza understood what Sergey Sergeyevich was thinking, and the thought terrified her. She said:

"You think… you mean that this is her final decision?"

"I'm afraid so."

"What a fool she is!"

"I can't help agreeing with you. What news with you?"

"Everything's fine, I've had an enchanting summer."

"I'm pleased for you. I'd very much like to say the same for myself, but that would be a lie. Anyhow, please explain to Seryozha that his mother is getting married, sooner or later. When should I expect you?"

"Soon, without much advance notice."

"Excellent. Take care of yourself."

"Goodbye, Seryozha."

Seryozha, who had been standing beside her, asked when Liza replaced the receiver:

"Who's a fool, Liza?"

"Everyone, my little one," said Liza with a sigh. "Everyone. But without a certain foolishness it wouldn't be worth living. Don't you think?"

Liza did not know whether to tell Seryozha that his mother was getting married. Strictly speaking, there were no particular reasons to hide this; however, Liza would have to make such an effort to initiate the conversation, because each of these matters would lead to another that had never hitherto been mentioned but was impossible not to have sensed. Nevertheless, she overcame her internal aversion to raising all these issues and told him about it that evening. Seryozha was shocked and distressed.

"I don't understand her," he said. "Of course, it's her own private affair. But we all love her so; she's so charming, and Papa has spent his whole life granting her every wish. So why this marriage?"

"Well, it's certainly not one of convenience, Seryozhenka."

"My dear mama—suddenly to marry another man! It's absurd, Liza."

"I think so too, Seryozha."

"I'll write to her today," said Seryozha. "She's probably thinking of me, too. I'll tell her that I'll still love her, just the same as before, that she's my mother and that's what matters. She is very charming, isn't she, Liza?"

Liza felt awkward; she had an unsettling presentiment, the reason for which was clear: she had to leave here, to come into direct contact, as it were, with every almost insurmountable obstacle awaiting her in Paris; she had to

241

be stronger than all this and set things up so that later she and Seryozha could be together.

"This is what we'll do, Seryozha," she said finally. "We'll go to Paris, then you'll head on to London. I'll say there for approximately one month, then I'll join you in England and we'll be together again. Do you see?"

"I see, Liza, but why a whole month?"

"It will be better that way, Seryozhenka. What's more, you must understand that no one should know about this."

"All right, Liza. And so on for the rest of our lives?"

"Perhaps our whole lives, Seryozha. Don't you think it's worth it?…"

"*O, si!* * Ten lives if needs be."

"Well then. To tell the truth, I'd rather not go to Paris or England. I'd rather stay with you here, my little one."

"Regrettably, I don't think that will be possible."

"Utterly impossible. Although we're lucky that there's another solution. Now close your eyes and let's forget that Paris and London exist, and we'll live like before, these last few days. These are our last days in the Midi," she said with inadvertent sadness in her voice.

"This year, yes. But we don't know what the future holds in store."

* Oh, I do!

THEY ARRIVED IN PARIS on the morning of the twenty-fifth of September; Liza did not want Seryozha to stay there with her and Sergey Sergeyevich for more than a few days. Since Sergey Sergeyevich had not been fore-warned, no one was there to meet them, so they took a taxi back to the apartment. At home they found only Sletov, who informed them that Sergey Sergeyevich would return late that evening, because he had been summoned to the provinces. In Paris Seryozha immediately felt an unbearable difference between the atmosphere of the Midi and the icy discomfort that reigned there. He had never thought that his house could seem so foreign and unwelcoming. In the course of the day he kissed Liza only once, when he went into her room. They both—despite their age and experience—exaggerated the danger of compromising themselves, and for that reason conducted themselves with mutual restraint, keeping an unnatural distance, so that even Sletov asked Seryozha:

"What's the matter, have you quarrelled with your aunt or something?"

"Yes, a little," said Seryozha, blushing.

Sergey Sergeyevich called in the evening to let them know that he had been detained and would return the following morning. Then Liza called Seryozha to her room.

243

"Seryozha," she said, almost breathless; he had never seen her in such a state. "I'm going out. Follow me in half an hour. Here's a key. Come to rue Boileau, number forty-four, first floor, on the left. I'll be waiting for you. Go now."

"What's there?" asked Seryozha perplexedly.

"You'll see," she said quickly. "Go, go."

When Seryozha arrived, he found Liza waiting for him on the other side of the door. She was wearing that same favourite dressing gown of hers with the embroidered birds; Seryozha wondered how the dressing gown, which ought to have still been in a suitcase, had wound up here.

"I have two, Seryozhenka," said Liza, smiling. "This is my apartment," she explained, "ours, if you like. Didn't you know that I had my own apartment?"

"No," he said in astonishment. "What do you need it for?"

"Every woman needs a place of her own," she said evasively. Had Seryozha been any other man, she would not have said this; however, Seryozha believed blindly in everything she said, and he found her every action remarkable. In any case, he should not have been initiated into this secret, but she could not help doing so: her desire to be alone with Seryozha was stronger than all other considerations. Late at night they left together; amid the cool air Liza felt a sadness that had not been there in the Midi. She sent Seryozha home, and she herself returned only an hour later; he was already sound asleep by then. The whole apartment was quiet. Only in Sletov's room was the light on; he was reading Casanova's memoirs, shrugging from time to time—he held a very dim view of this man, and

244

it seemed incomprehensible how someone could waste his entire life, swapping lovers almost daily: Sletov truly could not understand it.

The following morning Seryozha, having discussed trivialities with his father for a quarter of an hour, and in such a tone, as if it were only the other day that they had last seen one another (thus was always the case with Sergey Sergeyevich, for reasons unknown), obtained his mother's telephone number and rang her. In a voice choked with joy Olga Alexandrovna asked him to come immediately; she met him with prolonged embraces and kisses, as if he had been saved from mortal danger and it was a miracle that he was still alive. "My little one, my darling, you've grown so big, so handsome, Seryozhenka! You haven't forgotten your mother, have you?"

There was so much love in her words and intonations that tears began to well in Seryozha's eyes. He thought then that, whatever happened, he would always love this woman dearly, and suddenly the fact that she was getting married seemed entirely immaterial and inconsequential to him. As if apprehending his thoughts, Olga Alexandrovna asked:

"You won't stop loving your old mother because she's not behaving as she should, will you?"

"No, Mama," said Seryozha, kissing her warm hand. "No, I'll never stop loving you. You're the only mother I have."

"We'll see each other often, we'll go for walks together, we'll talk. You'll tell me everything, won't you, Seryozhenka? Are you going to London? I'll come to visit you.

You're all I have, too, but then you're such a good boy. You're growing up. Soon you'll really start living, and we'll talk about everything."

"Well, you know, Mama," said Seryozha, sitting on the arm of her chair and embracing her around the neck, "there's so much that I've come to understand recently."

"What have you understood, Seryozhenka?"

"Such very, very important things. And, you know, it's so strange—here we are, talking about it. You aren't rushing off, are you?"

"No, no, tell me."

"There are things we don't ever seem to think or talk about, but when we stumble across them for the first time, as it were, we find we already have a perfectly formed impression of them."

"Such as?"

"Such as a person's relationship with his mother. I love you dearly and I'm certain that, come what may, I'll always love you. No one else, only you. Of course, on the one hand, it's just a feeling, but it's a feeling that corresponds to a theoretical conviction, one that's unshakable, good and right."

"Oh, how clever we are!" said Olga Alexandrovna. "Well then, I'll also make a confession to you. You know I'm getting married?"

"Yes."

"Well, it's all the same to me what people will think. If somebody takes offence, that's a great pity, but what am I to do about it? The only thing that worried me was how

246

you would react. It's odd, isn't it? You're still a child, a boy, Seryozhenka, a babe in arms—and when you don't pay attention to yourself and put on airs with other people, you still have that darling little face of a baby. And to think, it's so important to me that this little baby doesn't stop loving me."

"You don't have to worry about that, Mama."

"I don't any more, I know," said Olga Alexandrovna. "Although I did tell you a fib; I do need to go out, but it pains me to part with you. We'll go together; you will accompany me, won't you?"

"Of course. Do you know I'm leaving tomorrow? I'm going to London."

"At what time?"

"In the morning, I think."

"Then I'll say goodbye to you. It will only be a week until I see you again. Goodbye, my little one," she said, kissing him several times. Then she made the sign of the cross over him three times in quick succession, repeating: "Christ keep you, Seryozhenka. Study hard, and be good."

"You always treat me like a child," said Seryozha.

"No, darling, it's just awkward doing it in the street."

They parted ways, their minds at peace: Seryozha was glad that this meeting had not changed his usual perception of his mother at all; after her conversation with Seryozha, Olga Alexandrovna let go of the sole unpleasant thought that had recently materialized, which was how her new marriage might affect her relationship with Seryozha.

247

ON THE EVE of Seryozha and his father's departure for London, dinner might have passed in silence were it not for Sergey Sergeyevich's chatter, in which he recounted his summer trips, how he had met a great many exceedingly lovely people during this time; as ever, all these exceedingly lovely people came off as complete idiots, in spite of Sergey Sergeyevich's preposterous appraisal of them. He took particular pleasure in describing one of his accountants who worked in Norway and was, according to Sergey Sergeyevich, an extraordinary man.

"In what way is he extraordinary?"

"Well," said Sergey Sergeyevich, "just imagine, he was the richest man in Russia, managed millions, was the head of a household, and so on. His wife committed suicide, his children all perished, his fortune too, and he barely managed to escape with his life. And this is what he says to me: 'Please, Sergey Sergeyevich,' he says, 'have the workers treat me as my rank and status demand.' His rank! Such an odd word, you know. And that's what preoccupied the old man. Isn't it touching? There you go, Fedya, a variation on axiology."

Sletov shrugged; both Liza and Seryozha, however, would scarcely have been able to repeat Sergey Sergeyevich's tale, so removed from the conversation were they. Seryozha had no appetite whatsoever and hardly ate anything; he kept thinking over and over that as of tomorrow he would no longer see Liza. Liza knew he was thinking about this and shared in his suffering. Subconsciously, however, he was more egotistical than she: he did not think the situation was all that bad, since it was equally difficult for both of them. Sergey Sergeyevich could not help noticing this suspiciously concurrent depression of theirs. He was, however, far from the thought that this might be explained by anything other than chance coincidence or, ultimately, a feeling of grief that was only natural. He considered Seryozha's having spent his entire life until now in the company of two women, his mother and his aunt, and that this must have had an effect on his character. He supposed, however, that Oxford, where he himself had studied in his time (before he began attending lectures at the university in Moscow), ought to steer Seryozha in the right direction. His son's sustained emotional emollescence, which he had inherited from his mother and which, until recently, Sergey Sergeyevich had not attempted to combat, nevertheless seemed to him a negative trait. After dinner, once he was alone with Liza, he mentioned this in passing, as usual. Liza answered him very sharply:

"A hunchback probably considers the absence of a hunch to be a deficiency."

"If, Liza—"

"If what?"

"If he's not only a hunchback, but also a fool into the bargain."

"I don't see what's so bad about the boy's having a good heart. From any vantage point, that's a positive attribute."

"You've never boxed, have you, Liza?"

"How is it that you fail to understand that one cannot reduce everything to that idiotic sport? We talk about the soul, you compare it with boxing; about love, with rational physical development; about misery, grief and misfortune… I don't know what you'd compare those with, perhaps football?"

"I'm afraid you don't follow, Lizochka. It isn't a question of a direct…"

"Out with it, for God's sake! A direct what?"

"Comparison, *voyons*.* But that's the point. You strike a blow of equal strength to one man and then to another. The first falls unconscious, while the second remains standing, as if nothing has happened. Why?"

"Because one is weak and the other is strong."

"No, they're absolutely identical."

"Why then?"

"Because the first is lax, and the second is well trained. But at the start they were both equally susceptible."

"So you mean to train Seryozha?"

"Precisely."

"Why?"

"Because, Lizochka, he's my son. Because I love him.

* Come now!

250

Because I want him to experience as little pain and suffering as possible—pain and suffering that will be inevitable if he remains as he is. Do I make myself clear?"

"What right do you have to do this? Let him live as he pleases. Leave your philosophy for yourself. Just think how many people, thank God, manage without it. It would strangle them."

"So they'll be strangled. But even if that's true: the weak ones will be strangled, the strong ones will live."

"What a primitive notion!"

"Nothing satisfies you, Liza, you don't like anything. What's happened to you lately? You're even defending softness, which isn't exactly in your nature."

"And who told you that?"

"It just seemed that way to me."

"Because you don't know me, my dear."

"You're shattering my finest illusions mercilessly, Liza. We'll talk more when you're in a better mood—if such a time ever comes. Perhaps I don't know you. *On aura tout vu,*[*] as they say. Goodnight, beautiful stranger."

He kissed her hand and went through to his study to work. He had been so gay and sarcastic, as was his wont. However, Liza, who had been observing him with hostility, to which was added a distant, almost forgotten but still very palpable feeling of regret, seemed suddenly to spot a fleeting look of affliction in his eyes, which hitherto she had never noticed; she suspected that Olga

* That would take the cake.

Alexandrovna's leaving was still a great blow to him, one that, for all his perfect "training", he could not help feeling much more acutely than one might have been led to believe.

Indeed, Sergey Sergeyevich was much pained by Olga Alexandrovna's leaving him, although his feelings were entirely different from those one might expect of a husband when his wife forsakes him. In life he always acted more or less in accordance with the aesthetic system he had devised for himself, in which principles that were exterior and ornamental, as it were, played the leading role. It was not based, as it ought to have been, on private emotions, and he himself would have been hard pressed to explain why, in fact, it was necessary to act one way and not another; nevertheless, he was firmly convinced that it was necessary to act this way. The system comprised many simply absurd and ridiculous things; he must have known this, yet he considered them essential all the same. There had to be a family; there had to be an heir to his name and fortune, and someone to continue the family line; there had to be a wife. But now, one aspect of his system had suddenly vanished, and this had been her grossest transgression. Of course, Sergey Sergeyevich knew that Olga Alexandrovna's departure marked not only the vanishing of this aspect: it also created a void where once there used to be her tender eyes, her caressing, quick patter and her enduring charm, which, objectively speaking, Sergey Sergeyevich prized greatly. However, the moral side of her departure was her own private affair, in which he considered himself unable to intervene. He recalled how still quite recently, only a few months ago, he had wanted Olga Alexandrovna finally to find a man on whom she could settle; his dream had come true, but not in the way he had intended. Now he found this discrepancy between his intent and reality unpleasant. What was more, he had imagined that Olga Alexandrovna would have stayed also because Seryozha's interests demanded this: not his immediate interests, since he was going to England, but those of tradition. In short, he allowed all deviation from private morals, but was an adherent of several almost patriarchal principles. Like many people lacking in robust, rigid convictions, he understood the poverty of political doctrines, which he scorned, and the questionability and often senselessness of those questions that were, at a particular moment, considered topical—and, moreover, in spite of his extreme scepticism, he was an advocate of so-called family values, the frailty of which he ought to have known better than anyone else. All his experience of life convinced him that there was nothing, or almost nothing, that one could rely on, that political opinions, principles of state, personal attributes, moral frameworks, even economic laws—of this he was certain—were the very essence of conditionality, understood variously by different people and being themselves almost devoid of any substance whatsoever. From this stemmed his broad tolerance of everything, his acceptance of many things that clearly did not merit it, in a word, what was ascribed to his magnanimity, generosity and perfect character, and what in actual fact was the result of uncertainty. He acted only when required, and would always do so reluctantly. There had been, however, few such instances in his life, yet he would always recall them with disgust. For example, there was a duel, happily lacking a fatal outcome, which Sergey Sergeyevich felt duty-bound to honour, although he would always say that he considered it to have been foolish. Naturally, there had been stock-market transactions in completing which he knew he would ruin certain people—but here he was dealing with figures, and so he felt more at ease. Generally speaking, however, he had no taste for action, although everything within him seemed to have been made for specifically for this: his alacrity of mind, his perpetual equanimity, the total subjugation of his faculties—spiritual, intellectual and physical—to his will; in this sense he was like a beautiful spring, whose qualities, however, did not go to waste. He would rise to the occasion in every tragic circumstance—thus had it been in the Crimea when the White armies were retreating; thus had it been when a second attempt was made on his life in a busy street, when he alone managed to spot the quick movement of a man whipping out a knife, and arrest his hand. Until the most dreadful conditions forced him to act, however, he would talk derisively about everything, delight in manifestly stupid people and remain invariably benevolent and passive. In this way, no one who knew Sergey Sergeyevich socially, apart from Liza, who, nevertheless, was also unsure of this, could have suspected that Olga Alexandrovna's second marriage was essentially the first defeat in his life—that is, in that narrow realm, beyond which he admitted everything, but whose inviolability he had hitherto managed to safeguard.

After the departures of Seryozha, whom Sergey Sergeyevich accompanied to London, where he stayed on for two days, and Olga Alexandrovna, there were only three left at home: Sergey Sergeyevich, Liza and Sletov. They would convene for lunch and dinner, but they each led a very different life, to the point that there was almost nothing connecting them. In the first days after Seryozha left, however, Sergey Sergeyevich could not help noticing that Liza was quite out of sorts, which is to say nothing of the fact that when he approached her he would meet with an invariably cold gaze, and it became apparent that no recommencement of their former relations was possible for the time being—she stopped taking care over her appearance, having her hair set, powdering her face and painting her lips, and there was always a fixed expression of concentrated melancholy on her face.

"What's the matter with you, Liza?"

"Nothing. Leave me in peace."

On several occasions she chose not to spend the night at home, but Sergey Sergeyevich did not even consider the possibility of a visit to rue Boileau—he knew Liza too well to have any illusions about how he would be met. Yet he found her condition almost alarming.

Once, at dinner, an argument about Seryozha flared up. Sergey Sergeyevich claimed that now, for the first time in his life, Seryozha was living more or less independently, that this was a fine thing and very necessary, so that he could develop in a new environment and become a man.

"By the way, I'll soon be going to England," said Liza, "I should see how he's getting on."

"I think that's absolutely unnecessary. All the more so, since I'm there often enough."

"You know that Seryozha has far less in common with you than he does with Lyolya and me."

"More's the pity. But this is a shortcoming that you and I have previously discussed."

"In my opinion it's a pointless argument. We have different views on upbringing."

"Undoubtedly. However, there's one detail that escapes you: Seryozha is my son, and it is I who bring him up."

"That's something of a belated realization."

"I do hope it hasn't come too late."

Liza received a letter from Seryozha every other day, sent to her apartment in rue Boileau. Seryozha wrote that without her nothing was of any interest to him, that his life was spent in anticipation of her arrival. "Everything is like a dream," he wrote, "everything is unreal, because you are not here. I know that I have to study, but I feel no desire to do that, and I learn a lot of useless things, which, perhaps, would be worthwhile if you were here with me. When I am alone, they seem entirely unnecessary." Liza would reply to him, asking him to wait a little longer and not to pine after her, but her letters lacked persuasion, since she herself always felt a deathly, unceasing ennui. Everything exasperated her; she slept little and poorly, ate little and poorly, and could not concentrate on anything or read. In a very short time she lost weight and her good looks, so much so that Sergey Sergeyevich said to her:

"I'm afraid, Lizochka, that if this continues, your radiance risks diminishing somewhat."

Left alone, he racked his brains over the meaning of this. In the end, he came to the conclusion that Liza must have had some abortive romance in the Midi and was now suffering the usual disappointment more strongly than she had done on previous occasions. To a certain degree this was only natural: she was no longer twenty, life was pressing on and she could not have failed to notice this. One day Sergey Sergeyevich even hinted to her that, in light of Olga Alexandrovna's marriage, it would perhaps be desirable to…

"I'd rather die than marry you," she said in a rage.

"How does one define romanticism?" mused Sergey Sergeyevich. "*Exagération du sentiment personnel?** Yes, it seems so. You were born almost a century and a half too late, Liza. You ought to have met Byron. He was a bit of a lame poet, but a very, very sweet chap, and capable of appreciating exaggeration."

"You're a clown," said Liza before leaving and slamming the door behind her. Sergey Sergeyevich's smiling face appeared behind the door, which immediately swung open again, and his voice said:

"You're like the heroine of some melodrama, Liza. You

* Exaggeration of private sentiment?

don't know just how enchanting and classic you are! *C'est de la Comédie-Française le jour des abonnés.*"*

However, he in fact found Liza's condition almost as unpleasant as Olga Alexandrovna's behaviour. In essence, what had happened was what he had always expected— the gradual departure of those nearest to him. Solitude clearly awaited him in the future. Several times Liza had spoken of a trip to England; perhaps the object of her desire was there and for some reason unable or unwilling to come to Paris.

More and more often he would go out for a stroll around Paris, wandering through the streets with uncustomary aimlessness. Since many of his acquaintances lived in more or less the same area, he would often come across them; he once spotted Lyudmila in a very solid automobile that was passing by, sitting beside a pleasant-looking elderly man, the very one for whom she had divorced her first husband. Another time he saw the latter, plodding along the street, hands thrust in his pockets and looking straight ahead with dull, vacant eyes.

One day he set out on his usual Sunday stroll towards evening. It was the end of October and the weather was surprisingly mild for Paris at this time of year. He walked in the Bois de Boulogne, then went up to the place de l'Étoile, exited at avenue Victor Hugo and turned onto rue de la Pompe. There was scarcely any traffic; it was rather warm,

* It's straight out of the Comédie-Française, on season-ticket holders' day.

but in the light breeze that got up from time to time there was a distinct, deceptive scent of winter. As he walked, he thought that by now it was already too late, perhaps, to change anything about this essentially absurd guiding principle that he had imposed on himself and that he had unswervingly adhered to his entire life—that of *la bonne mine à mauvais jeu!** In the long run, it usually did more harm than good. Why was it necessary, he thought, to feign this all his life and to play it out as though upon a stage? These thoughts, however, were almost devoid of bitterness—rather they were meditative. This could be attributed to the fact that the weather was still very fine, that the air was gentle and fragrant. On reaching the corner of rue de la Pompe and rue de Passy, Sergey Sergeyevich thought to himself that he would very much enjoy a cup of tea. He went into La Marquise de Sévigné. All the tables were taken. Not far from the entrance, with her back to him, sat a very elderly lady in mourning. There was something familiar in the shape of her back and shoulders. Sergey Sergeyevich drew nearer. The lady turned to him—it was Lola Aînée. It was he who recognized her, for all that she had changed. Those old, tender, nonchalant eyes of hers stared at him and she bowed her head, smiling. Sergey Sergeyevich recalled that since her visit to him, soliciting financial backing for her music hall, her husband had died—he had sent her a letter of condolence immediately, but since then had heard nothing of her.

* A smile in the face of adversity!

"May I?" he asked, approaching her table.

"Yes, yes, by all means," she replied.

After exchanging a few words, Sergey Sergeyevich found that the Lola he was now talking to was divorced by an entire life from the one who had come to him before. Now it was impossible to think of her as anything but a very old woman. When the conversation turned to her late husband, her eyes momentarily filled with tears, which very much surprised Sergey Sergeyevich, who had, like everyone else, known full well that her conjugal life had been difficult and unsuccessful. Neither of them mentioned the music hall—it seemed as unnatural as, for example, a conversation about Lola's planning to return to school would have done. Thus, Sergey Sergeyevich, just like the rest, could not fail to notice an astonishing inward change in Lola. She told him, as she did others, what a wonderful man her husband had been and how she had loved him, adding that she had nearly finished her memoirs. Sergey Sergeyevich did not ask about her plans for the stage; it would have been an obvious gaffe. She did mention, in particular, that in a few days' time she planned to travel to London on business, but that she would quickly grow tired and worried about the fatigue of the journey.

"You travel a great deal," she remarked. "Which means of transport do you recommend?"

Sergey Sergeyevich replied that in his opinion the least fatiguing option would be a journey by aeroplane—she could be in London in less than two hours.

"*C'est une idée*,"* said Lola. "I may well heed your advice."

Sergey Sergeyevich left the shop, wholly impressed by this meeting and the astonishing change that had taken place in Lola. The late-autumn sun was shining. Two well-dressed ladies were walking ahead; one of them drawled in Russian:

"It's all the same to me what they say. They're just swine, my dear, that's about the size of it."

Sergey Sergeyevich set off down avenue Mozart. At first he seemed to be wandering without any destination in mind. Then it occurred to him that he ought for once in his life to speak to Liza about everything without any irony, exhaustively and in all earnestness. He ought to tell her that she was all he had left, that essentially he had never loved anyone but her, save for a fleeting infatuation with her elder sister. He ought to tell her that he was prepared to do anything to become the man of her dreams, and that he would succeed in this. What was more, he ought to tell her that he would be kinder and more sensitive, that he understood now, since only very recently, what the most valuable thing in the world was—love—and, however much people might mock him, it would always be so.

On reaching rue Boileau, he paused for a second outside number forty-four, went up to the first floor and opened the door with his key. The shutters were lowered and the apartment was in semi-darkness. Liza's voice said:

* Now there's a thought.

"Seryozha?"

Sergey Sergeyevich paused momentarily. Liza had called his name, but there could be no mistaking the tone of voice: she had never spoken to him like this. An improbable thought flashed through his mind. On the floor in the hallway he noticed a little leather suitcase.

"It's me," he said, walking in.

Liza was lying on the bed; her hair was dishevelled, her face in the half-light seemed even darker than usual. In the doorway she saw the familiar broad figure. Raising herself on her elbows, she said in a strangled whisper:

"Go, go at once, do you hear me? I beg you, please, go!"

"I don't know that I must," said Sergey Sergeyevich. His heart ached; he felt cold and unwell, and with surprise he thought that this was the first time in his life that he had experienced such feelings.

"Go, you'll be the ruin of me!"

He could hear tears in Liza's voice.

"Seryozha," she repeated, "darling, please, go!"

Sergey Sergeyevich thought he heard the click of a key at the door in the hallway, but perhaps it was just his imagination. In a measured voice he said:

"Liza, you've been my mistress for many years…"

Liza sobbed, burying her face in the pillow. Sergey Sergeyevich heard movement in the hallway, turned and saw Seryozha, who was standing with a parcel in his hands and had heard what he had just said.

"I thought you were in England," said Sergey Sergeyevich as though in a dream. But Seryozha was no longer there; he had thrown down the parcel and run out of the apartment.

"My God, this is horrible!" said Sergey Sergeyevich.

He sat in the armchair and said nothing for a long time. All the while Liza's shoulders jolted and trembled. Sergey Sergeyevich looked at her with unseeing eyes. Finally he said:

"Liza, how could you?"

The room was getting dark; dusk was quickly falling on the other side of the window. It was quiet, and only the sound of Liza's rapid breathing could be heard. The despair that had seized her from the moment Sergey Sergeyevich appeared in the doorway had not left her; she was unable to speak. Finally it struck her that her only chance of salvation was to tell Sergey Sergeyevich everything and then to find Seryozha and explain to him that nothing mattered apart from her love for him, that however irreparable some things might seem...

She told Sergey Sergeyevich—the room was now completely dark, neither of them thought to turn on the light—everything that had gone on in the Midi, in every detail, and added that nothing in her world existed apart from her love for Seryozha. She said she knew all the impediments to this—the terrible relationship, the difference in age, the fact that it seemed wholly impossible and monstrous—yet, despite it all, were it not for this, her life would surely lose all meaning.

"Very well, Liza," came Sergey Sergeyevich's voice out of the darkness, "but all this has to do with you. I understand you're in a very difficult position. But you must think of Seryozha first and foremost."

"He feels just the same as I do; he cannot imagine life without me."

"I understand. But he's seventeen years old; you're the first woman in his life. Remember your first affair—what is left of that? No, to sacrifice Seryozha, even for you, is impossible."

Sergey Sergeyevich expressed the opinion that it was necessary to explain everything to Seryozha, to convince him that it was impossible to build a life on an unwitting crime and that he must forget about it.

"So you want me to give him up?"

"I demand it," said Sergey Sergeyevich. "You aren't accustomed to my making demands, but here, for the first time in my life, I'm demanding this of you."

"You don't know what you're saying."

However, Sergey Sergeyevich insisted. He said that any real man, and particularly one in love, ought to find the strength within himself to make a personal sacrifice, to renounce his own needs in order not to ruin the person whose existence seems most precious to him.

"You're saying this, you're able to say this only because you don't understand what love is. Love means that you're unable to live without this man, that you don't want to live, that you want to die, do you understand?"

"I do. You must give him up."

"It's easy for you to say!"

"No, Liza, it isn't. I've loved you for many years,

and, you see, I'm giving you up. I'm granting you full freedom—whatever you want, whomever you want—only not Seryozha."

Liza realized that the moment she always feared had finally arrived, the moment when this rational machine was set in motion. She sensed that any entreaty to Sergey Sergeyevich would have no effect. But still she said:

"No, you cannot forbid me from doing this. It's my life; I have the right to be in control of it."

"Yes, of your life, but not of Seryozha's."

"The two are one and the same."

Suddenly Sergey Sergeyevich said with genuine amazement and ire in his voice:

"How so exactly? Are you really so incapable of this? What then is the value of your love?"

"Don't speak of love, you don't understand it."

"So you and your sister have been saying for many years. I don't know what it is—probably because to love in your definition of the word is to sacrifice everything in the name of sensuality. Nothing exists: not true love, not care for the person you love, not his interests, not your obligations, not shame—nothing! Not even the possibility of ridding yourself of this physical languor for a while, to comprehend in the slightest measure what is just. Yes, in this sense I do not know what love is, truly I don't. I would not leave my house, wife and son to the mercy of fate—simply because I find it pleasant to spend time in the company of a lover. Yet true love I do know: you do not. Lyolya is better than you; she would understand me. She's sensitive and frivolous, but she has a beautiful heart and would sacrifice herself ten times over if it were necessary. You can't even do that."

"I will not listen to this!" cried Liza. "You have no right to say this to me; you have no right to say anything at all. I've hated you for so long," she thundered, "because you're a machine, an automaton, because you're incapable of understanding a single human emotion. Can't you see how everyone is deserting you? Lyolya has gone, I've gone, Seryozha has gone. You demand this sacrifice of me—it means my life! Yes, of course such a sacrifice would be easy for you."

"Everything you say is unfair, Liza," replied his measured voice amid the darkness. "Don't you know what suffering, sacrifice and unhappiness are? You haven't the faintest idea of these things, and you consider everyone who isn't like you unworthy of attention and compassion; you've never made a single effort to understand—just like poor Yegorkin, who, however, for all his naivety and *absurdity*, is of more human worth than you. I know you very well."

"You're a fine one to talk."

"Look, Liza, what comes first for you? Avarice and egotism. What is it to you if an unhappy and trusting boy ruins his life because of you? You don't think about this. Instead, you'll have a pleasant time—until you meet someone you like more than Seryozha—and then you'll forsake him with uncommon ease and offer up this sacrifice."

He was silent. Liza said nothing as she collected her thoughts. Suddenly he said (and in his voice she could detect an involuntary and unexpected smile):

"And still I love you."

"I know," Liza said with hatred. "You're a machine, but a perfectly made one, just like a human being."

"Another gross error, Liza. Understand that I'm not at all a machine. You and Lyolya always think so, because you can't fathom what it is that forces me to be this way. Haven't you ever thought about it? I pity people, you see. I've always pitied Lyolya—why should I have made her suffer, harassing her on account of those never-ending affairs? I let her live as she pleased—and all the more unselfishly, because I knew that I'd receive no thanks for it, that she would continue to think I had no heart. I pitied you—you must know that. I pity everyone, Liza, and for that reason I do not oppose others, I do not prevent them thinking what they like and living as they please, although they almost always act wrongly. So here's another proof that I'm no machine—this pity has its limit. You and I reached that today."

Liza heard him get up from the chair.

"I'm leaving," he said. "I need to find Seryozha. Matters between you and him are finished. I'll do all I can to make sure you never see him again."

"I'll kill you," said Liza with total equanimity.

"You won't, because then Seryozha will be lost to you. Moreover, you know it doesn't frighten me; I do not fear death. And if you think that I value my life greatly…"

267

He flicked the switch. Liza, squinting because of the harsh light, saw his tall, broad frame and motionless face with a strange, angry, melancholic expression. He took his hat and gloves, and, without adding a single word, without saying goodbye to Liza, he left. A second later the door in the hallway clicked. Without even burying her tear-stained face in her hands, Liza began to wail.

SERYOZHA RAN OUT of the building in a complete frenzy, almost unconscious of what he was doing, or, rather, his comprehension of the action came some time after the event itself. The street was empty. He walked quickly, reaching avenue de Versailles unawares, and, spotting a bench, sat down on it. Tears smothered and stifled his thoughts. His father's words still rang in his ears: "Liza, you've been my mistress for many years..." What did this mean? Of course it must be true, for his father had known about her apartment. But how could this have happened? How could Liza not have told him about this? "My God, what happens now?" he said aloud. So now Sergey Sergeyevich knew about his relationship. Seryozha no longer had a home. Liza had also lost him for ever. Liza, remarkable Liza! So this is how it really was. Everything—his childhood, her dark hands, everything that was warm, splendid and his own, all his sixteen years and their astonishing, dazzling culmination—all this had been a monstrous and cruel deception. Why had he been in such a hurry? He had been unable to go on living in London, and that morning, without any forewarning, he left for Paris, to see Liza—as it transpired, to step out for a quarter of an hour (after having savoured her impassioned embraces) to buy something for tea, then to return only to hear this merciless phrase uttered by the typically calm voice of his father, which left absolutely no doubt. Everything was at an end.

Then he recalled his mother. She was all he had left—but he could never tell her about this. He thought about it all over again. Everything had come crashing down. No father, no Liza—his love was impossible. What would he do now—and to what end?

The family of a factory worker passed by—a father, a mother and a little boy of around six. Then a pair of lovers walked past in a snug embrace. Unconsciously, without seeing, he followed them with his eyes. It was getting cold. He pulled his coat more tightly around him, and felt something firm in the side pocket: it was his passport. Then he got up and set out for the station.

By evening he was in London, in his father's cold, empty apartment. He went into the study, opened several drawers, and in the last one, at the bottom on the right, he found a revolver lying cornerwise. Everything was still. He sat at the desk and wrote on a slip of paper which he tore out of a notebook:

> Dear Mama, forgive me for the pain I am causing you. I love you more than anyone in the world. I cannot live any longer. I am sorry that I cannot see you now. Forgive me for everything. Your Seryozha.

He took the revolver and placed it to his temple. He felt faintly nauseous; he was terribly afraid. He thought that it would be awful if they were to find his body with a mutilated head, and so he placed the revolver to his chest, at the spot just below the dull, desperate beat of his heart. Then he closed his eyes and pulled the trigger.

It was a cool, quiet evening; stars hung high above in the dark sky; the dark Thames plashed faintly in its stone banks.

Just as it was impossible to imagine Sergey Sergeyevich's villa in the south of France without Nil, so too could one not imagine his house in London without Johnson, who was around sixty years of age and had been in Sergey Sergeyevich's employ for a very long time, since the year that he first came to England in the wake of the Russian Revolution. Just like Nil, Johnson knew all Sergey Sergeyevich's family, and he had known Seryozha since he was a little boy. He was an honest and exceedingly decent man, who valued his position greatly, executed his duties with exceptional punctiliousness, but was possessed of a single fault: in spite of his venerable age, he was a very heavy sleeper—a condition that he vehemently denied and invariably served as the basis of Sergey Sergeyevich's jokes, which was all the more gratifying because Johnson, despite appearances, was truly convinced that he slept lightly. On this occasion, however, there could be no denying it: that night he heard no shot.

By force of long-held habit, he rose exceptionally early—in autumn and winter it would still be dark at the time. On this day he got up earlier than usual. When he stepped out of his room, he was surprised to notice a light behind the door to Sergey Sergeyevich's study, which was ajar; that instant, he heard a faint wheezing. He rushed in and, throwing the door open, saw Seryozha's body lying on the floor next to the revolver he had dropped, specks of blood on the carpet and pink foam on the youth's lips. He immediately went to the telephone and summoned the doctor on call. Then he noticed atop the table a slip of paper with some writing on it in Russian, and he hid this in his pocket. With a certain difficulty he then lifted up Seryozha's heavy body and laid it on the divan. These events had so affected him that he forgot about everything and, the moment after he called the doctor, despair gently took hold of him. With tears in his eyes, he silently watched a choking Seryozha, who continued to wheeze heavily, while bloody foam bubbled at his lips as before. Only then, after the doctor's arrival, did he recall that Sergey Sergeyevich had telephoned the previous evening to ask whether Seryozha had returned, and ordered Johnson to let him know the moment he arrived. The doctor, with Johnson's help, quickly undressed Seryozha, placed his stethoscope to his chest, blood caked around the wound, and said that he had to be taken to the clinic immediately.

"Will he live, Doctor?" asked Johnson.

The doctor shrugged, sighed and replied that he hoped so: the bullet had missed his heart.

Only after Seryozha had been taken away—it was already around eight o'clock in the morning—did Johnson, returning to his senses, remember that he had still to call Sergey Sergeyevich. He ran once again to the telephone. It took a long time to connect the call; then finally, when he heard Sergey Sergeyevich's voice, he was in a state of such agitation that in the first seconds he was unable to explain anything. Then he somehow managed to relate, not without getting in a muddle, everything that had happened.

"Is he alive?" asked the unfamiliar voice from Paris, which Johnson would never have recognized, had he not been so absolutely certain that he was speaking with Sergey Sergeyevich.

"Yes, and the doctor says he hopes… He says the bullet missed his heart."

"I'll be on the first aeroplane to London," said Sergey Sergeyevich. "Send the car to Croydon immediately."

After leaving Liza the previous evening, Sergey Sergeyevich had telephoned Olga Alexandrovna, asking her whether she had seen Seryozha; then he had called London. Seryozha was nowhere to be found. He had lain on the divan all night without bothering to undress, slept soundly for three hours and awoken not long before Johnson's call. He learnt from the aerodrome that take-off was scheduled for half-past nine.

At that moment, Liza came into his study; she was dressed for travelling. She had come to Sergey Sergeyevich because he had her passport—with the firm intention of going to England. However, when she saw Sergey Sergeyevich, the words she had prepared suddenly caught in her throat. Despite the fact that he was just as cleanly shaven and well dressed as ever, his face was so changed that for a second she thought she was looking at another man.

"What's the matter, Seryozha?" she said with a tremble in her voice that a moment ago would have been entirely unthinkable.

"He's shot himself," said Sergey Sergeyevich.

"What?" asked Liza, failing to comprehend. She felt unwell; her vision dimmed; in the grey light of the October morning Sergey Sergeyevich's study melted and pitched. "What?"

"The bullet missed his heart, there's hope that he'll live," said Sergey Sergeyevich.

The melting objects momentarily took solid form. Liza began to breathe rapidly.

"I need to go there, I will go, you can't tell me now that I can't go."

"The main thing is that he pulls through," said Sergey Sergeyevich, "come what may—even you, Liza. Just let him pull through."

There was a knock at the door; in came Sletov. Sergey Sergeyevich told him that Seryozha had shot himself. Sletov made the sign of the cross. "I'll come with you," he said. "Are you ready?"

"No," said Sergey Sergeyevich. "I don't want to tell Olga Alexandrovna what has happened over the telephone. Drive to her apartment: tell her that Seryozha has fallen ill, and bring her to the aerodrome. The aeroplane departs at half-past nine; I've reserved a seat for her."

A moment later Sletov was gone.

"Let's go, Liza," said Sergey Sergeyevich. "Here, take your passport."

O N THE WAY TO le Bourget, Sergey Sergeyevich's long motor car first overtook the taxi in which, wrapped up in a new fur coat, Lyudmila was travelling, and then Lola Aînée's Delage, which was speeding along—he had said to the driver: *"Allez à toute vitesse!"** When Sergey Sergeyevich and Liza arrived at the aerodrome there were still twenty minutes before the flight. After a while, they watched as Lola Aînée laboriously mounted the narrow metal staircase. A sharp cold wind was blowing. Several minutes later Lyudmila quickly made her way up those same steps and disappeared into the depths of the aeroplane. Meanwhile, Sergey Sergeyevich was looking at his watch: Olga Alexandrovna and Sletov were not there. There were only a few minutes left; the propeller had already been set in motion and the engine roared, warming up. At the last minute, a plump, jolly man ran up to the aeroplane, panting from vigorous exertion, his hat askew. Without addressing himself to anyone in particular, but smiling amiably to Sergey Sergeyevich and Liza as though he had been long acquainted with them, he said gaily, still panting,

* Drive as fast as you can!

"*Ah, j'ai de la chance!*"* and boarded the aeroplane. Olga Alexandrovna was still not there.

"What's to be done, Liza? Let's go—she can catch the next one," said Sergey Sergeyevich.

They went inside. The aeroplane taxied quickly, and smoothly took off into the air. At that moment, Olga Alexandrovna and Sletov ran into the aerodrome: they were just in time to see the aeroplane climb and disappear.

* Ah, I'm in luck!

A SERIES OF FORTUITOUS and vast-ranging circumstances, infinitely removed from one another, united in this autumnal Paris–London flight such different people, all of whom, however, would meet with the same, simultaneous fate. There was nothing at all in common between Lola Aînée, who was travelling to London to receive the money left to her long ago by her deceased lover, and Liza, who was flying to Seryozha, that most precious and dear person, without whom she could not imagine her life; between Lyudmila, who after many long and arduous ordeals and journeys had attained what she had been so vainly searching for her entire life, and Sergey Sergeyevich, who for the first and final time in his life was wholly consumed by a single thought: that Seryozha must be saved at whatever cost. In just the same way, none of these people had the slightest notion about their chance fellow traveller, that plump, jolly man who had said as he boarded the aeroplane: "*Ah, j'ai de la chance!*" Far below, the earth loomed dark; the aeroplane shuddered and pitched slightly, and the lofty, cold, airy expanse floated infinitely around it.

Lola Aînée sat dozing—this was now an almost permanent state, so long as she was sitting and not walking— waking every now and then, and detecting, as usual, an unpleasant taste in her mouth. From time to time she would feel ever so slightly nauseous, but slumber proved more powerful than mild nausea. Waking for a moment, she began to think how she would return to Paris with her money and walk into a modest, new, just-let apartment on a quiet street in her beloved Auteuil—she would no longer have to go anywhere, unless during the summer she took the motor car and, taking long stops in each village, set out on the smooth road leading from Paris to Nice to spend several weeks there, on the shore of the warm summer sea. All her journeys and tours, all these Rumanias, Hollands, South Americas, Greeces, and the constant strain of work in the theatre, the eternal fear that her legs would suddenly give way, that her rheumatic shoulder would crunch audibly and painfully, or that in the middle of an act fiery circles would suddenly float up before her eyes and the floor would begin to slip away from under her feet—as had happened to her several times recently—all this now receded into the past and vanished with astonishing speed: only this blessed slumber, this almost pleasant weariness lay ahead—right up to the day when it would rise up and leave her breast for the last time, letting out her last breath of air—and there would be no more. However, she could not know that this day was nigh, that this very minute, with monstrous speed, it was swirling and hurtling towards her. She continued to dream.

Liza seemed to be thinking only about Seryozha. After Sergey Sergeyevich said, "The bullet missed his heart," she felt almost certain that he would live. Yet despite her wishes, this one unrelenting thought was infiltrated by other reflections, other words that were nevertheless connected to it and essentially constituted an extension of it: the scene in her apartment, Sergey Sergeyevich's appearance and the sense of deathly ennui and hopelessness after Seryozha left. As illogical as it seemed, she no longer had any doubts that her life with Seryozha would begin anew, though he would still be aware of the fact that impeded this, the one of which he had just learnt and which no shot could ever eliminate. However, Liza did not dwell on this; she was unconsciously confident that if Seryozha survived, all would be as it was before. Nevertheless, she fancied that for the first time in his life Sergey Sergeyevich had been exposed to human emotion. Yet she was unable to feel any gratitude towards him, since she had been much hurt by his words: "Come what may—even you." She could not forgive this "even you". "Even you"—after so many years of intimacy, in the course of which he had never spoken a harsh word to her. Yes, of course, she ought to have expected it. After what he said to her in her room, after Seryozha's leaving: this was not the result of anger, this was what he had always thought. But she could not even bring herself to hate him; indeed, she almost forgave him. She saw that the incident with Seryozha had been a terrible blow to him, one that was capable of transforming all his sceptical and derisive theories once and for all, and perhaps it would allow him to comprehend the strength of her love for Seryozha. Several times she glanced at him, continuing to think of Seryozha and uninterruptedly imagining his head on a white pillow, those beloved dark eyes, and his chest bandaged in gauze.

Sergey Sergeyevich sat motionlessly in his seat, never once turning his head to her.

He felt a strange weariness; it was as if he wanted to sleep the whole time. Whenever his thoughts returned to Liza, who was the cause of this terrible catastrophe enveloping Seryozha, he experienced a strange aversion towards her: she had borne that blind, egotistical passion, ruthless in regard to its victims, whose blood was on her hands; all the actions and betrayals of her sister paled in comparison with this. If Seryozha survived—and he had almost no doubt that he would—he would explain everything to him, and Liza would leave, going almost as far away as Seryozha had nearly gone. He felt something like gratitude when he thought of Olga Alexandrovna; she was not to blame for having passed on to Seryozha her rapturous, trusting nature, which had ruined him. Since the moment he first felt attracted to Liza—Sergey Sergeyevich had no doubt that it was Liza who had seduced him—his childlike defencelessness had prevented him from putting a halt to these events: how could he have known that Liza would inveigle him into her monstrously cruel world, where there was no place for him, and whose slow poison Sergey Sergeyevich—even Sergey Sergeyevich—would at times feel acutely, despite being armed against it a thousand times better than anyone else.

Lola and Lyudmila sat in front of Sergey Sergeyevich and Liza; both of them at the beginning of the flight turned and bowed to Sergey Sergeyevich, who replied with his unvarying smile, which had lost, however, its usual

281

persuasion, for his eyes did not smile. He thought about them for a moment, and his memory obediently and instantaneously recalled everything: the conversation with Lola at La Marquise de Sévigné, when he had advised her to go to London by aeroplane, Lyudmila's letter and his having spotted her in a motor car with her grey companion. He recalled all this and ceased thinking about them.

Lyudmila had parted with MacFarlane only a week previously, but this had provided ample time for her to feel his absence. Just before she set out, she received a telegram from him: "Darling, I'll be waiting." This telegram sat in her handbag, along with the divorce papers she had finally received and all the necessary marriage documents. She was certain that MacFarlane's motor car would already be waiting for her at Croydon. She thought the aeroplane was not going nearly fast enough.

WITHIN THIS SMALL space inside the aeroplane flying over the English Channel, there was concentrated in these final minutes a whole world of diverse and unique things, several long lives, a multitude of correctly and incorrectly understood emotions, regrets, hopes and expectations—it was a complex system of human relations, a vain account of which would perhaps take years of persistent toil. Their convergence, precisely here and now, was in turn the result of a million accidents of chance, the innumerable wealth of which was beyond human comprehension, for, in order to know the exact reason that had led each of these passengers to the aeroplane, it would be necessary to know everything that had come before this flight and to establish thus amid an evolution of sequential circumstances almost the entire history of the world. The reasons that had brought each of these people here perhaps originated from a mistake made long ago, under conditions of which we are ignorant—that is, if the word "mistake" here has any meaning at all. Yet just as we see the sky as a semicircular vault owing to an optical fault of our vision, so too we strive to examine all human life and any exposition of events as a closed circuit, which is all the more astonishing since the most superficial analysis convinces us of the clear futility of these efforts. Thus, just as that visible semicircle of sky hides an infinity beyond our comprehension, so too the external facts of any human existence mask the deepest complexity of things, the sum total of which is too vast for our memory and escapes our understanding. We are fated in this way to the role of impotent contemplators, and those moments when we suddenly seem to grasp the essence of the world can be wonderful in themselves—like the slow race of the sun across the ocean, like waves of rye in the wind, like the bound of a deer from a rock in the red of the evening sunset—but they, too, are fortuitous; and essentially almost always unpersuasive, like everything else. Yet we are inclined to believe them, and we prize them especially, for in every creative or contemplative effort there is a consoling moment of illusive, transient extraction from that single indisputable reality that we know and call death. Its constant presence everywhere and in everything seems to predispose to failure all attempts to imagine the material of life, which alters by the minute, as something bearing a definitive meaning; the futility of these attempts is perhaps equalled only by their allure. But if we allow that the most important event in the history of one or several lives is that last act, which occurs only once in a lifetime, then the flight of this aeroplane carrying Sergey Sergeyevich, Liza, Lola Aînée, Lyudmila and the jolly man whose hat was askew was just such an event, for when it was midway over the Channel, the people in a steamer below saw it come crashing down, enveloped in a black-and-red vertical whirlwind of smoke and fire.

Sletov had driven Olga Alexandrovna to le Bourget after waiting for almost a whole hour in the reception of her hotel, and they were in time to see the aeroplane only as it was flying away. She passed another torturous hour at the aerodrome, waiting for the next flight and being so insistent to know the truth that Sletov finally told her what had happened. After this she lost her head entirely. Her face stained with incessant tears, she at last boarded the aeroplane and flew off alone. Sletov was unable to accompany her since he had no visa; Olga Alexandrovna, like all the members of Sergey Sergeyevich's family, held a British passport. When she disembarked from the aeroplane at Croydon, there was an extraordinary commotion. The word "catastrophe" reached her ears, but she was unable to understand it. Johnson, who had set out for Croydon together with the driver to meet Sergey Sergeyevich, was the first to see her.

"Take me to him," she said without even greeting him, and in such a voice that Johnson was unable not only to ask her anything but even to make any reply. At the clinic she could not wait for the moment when they would let her in to see Seryozha; finally, accompanied by a doctor, she entered his room and leant over him. He opened his eyes.

"Mama!" he said. "Thank God I've seen you; now I can die."

Olga Alexandrovna looked at the doctor in despair. The latter smiled and said that the danger had passed.

In one rapid movement, she fell to her knees in front of his bed and kissed his hand. He made an effort to smile.

"There…" he said with difficulty. "When I came to, I hoped just for this… only for your face, Mama, only for your eyes… I've nothing left… And for you to say, 'My little fair-haired one'."

In a voice altered and slightly absurd because of the tears, Olga Alexandrovna said:

"My little boy, my Seryozhenka, my little fair-haired one, everything's going to be fine, you'll see."

It was a cold and windy day. At around two o'clock in the afternoon, in Sergey Sergeyevich's study in Paris, Fyodor Borisovich Sletov, who had just received a telephone call, sat down, dropping his head onto the former's writing desk, and sobbed uncontrollably, like a child.

Pushkin Press

Pushkin Press was founded in 1997, and publishes novels, essays, memoirs, children's books—everything from timeless classics to the urgent and contemporary.

This book is part of the Pushkin Collection of paperbacks, designed to be as satisfying as possible to hold and to enjoy. It is typeset in Monotype Baskerville, based on the transitional English serif typeface designed in the mid-eighteenth century by John Baskerville. It was lithoprinted on Munken Premium White Paper and notchbound by the independently owned printer TJ International in Padstow, Cornwall. The cover, with French flaps, was printed on Colorplan Pristine White paper. The paper and cover board are both acidfree and Forest Stewardship Council (FSC) certified.

Pushkin Press publishes the best writing from around the world—great stories, beautifully produced, to be read and read again.

STEFAN ZWEIG · EDGAR ALLAN POE · ISAAC BABEL
TOMÁS GONZÁLEZ · ULRICH PLENZDORF · TEFFI
VELIBOR ČOLIĆ · LOUISE DE VILMORIN · MARCEL AYMÉ
ALEXANDER PUSHKIN · MAXIM BILLER · JULIEN GRACQ
BROTHERS GRIMM · HUGO VON HOFMANNSTHAL
GEORGE SAND · PHILIPPE BEAUSSANT · IVÁN REPILA
E.T.A. HOFFMANN · ALEXANDER LERNET-HOLENIA
YASUSHI INOUE · HENRY JAMES · FRIEDRICH TORBERG
ARTHUR SCHNITZLER · ANTOINE DE SAINT-EXUPÉRY
MACHI TAWARA · GAITO GAZDANOV · HERMANN HESSE
LOUIS COUPERUS · JAN JACOB SLAUERHOFF
PAUL MORAND · MARK TWAIN · PAUL FOURNEL
ANTAL SZERB · JONA OBERSKI · MEDARDO FRAILE
HÉCTOR ABAD · PETER HANDKE · ERNST WEISS
PENELOPE DELTA · RAYMOND RADIGUET · PETR KRÁL
ITALO SVEVO · RÉGIS DEBRAY · BRUNO SCHULZ